WHITE RAVEN

SNOWS OF WAR – PART I

CATHERINE DOUGLAS

Dedications

First and foremost, to my husband. You aren't the biggest fan of fantasy, but you supported me the whole way through the writing of this book, and helped me turn it into a series. Thank you for double and triple-checking my work and spending long hours discussing historical accuracy and random ideas at all hours.

Second, to my sixth-grade reading and English teacher. I would not have come this far without you encouraging me to keep writing, even though I wholeheartedly admit that what I was writing in sixth grade was not good. You still supported me, and I managed to grow out of the bad writing phases over the next several years. Thank you for helping me start a library of World War II fiction, for discussing episodes of *Hogan's Heroes* over hot chocolate and cookies during my lunch period, and for the birthday and Christmas cards—I still have and treasure them. I can still remember you telling me that you want to see me move past magazine-length work… and here it is.

Chapter 1

September, 1955

Over the last several weeks since returning from Washington, I watched my fellow New Yorkers walking around far below my window gradually put on more and more layers of clothing as the weather grew colder and colder. Their clothes seemed to change with the leaves. Gusts of wind from Central Park blew shades of red and yellow and orange and brown around the street. In the past, I associated this time of year with the approaching holiday season, baskets of apples, pumpkins, cornfields, and Mother's Thanksgiving dinner. That changed thirteen years ago, when I was approached for a secretive mission over in Europe during World War II.

At the moment I'm not allowed to publish or talk about anything I did during and after the war because it's all still classified, but I can write as much as I want in the privacy of my home as long as I don't show anyone and I keep everything in a secure place. If it takes decades for the information to be declassified, I would like my memoirs written just in case I'm no longer around to publish them. What I did was important but it was also a fascinating story, and everyone loves a good story.

I'm not a prideful person. I try not to brag about anything, but it would be silly of me to say I didn't take part in anything extraordinary during the war. Then again, a lot of events were extraordinary, strange, or miraculous. Many people, Conjurus, Magicless, and witches can claim they were part of these events. Even though the Magicless see me as an extraordinary person, I don't like to think so. I'm not extraordinary among my own people. In fact, I'm a perfect example of what an average ice-variant Conjurus looks like. I don't even have any powers that are considered rare or extraordinary.

Life is composed of successes and failures. I experienced a failure I thought I wouldn't recover from before I took part in the war effort. It still haunts me, and I still miss the people I lost. I wish they could have seen my successes later on. Then again, if they had survived, would I have even had the chance to do what I did? Would history look a little different? There are times when I do wonder if certain things are simply meant to happen, even if the reason isn't always clear.

August, 1942

In New York City, it didn't take long for everything to change when war was declared after Pearl Harbor, but in some ways it was a good change. Places and businesses that had come to a standstill during the Depression suddenly became hubs of activity for scrap drives and mass production of every little thing a soldier needs on the battlefield. Everyone was active, even the Conjurus.

I was a worker at a refrigerator factory here in Manhattan. Electric refrigerators were still fairly new then and ice-variants were gradually turning to the field as we no longer needed big blocks of ice to store food. It's not particularly glamourous or exciting, especially when one considers that I used to be an explorer in Antarctica.

My uncle Redvar ran a stand he set up literally overnight to collect scrap metal and rubber as soon as war was declared. At the end of every day he drove everything to the shipyard. Redvar embraces both Conjurus and Magicless cultures, which is something I've also tried to do, especially since he raised me alongside my mother when my father died.

I tried to give him something each day since he opened that stand. Sometimes it wasn't much, but I always did my best to have something for him. He was organizing crates of metal pieces when I arrived at the stand, hardly waiting for my motorcycle to stop before getting off.

"Whatcha got today, Jay?" Redvar asked, a half-smoked cigar hanging from his teeth.

"Ah, not much," I replied, taking a small cardboard box from the back of the motorcycle. "Some nails and bicycle gears. That's it."

"Better than nothing," he said. "Just drop it by the counter." He opened his makeshift cash register. "How much you want for it?"

"I'm family. No need to pay."

"Aw, come on, even you need a little cash."

I shook my head. "Keep it. You have Aunt Lucille to think about."

Shrugging, Redvar closed the register. "Your choice, Jay." He wiped sweat from his forehead. "How was work?"

"Alright. Lost a bunch of workers to the draft. They're gonna start hiring women to fill spots." I probably shouldn't have added what I said next, but I did. "Even most of our ice-variants left."

Redvar gave me a sympathetic look and gestured for me to come closer so we could speak more privately. "I know how badly you want to put your name in for the draft, but the second they see your name—"

"They'll tie me to my father. I know."

"Yeah, plus, we're not allowed. I know many of our people are going because they can pass as Magicless, and they don't care what our representatives say. Look, there are other things you can do. Didn't you mention your place is putting fridges on Navy ships?"

"Yes, but that's not enough for me. I'm still young. I can pass the military's physical. I can pass as a Magicless if I really want to."

"That's not what our representatives are concerned about. There are thousands of Conjurus who are able to join the military and pass as Magicless, but because of what Morgan did, we could get in serious trouble if our representatives found out or if someone from an enemy country found out."

"Dad tried saving the last of his unit. I think this is absurd."

"German officers saw. I'm not saying he was wrong, but it made things at the signing of the Treaty of Versailles more complicated. The Germans thought—no, accused—the United States of using Conjurus as weapons."

"I know the story. There was a private meeting with Conjurus leaders about changing our status for the draft. They agreed with the military that it'd be better for us so we avoid capture and abuse by an enemy power. I *know*. I still want to go. Even if our leaders are too cowardly to send some of us overseas."

"They're not cowardly. They have good reason for sticking with their decision because they know about what's going on in Europe through refugees who came in months ago."

I raised an eyebrow. "And what's going on?"

"Do you really want to know?"

"I do."

Redvar sat behind his counter, taking his cigar out of his mouth and tapping it over an ashtray. "Germany is not exactly doing well in Russia."

"I've been seeing that in the newsreels."

"Yeah. They're going to find themselves on the defensive sooner or later and they're desperate for a solution to get the Soviets out of their way. So, what's the solution? Kidnapping ice-variant Conjurus. Nobody knows where they're being taken or what's being done to them, just that they're disappearing."

"The only thing coming to mind is that the Germans could be making a magical army," I said. "Made up of people who can survive winter with minimal effort and wreak havoc on the Soviets." I shook my head. "I can't see the Germans being successful with making an army of Conjurus. Didn't they deport most of their Conjurus several years ago?"

"They could still try, given how many countries they occupy. It might not be as large as their regular army, but it's an army of beings with supernatural powers. That could be enough to scare the Soviets into surrender."

"And it could convince Italy and Japan to do the same thing."

"Yeah. That wouldn't be a force anyone wants to face. Our representatives don't want any of us being captured because of this. That's why they're not going to let us volunteer or be drafted. You do understand that, right?"

"I do, but that doesn't mean I still don't want to go."

A look of defeat crashed over my uncle. He looked up, as if trying to ask God for advice, then looked back down at his counter. "Jay, even if you could go... we'd all be worried about you. Trust me, I don't want to hold you back, but it's too big of a risk."

"If there's nothing you can do, don't feel bad." I turned to head back to my motorcycle, then looked over my shoulder. "Tell Aunt Lucy I said 'hello.'"

"I will. Have a good night, Jay."

I found a pair of newspapers, one from a Magicless publisher and the other from a Conjurus one, on my doormat when I arrived at my apartment. I set them both on the kitchen counter as I entered, unsure of whether or not I was going to bother reading them. I've only gotten my name in the papers once, and it wasn't for a good reason, just like my father. Although my instance had far less severe consequences than his had.

Around nine I left my study and went out into the kitchen to make a cup of tea before bed. My gaze fell on the newspapers on the counter as I waited for the water to boil. The Magicless paper contained more stories about the war. The Conjurus paper was largely the same, and the stories were mainly about the refugees coming in from Europe and their accounts of the German occupation of France and the Low Countries.

My uncle was right about the Germans rounding up ice-variants. That was one consistency I found in these stories. Those who were able to flee before they could be captured didn't have the slightest idea where these people were being taken.

What was strangest was that the Germans were taking everyone—men, women, children, young, old, sick, and injured. Redvar had suggested the kidnappings were to build an army that could withstand the elements, but this didn't look like they were searching for those who were fighting fit. Unless they were trying to get every ice-variant in one location to prevent escape of those who could or were threatening entire families to coerce the healthy men of fighting age into serving.

The articles continued with statements from Conjurus representatives. Most were claiming that now they would never let us put our names in for the draft if this was what was in store for us if we became prisoners-of-war. Others were considering sending in their own army, but that would require a vote, and I already knew a war declaration wouldn't pass. That and no one could be sure how the rest of the Allies would respond. An army purely made up of Conjurus would be far too small. Those who chose to go could be cast out from their families like my father was.

I closed the paper, tired of reading about the cowardice. It's no wonder many Conjurus have been choosing to live more closely to the Magicless and more like them. I glanced over at a photograph of my father hanging on the wall over my desk. I had been told by some of my relatives that I look almost exactly like him. The most noticeable difference is that he's always smiling in the pictures, like he's thinking about something so delightful he can't wait to share it. He was the one person anyone could count on. Selfless, loyal, and possibly the world's gentlest soul when he courted my mother. Redvar said it took two years before they were married.

I was only two when he died. I hardly have any memories of him, but I grew up thinking he was a hero, a legend, in a way. Redvar thinks so. My mother thinks so. It's hard living up to that, and it's equally hard knowing I'm never going to speak to him.

Unlike him, I generally don't smile. I do try sometimes, and Mother and Redvar claim it's because I think more than I speak. Smiling for me became rarer when I returned from my last trip to Antarctica. What had happened was something I still hadn't been able to accept.

My gaze remained on my father's photograph. I wished I could have one chance to talk to him, one chance to learn from him. He knew his place in the world. I had thought I found mine but in the end I turned out to be dead wrong.

It can be hard to find a quiet place to sit and think in Manhattan, aside from the libraries. I decided to walk to Central Park the day after talking to my uncle. The leaves were beginning to change colors. Some trees had already transformed into a bouquet of red, yellow, and orange. Others were still only tinged with color, but they would turn in time.

The sound of automobile horns mixed with the birdsong and wind rustling the increasingly dry leaves. An elderly man was raking the leaves that had fallen on the paths. He turned to say "hello" and tip his felt cap, and I responded in kind.

Up ahead I could hear the cooing of pigeons and I spotted a familiar young lady throwing seed and crumbs from a small pail. Laurel Wendaline. She was a fire-variant, and I had known her for a long time. We had met shortly after when I was taken up to the Adirondacks to hone and train my abilities, at a party celebrating the initiation of us and several other young Conjurus into our training. At the time I thought she was lovely, and we both had stories of our time away from civilization to train, although hers sounded much more fun; needing heat, her father had taken her to an isolated beach on Cuba sheltered by the jungle. She told me that she used to be a bit of a brat, and her experience gave her a chance to learn and better herself. Nowadays you would never suspect her behavior used to be so terrible, and she has grown into a much quieter, calmer, more patient young woman. I liked her for her patience, and it amazed me that we had remained friends after the Antarctic disaster when I became distant from everyone. She visited often and brought food, advice, and kind words. It took me a while to thank her for all she did, but when I did, I knew Laurel was someone I wanted to stay in my life.

It was nice to see her that morning. Her brown hair was almost shoulder-length and slightly curled at the ends, and her bright, twinkling eyes were just a few shades lighter in color. Her complexion and clothing always make her seem like the embodiment of autumn coziness. It took a moment for her to notice me walking toward her, but when she did she stood up straight and smiled. "Good morning, Jay."

"Good morning, Laurel," I replied, then gestured to one of the benches by the path. "May I?"

"Of course." Laurel pitched another handful of crumbs and seeds before covering the pail and sitting next to me. "What brings you out here?"

"Just wanted some peace and quiet. Off work today," I said, looking over at the pigeons strutting around the sidewalk. "Making new friends?"

Laurel smiled slightly. "Not particularly. This bread deflated in the oven last night and I didn't feel like throwing it out."

"Ah, so, you're clearing your head today."

"Yes." Laurel tipped her head back and sighed. "I've never been so busy."

"Feels good, doesn't it?"

"Oh, yes, but one weekend to myself would be nice."

I grinned a little. "The Germans and the Japanese aren't going to put their plans on hold for a weekend."

Laurel smiled. "I'll put someone else in my place, that way things still get done." She looked up at the cold blue sky and then back at me. "Why don't you come work with me? I think you'd be happier there."

I shrugged. "I still have my place at the refrigerator factory. Besides, the most I could do is keep the freezer running. I could never stand in the heat of the kitchen for hours at a time."

Her smile widened. Laurel picked up my hand. "No, but the customers would surely love your flowers made of ice."

"Now, how did I know you were going to mention those?" Laurel absolutely loves my ice roses. I've never been sure why, but I have a hypothesis, especially with the symbolism of roses. I held my hand out slightly, palm up, and with a slight effort, made a small cloud of white mist form around it. A slight cracking sound could be heard and a rose completely made of ice appeared. My ice roses are extremely fragile, and so detailed that no professional sculptor would be able to replicate them. Laurel is a fire-variant. To trust her with just holding the ice rose is a bit of a risk, but I trusted her regardless and carefully placed the rose in her palm.

"Thank you," she whispered, as though anything louder would shatter the rose.

"I will make bouquets for the diner, but that is all," I said.

"They'll be good for morale. I appreciate it."

I offered her a slight grin. "No problem."

There was silence for a few minutes until Laurel looked at me as the rose began melting. "Why don't you go back to Antarctica? They're still sending expeditions there. You've definitely changed for the better since that accident, but I can sense you're... not as happy as you once were."

I bit my tongue, my gaze turning downward to my boots and the sidewalk, my happiness from a second ago melting like the rose. Dead, dry leaves blew across, making scratching sounds as they bounced on the concrete. "Well..." I sighed, then paused. Going back isn't possible. I can't be trusted with another crew of explorers. "No. I can't."

"Why? You learned from last time. I know you can prevent another tragedy."

"The next group will know who I am, and then how am I supposed to convince them to trust me?" I squeezed my hands together. "It's like my father all over again. I wouldn't be surprised if the Loalin name is cursed."

Laurel gave me a sympathetic look. "That doesn't mean things can't change. Look at me. My parents thought I would never grow out of being a brat until the trip to Cuba. Looking back, I was quite an embarrassment to them. It was strange coming back and going to school and seeing people look at me differently. Change is part of life, even unexpected changes."

Nodding, I relaxed my fists. "That's true. It also means it could take years for things to change. I would rather wait until after the war, but that doesn't mean I'm going to do nothing now. I'd like to see other places." A sense of excitement began building in me again upon changing the topic. The wonder and thrill that came with travel. That wonder was tinged with soreness. It was traveling that gave me happiness, but it also had given me tragedy.

Laurel raised an eyebrow. "How exactly are you going to do that? There's nowhere to go that's safe now."

"That doesn't matter. I don't want to sit idly by. I'm sure the British aren't having their Conjurus do nothing."

"They're in a completely different situation than we are. Jay-" Laurel gently took my shoulders, "I don't think you're understanding just how dangerous things are."

"I completely understand, but no one ever stopped me from going to Antarctica, did they?"

"No, but-"

"The danger is just as great, but I would rather face soldiers than Antarctic weather. Soldiers can be outsmarted. Antarctic weather can't."

Laurel sighed. I could sense she felt defeated. There really was no talking me out of trying to go to Europe or Asia. "What if you're captured? I'm sure you've been hearing about what the Germans are doing to their Conjurus."

I wasn't sure how to answer that. I certainly don't think I'm capable of effortlessly avoiding capture. Despite the powers we possess, anyone can catch a Conjurus if they're intelligent. Magicless Germans have clearly been able to do it. "It's a risk I would have to live with until coming home. I'm not denying your fears or Uncle Redvar's or anyone else's, but I'm tired of feeling held back. I want to see what my place is in the world, and I'm not convinced Antarctica is it anymore."

I returned to my apartment feeling like all I had been doing that day was alienating everyone I knew. Every other Conjurus at work had accepted the fact that they weren't allowed to register for the draft or enlist and didn't feel like discussing it with me. Even when I mentioned the fact that there were already Conjurus secretly enlisting, I was told to stop daydreaming and keep working. We were doing our part for the war effort by building and maintaining refrigerators.

It was times like this where I felt like I needed someone to talk to. The only person I could think of was my father, even though he's dead. I needed someone who was just as adventurous as myself.

My thoughts turned to my old team in Antarctica. They were all just as daring. After preparing a hot drink, I went into my study and dug around my cluttered desk for photographs from my time as an explorer's assistant. On top of them is a framed one from my last team. I had been commissioned to be both a survival guide and a "last survivor". A "last survivor" is exactly what it sounds like. An ice-variant has a higher chance of surviving in Antarctica than a Magicless, so we head back to where the expedition started if the rest of the group dies. It's our job to get the news back home about what happened.

I didn't think I would ever have to take on that role. I always made sure the team returned home safely. Frostbite was an issue, but I never had anyone die on my watch. I never let it happen.

I looked through those photos when I returned from the park, thinking hard about what Laurel said. Everything she said was true: I'm a good explorer, I did love my job, and I tried harder than anyone could imagine. I had grown familiar with certain locations in Antarctica, including places I suggested landing. The problem with Antarctica is that it's unpredictable. A perfectly suitable harbor can become treacherous in a matter of hours. I constantly revised maps and guides and it was tedious up until Duncan Barlow, one of the men I worked with for several years, suggested using the maps and guides to study patterns in the Antarctic ice and weather. After that I never felt more crucial to anything. I was the only member of the team who could stand out in the cold for hours to gather whatever information we needed.

I only saw Duncan a few times out of the year. He lived in Maine, but we kept in touch through telegrams and letters. When an expedition was planned, we met up in Washington and boarded a ship for South America. The weeks just spent on traveling were some of the best I experienced. Duncan was much older than I am. Like my father, he was a soldier in World War I. They didn't know each other, but he did hear about the incident my father was involved in.

"It was impossible not to hear about. Every soldier, sailor, and Marine heard about it," Duncan told me one morning as our ship was leaving a port in Cancun.

I nodded. "What exactly did you hear in terms of... the incident with my father?"

"A platoon was sent as backup for your father's when they learned about the German ambush. When they arrived, there was a field of ice stretching for nearly a mile. Your father had been shot dead, and the ice started right in front of him. Not too far off, every German soldier had been frozen solid. They were said to look like sculptures. They either died from shock, hypothermia, or icicles driven through their bodies. No one had ever seen anything like it."

"How did the Germans even find out about this if there were no survivors?"

"There was one. A sergeant. I think his name was Wahler, according to what I read. I don't know how he escaped, but he managed to tell his commanding officer and, well, you know the results of that."

"The Germans thought we were being used as weapons."

"The men who found your father were every bit as shocked as the Germans." Duncan took a sip of his coffee. "That was an interesting day. Word spread quickly about what happened, and they told everyone not to tell our families when the Conjurus representatives heard about the German accusations. They didn't want a big fuss about it."

"Did you?"

"I wasn't married at the time. Didn't meet Margaret for another two years. I did tell her when I knew I could trust her. Turns out she already heard from her brother, and he knew your father during the war. He had been seriously wounded during the battle—survived, but had his right leg removed—and he's forever grateful that Morgan did what he did."

"It sounds like something he'd do. Mother always said he was extremely selfless."

"And what he did was one of the most selfless things a man can do."

"He wasn't given a hero's funeral, though." I bit my tongue as I thought, remembering what my mother told me about one of the representatives coming to the door a few days after my father's body was brought back to the States. "We were told not to talk about it outside of family."

"That had to be difficult. I can tell you many of us thought he deserved better, but when all mention of him disappeared once he was returned to his people, no one brought it up again." Duncan smiled at me. "I'm very pleased to have his son on my team."

For the longest time, I was certain I could be the man I knew my father would want me to be, and every expedition to Antarctica proved it until four years ago. After that, it wasn't just him I let down, but Duncan too. Everyone in that expedition.

I closed and locked the drawer after putting the photographs back. I couldn't look Duncan in the eye, even in a picture. A sudden swelling of pain had formed in my chest and tears started running down my face. The last thing I wanted to do was go back to the state of mind I found myself in for several months after coming home from Antarctica.

The apartment was silent that night. I kept the lights dim except for the one by the radio and sat with a cup of cocoa, pulling back the curtains to peer at the city. Brightly lit spires and towers stood against the dark, bluish-violet sky, and the half-moon shone above them. As tired as I was from revisiting old memories, I wanted to finish my drink before I went to bed.

A jolt passed through me when I heard three knocks on the door. The surprise was followed by confusion. *Who could it possibly be at this hour?* Standing, I set my mug on the counter before going to the door. "Who is it?"

A man's voice replied, "Lester Halcomb. I wish to speak with a Mr. Jay Loalin."

I didn't know any Lester Halcomb. Suppressing my nerves, I opened the door to see a man in casual clothing. He was short, skinny, had unusually prominent cheekbones, and his thick, black hair was tucked under a gray hat. He had a manila folder in his hand and I noticed the gold chain of a pocket watch wrapped around his index finger. He smiled and held out his free hand. "You must be Mr. Loalin."

"I am," I said. "And... who exactly are you?"

Halcomb gestured into my apartment. "I will explain in private."

I closed the door after he walked inside, and watched him study the room before I said, "Have a seat. Would you... like anything to drink?"

He shook his head. "Not at the moment, thank you."

I sat across from him, holding my mug. "Alright, then, what is this private business you came here for?"

Halcomb set his folder on the coffee table. "You are an ice-variant Conjurus, correct?"

I nodded.

"Son of Morgan Loalin?"

Another nod. "Please, don't tell me you're here to talk about him."

"No, but his name did lead me to you. You were a team member for expeditions in the Antarctic, right?"

"Yes. I... don't want to talk about that, either."

"I can understand, but I also hope you understand why I chose to approach you."

I raised an eyebrow. "Your point?"

"You've heard of the OSS?"

I nodded. "Recently formed, right?"

"Yes. We're looking to recruit Conjurus agents for specialized tasks in Europe and the Pacific. I was in the process of putting papers together when this intelligence came across my desk." Halcomb looked at the folder. "With the Soviets pushing back as hard as they can, the Germans have been struggling, to say the least, and their logistics have rendered them unprepared for to fight a drawn-out defensive war. Not that long ago, one of our spies found this facility in Poland—" He opened the folder, pointing to a photograph of a plain-looking building in the middle of nowhere, "and inside, they found a dozen cells, all holding ice-variants." He turned to another photograph and his face paled. "They also found a cadaver. It looks like the Nazis are conducting experiments, or studying them like you would a rat in a lab."

I found it hard to look at the picture. My stomach was starting to turn in on itself. The man on the table was naked, and his torso had been opened from the base of his neck all the way down to his genitals. His hands had been flayed. The skin on his palms and fingers were pulled away neatly. "It looks like they're trying to find the source of our powers."

"We're still missing some pieces of the puzzle, but everything we do have points to them doing what they suspected the Allies of doing back in the First World War."

I turned over the photograph before I could be sick. "This is different. Very different. Did your spy find anything else? What exactly do the Nazis want to accomplish with this?"

Halcomb shook his head. "All we found is the facility, and the man in charge." He turned to another page in the folder. The next photograph was of a very thin, uniformed man with sharp facial features. "SS *Standartenführer* Fritz Wahler." Halcomb looked me in the eye. "The same soldier who fled your father's last stand."

Now I felt sicker. If this really was the same man, was he doing this because of what he witnessed? "My uncle had heard rumors that the Germans were going to use captured ice-variants as soldiers. This... doesn't look like it. This... is sick and twisted."

"It is, and we can't figure out what their goal is. Making their army less susceptible to the cold, creating ice-based weapons, no one knows, but this isn't going to continue."

My thoughts came to a screeching halt. "Are you trying to get *me* to go?"

"To put it bluntly, yes."

I couldn't believe what I was hearing. "I'm in."

Halcomb grinned, but he also looked puzzled. "That was easier than I thought it'd be."

"Pardon?"

"No one I've ever recruited said 'yes' immediately. Most took some time to think about it. This is incredibly dangerous work. Are you really sure about this?"

"Positive."

"I do mean more dangerous than Antarctica."

"I'm aware. Train me and send me. I'm ready."

Halcomb frowned. "You're not exactly going alone, Mr. Loalin. Once you complete your training, someone will be accompanying you to Europe."

My heart was sinking. I'd be a lot happier going on this mission alone. That way, there's no risk of anyone other than me getting hurt. That way, I don't disappoint anyone. I couldn't say that to Halcomb, though. Of course, I still had the option of not going, but going would be better than staying here and doing nothing. I just can't do *nothing* anymore, especially now that I know what's going on.

"I'll arrange for you to fly down to Washington." Halcomb stood, closing the folder. "Any questions?"

"What do I tell my family?"

"Make something up."

"I can't lie to them."

"I'm sorry. You can say nothing, but I prefer something, even a lie, to them thinking you've disappeared without a trace."

Chapter 2

Going on a top-secret assignment was the last thing I expected out of that evening. The fact that I couldn't tell anyone what I was doing made it a lot harder, but the determination to just *go out there* and *do something* burned intensely.

The morning after Halcomb's visit, I paced my apartment. I was struggling to think of what I would say to Mother, Uncle Redvar, and Laurel. I couldn't stand the thought of lying to them. I knew in my heart that none of them were spies for Germany, but the last thing I wanted was to dig myself into a hole for telling classified information to people without clearance.

My flight was in three days, and Halcomb had already arranged for someone to go to the refrigerator factory and let my boss know I would be leaving for an undetermined length of time. Frankly, I was glad I didn't have to do that, especially since I already had to lie to my closest friends and family.

Redvar was sorting crates of scrap when I approached his stand that afternoon. He smiled, setting down the crate in his hands. "Jay! Nice to see you today."

"Nice to see you, too, Uncle." I bit my lip, realizing I was about to lie to my own uncle, the man who practically raised me and trained me, who told so many stories about my father that I aspired to be like him, follow in his heroic footsteps. "I..." I stopped, mouth hanging open, already embarrassed even though I hadn't said anything. "I'm going away for a while."

His smile disappeared. "Excuse me?"

"I'm going away for a while. I'm sorry."

Redvar pursed his lips and tilted his head. "And... can I ask where you're going? Are you going back to Antarctica?"

"No. Right now, I'm not allowed to say, just that I'm not sure how long I'll be gone."

"Jay—"

"I can't answer any more questions." I felt like I had been punched in the stomach. I couldn't believe I was saying all this.

Redvar drew in a breath, like he was going to argue with me, but a look of defeat crashed over him and he sat down. "Alright." He looked up at me. "Perhaps I was wrong in painting your father like a legend. I should've done more in encouraging you to just be your own person."

I shook my head. "I already know the differences between us. I am my own person."

"So, it's a coincidence that I look at you now and see Morgan. I didn't want you living in his shadow. I didn't want what happened in Europe to be something that you want to emulate."

"I don't want to emulate what happened!"

"Well, you're awful quick to put yourself in danger! What, are you hitchhiking on a ship to Europe? Go off and kill Germans all by yourself like Morgan did? Is that what you're doing?"

Something boiled inside me at Redvar talking to me like a child.

He folded his arms over his chest. "I'm right, aren't I?"

"I'd tell you everything if I could."

"Right. Because you're getting on a ship and sneaking into Europe, thinking it'll make you just like your father."

Unable to say anything to put his assumptions to rest, I turned to walk away, saying, "I'll let you know when I return."

Redvar was going to tell my mother, and given his reaction, I didn't care. He had always been supportive of me and I couldn't understand why he turned right then. It took a little while for me to come to the conclusion that he was afraid for my safety, but I think he could have expressed that better. I didn't want to think of it as a betrayal. That would be childish of me.

My next stop was to see Laurel. When I stopped in at the restaurant where she worked, it was empty except for a pair of customers sitting at a corner booth and a young waitress wiping down a table. "Excuse me, is Miss Wendaline here?" I asked.

"She's in the kitchen, sir," the waitress replied. "Do you need her?"

"Yes, there's something I need to discuss with her in private."

Nodding, the waitress walked behind the counter and disappeared into the kitchen. A minute or two later, Laurel came out. "Hello, Jay."

"Hey." I swallowed. "Could we... go somewhere alone?"

"Of course." Laurel turned to the waitress. "Could you tell Rebecca to take charge for a while? Thank you."

She followed me outside and we walked into the alley, which was slowly filling with dead leaves that were being raked in to avoid cluttering the sidewalk. I wasn't sure what to expect from Laurel so I got right to the point.

"I'm going away for a while. I can't say where I'm going or what I'm doing, just know that I'll return someday."

Laurel looked down. For a moment, I thought she was going to cry. "How long will you be gone?" she asked.

"I don't know. All I can say is that this will take me many places, and that I will come back."

"Is there a reason you can't tell me?"

"It's secret. If I told you what I'll be doing, people could get killed." I gently took her hands. "I will come back, I promise."

Laurel squeezed my hands back. "Please. And... please be careful."

I could sense she was holding back. We had been close friends for years, and I had considered the idea of us becoming more. The Antarctica disaster put a pause on that when I retreated into myself, and now I wasn't sure how to bring up the topic of love with her. It seemed pointless to bring it up when I could be going on a mission I might not come back from. I couldn't leave her with pain and regret. On the other hand, I didn't want to regret not telling her. "I'll be as careful as I can be."

"Thank you."

We let go, and I left the alley. This had been far from satisfactory, and I wanted nothing more than to tell everyone the truth.

"Have you ever been to Washington, Mr. Loalin?" Lester Halcomb picked up one of my suitcases as we boarded a plane early Friday morning.

"Several times. The team I used to work with in Antarctica used the city as a meeting point," I replied. "I... haven't been here since the accident."

"Sorry." Halcomb looked unsure of what to say next. He opened his mouth to say something, presumably about what had happened, but then closed it. "So, I take it you know your way around?"

"Intimately."

"Good. I have you booked at the Willard for the next few nights. As of now, that's all I can tell you until we arrive."

I couldn't ask many questions because nearly everything I wanted to discuss was classified, but I could wait. The flight was only supposed to be three hours, and I spent that time thinking. The last time I had taken a plane was to Key West four years ago, when I met up with Duncan and the rest of the team to make the long trip to Antarctica. I'm the only one who came back.

"I know I read your file on what happened, but... what exactly went wrong?" Halcomb asked.

I had been hoping he wouldn't ask anything about Antarctica. The only two people I ever confided in about it were Uncle Redvar and Laurel. I never dreamed about telling a stranger. Then again, I had a feeling I would be getting to know Halcomb very well on this journey, so I figured it would be best to trust him with this. It took a long couple of minutes, but eventually I told him.

It was Duncan who suggested we join the ranks of explorers who have reached the South Pole, and he pointed out I would be the first Conjurus to reach the Pole. I felt that would be my chance to be as legendary as my father, which I expressed to Duncan in private.

"I think he'd be proud of you even if you didn't get to the Pole," Duncan said, gesturing to a thick, worn manila folder containing my reports on Antarctic weather. "Your work is impressive."

We were set to meet in Key West and take a ship to Cancun and then to our remote camp at the very edge of Argentina, from where we'd sail on to Antarctica. We had a new team member, a young man by the name of Archie Marsden.

"It's a pleasure to meet you, Mr. Loalin," said Archie, taking my hand in a firm grip. We met up in Washington before the flight to Florida.

"Pleasure to meet you, too," I replied. "First time to Antarctica?"

"Yes. I was in Greenland four months ago and Ellesmere Island before that."

"I picked him for his experience," Duncan said, hefting some of our bags into a cart.

"Only after I put in a request two times," Archie added.

I gave a sheepish grin. "What about our team is so appealing to you?"

"Well, I was looking for an opportunity to reach the South Pole and came across your records. Frankly, what impressed me is your team has had no deaths in the six years it's been active."

"I pin that all on sheer luck," Duncan said. "We've come close to losing people a few times."

"Up until I joined four years ago," I replied.

"Oh, we've still had close calls after you joined. Remember when Tallor fell through the ice?"

"Yeah. I was trying to freeze the water around him so he didn't get dragged away while you and McIntyre were pulling him out. I'm just happy I didn't kill him in the process."

"I think he was happy he managed to keep all his extremities afterward."

Archie's face paled. "My team... up in Ellesmere... lost someone under ice."

"I'm sorry," said Duncan, reaching out to pat Archie's shoulder. "Antarctica can be unpredictable at times, but we'll do everything in our power to keep each other alive."

"We've aborted several expeditions to prevent deaths," I added. "If we have to scrap this one at any point, we will."

Archie nodded, but he still looked a little uncertain. I shared a glance with Duncan and saw he knew as well as I did that it would take some time for Archie to be convinced that this trip would be alright.

We met up with Tallor and McIntyre in Key West. Lyle Tallor was our navigation specialist, formerly a quartermaster in the Navy. He was tall and a little on the thin side. His hair was coal-black, and he was usually clean-shaven. I had the pleasure of spending a summer with him in his home down in Pennsylvania putting together a map of Antarctica for *National Geographic*. His library was full of atlases from all over the world in French, German, Chinese, Spanish, Arabic, Russian, Italian, Latin, Turkish, and every language you could think of. I felt like a child in a candy store.

Vern McIntyre, like Duncan, was a Great War veteran. Red-headed with turquoise eyes, he was muscular and the tallest of the team. He was our general fix-it man. Broken generator? He could repair it. Sled boards cracked? He could fix it. He also knew basic first-aid and had built more than his fair share of splints in the six years he had been on Duncan's team. I swear half our luggage every trip was his tools.

Archie was a biologist. His time in Greenland and Ellesmere was spent mainly with Arctic foxes, and he was compiling his research into a book. When we boarded our ship to Cancun, he showed me his research. He had everything from sketches to journal entries to photographs, and his passion showed in each. I was impressed, and it made me look forward to having him on our team even if he'd mostly be drawing just penguins and seals.

"This isn't everything I've ever done. Back home I've got whole books full of wildlife sketches. I took a trip to Africa a few years ago and came back with drawings of lions and elephants and cheetahs and monkeys. I'd love to do it again." Smiling shyly at me, Archie handed me his sketchbook. "Take as long as you like with it." He followed me as I took a seat near Duncan. "Mr. Loalin—can I call you Mr. Loalin?"

"I have no preference," I said.

"Alright. Could I ask you... how did you come across this job?"

"I volunteered. I'm the team's last survivor." I made eye contact with Archie. "Your team in the Arctic didn't have one, did they?"

"No. I'm thrilled to be meeting a Conjurus. I came from a town where they weren't common. Duncan speaks so highly of you."

I waited for him to say something about my father, but I figured Archie was too young to have known about that. Perhaps I've just gotten used to hearing people I've never met, but were old enough to have served in the Great War, bring it up when they hear my last name.

When we docked in Cancun, I was happy to get another chance to explore the streets of that lovely city, even though the tropical heat isn't the best for me. I sweat profusely in higher temperatures, but it was worth it to be out with the people I had come to call my friends and brothers.

"We do have enough supplies to reach the South Pole, right?" Archie asked when the five of us sat out on the patio outside a restaurant we always stopped at.

"Yeah. Wouldn't have made the trip if we weren't ready," McIntyre replied. He studied Archie's face. The younger man was looking increasingly worried the further we got from home. I shared a glance with the others and got the sense that everyone was trying to think of ways to reassure him.

"Vern's right." Duncan broke the silence. "I double-checked everything before we left Key West and I'll check everything again when we get to the camp in Argentina. If anything is out of sorts, we won't proceed until it's fixed. Don't worry."

Archie nodded, looking down at his menu. Somehow, I had the feeling it would take a lot more to help him relax.

We had a long way to go before we reached Argentina. Over a week, actually, especially when you took into account the fact that we were stopping in Salvador, Brazil. Archie joined us for meals, but he spent most of the time in his compartment. When we weren't going over checklists for Antarctica, I was on the deck sitting by the railing and staring out at the ocean. In that part of the world, it's not unusual to see dolphins, and if you're lucky, humpback whales.

Passing by the many tiny islands that dotted the sea never got old. It broke up the endless blue horizon with the whitish tawny sand and vibrant green of the exotic trees and shrubs. I had made that trip so many times that I knew when we didn't see any more islands, we had left the Caribbean and entered the vast Atlantic.

Having never crossed the Atlantic, I found myself fantasizing about going across the ocean and seeing what life has to offer. Maybe I should go to Africa like Archie did. Perhaps Europe. Asia. Australia. There's more of South America I haven't seen yet, and so much even in North America I've never explored.

When we left Salvador, we continued southward to Argentina. On some trips we would make a stopover in Buenos Aires. Other times, like this particular journey, we didn't. We just kept going. The ship stopped several hundred miles north of the island and from there, we took a separate vessel and kept going south. Archie had been quiet for the majority of the trip. I noticed he had taken to drawing in his sketchbook to alleviate boredom and avoid pestering us with questions and concerns. A part of me had wanted to tell him to just trust Duncan as I had, but I knew saying such a thing wouldn't work with everyone.

The further south we went, the more I could sense the cold. The island we prepared on was almost barren. Its northern half was speckled with hardy conifers and inhabited only by migratory seabirds and seals. Permanent settlement would be impossible there. It's too rocky to farm and the weather, dictated by Antarctic winds, is awful for most of the year.

After docking the ship, we hiked up to the cabin where Duncan ordered us to double-check our supplies. Once Archie saw everything laid out, I got the impression that he had relaxed a little. Then again, we were all thousands of miles away from home. There was no turning back now.

We took a day to rest up before boarding our ship again and setting a course south to the Antarctic Peninsula. It didn't take very long for us to start seeing icebergs and broken sheets of ice floating toward us. I did my best to give Duncan a clear idea as to where to steer the ship and avoid the ice. In warm water it would have been a straightforward trip, but in that region it can take several hours to navigate around the ice. The place truly is a deathtrap.

Depending on the time of year, Antarctica can be completely engulfed in darkness. Sometimes we had to trek over hundreds of miles of pure ice before reaching the continent itself. Even I, who can survive a place like that with greater ease than my companions, found Antarctica to be a truly terrifying place. Perhaps it's because Antarctica is uninhabited and you can feel the oppressive loneliness. I can't imagine anyone, even the most devout introvert, would want to live there. Worse yet, imagine dying there alone.

We had several months to complete this, but we were cutting it close to the winter solstice for the southern hemisphere. We were projected to return to the ship by the end of June.

I had thought we would reach the Pole and go back before the weather got too bad. I was confident about that, and Duncan trusted me. If he trusted me, so did the others. That was how it had been for the last several years.

There are no paths or trails in Antarctica. We can't even rely on landmarks because they can change on a dime here, so we have map after map of latitude and longitude and scale measurements and calculations on how long it takes to walk a mile. The fact that we had been able to reach a certain point and make it back home is impressive.

The winds were fairly calm when we anchored the ship and loaded our sleds up with supplies. We walked single-file, tethered to each other so no one wandered off if they became disoriented, and each of us towed a sled. I always led in case we come across patches of thin ice. Duncan was behind me, followed by Tallor, Archie, and McIntyre.

There isn't much to describe with the Antarctic landscape. It's colorless, desolate, and the feeling that you're far away from civilization is ever-present. The sky was pale-gray and we could see faint rays of sunshine peering through cracks in the clouds. The snow was frozen beneath our boots.

I looked over my shoulder at the others. "Everyone alright back there?"

"All good, Jay! Keep going!" Duncan called back.

It was easy to become exhausted in this environment. We stopped walking after several hours to set up a pair of large tents—one for us and one for our supplies. After setting up a pair of firepits, we set up shifts so we could keep an eye on the weather and make sure the sleds didn't accidentally catch fire from a stray ember.

I took longer watches than the others. At the end of the third hour, Duncan approached me after leaving his sleeping bag. "How's it looking, Jay?" he asked.

"So far, it's been calm, and I'm not sure I like that," I replied. "It's always calm before bad weather."

"You think we should just head out now?"

"Frankly, yes. Give the others another two hours to rest and we'll start walking."

In the four years I had been traveling in Antarctica, my decisions were never made lightly. I've made some that could have gotten people killed, but somehow, everyone had managed to survive. I pinned it on luck.

That trip was where that supposed lucky streak broke. We had been hiking for around two weeks, and, as one can imagine, we were still thousands of miles away from our destination. Snow started falling gently on the beginning of the fifteenth day, and it didn't take long for it to get worse.

Duncan, Tallor, Archie, and McIntyre were completely reliant on me to get them through when the whiteout worsened, especially when we had to cross a bridge of ice floes over a steadily freezing sea. That was nothing new. All I had to do try to connect some of the floes together to form a bridge.

Magic doesn't mean perfection, and any mistake out there can get someone killed. I felt someone yank on the tether, and whirled around to see McIntyre falling off an ice floe that had shifted. Duncan let go of his sled to help him.

"Jay!" Duncan shouted.

I jogged over, narrowly avoiding falling into the water myself. Tallor held tightly onto the ropes to keep the rest of us from falling as the ice began shifting from our movement. Grabbing McIntyre's hand, I tried pulling him back onto the ice. He struggled to get back onto the floe.

"Don't flail!" I barked.

Duncan took one of the straps on McIntyre's backpack and pulled hard. Grunting, the two of us hauled him back onto the ice. "Get him on one of the sleds!" Duncan ordered. "Jay, get us off this damn sea!"

Wind whipped and howled around us as I led the team to the frozen shore. We immediately put the tents up and made a fire to start warming McIntyre. As soon as he had been pulled from the water, a thin layer of ice had formed over his entire body. Duncan broke the ice and roughly rubbed McIntyre's clothes together. "Get some dry clothes from his bag, Jay."

Nodding, I unhooked the straps on McIntyre's sled, searching frantically for a set of dry clothes.

"How the hell are we supposed to undress and redress him?" Archie asked. "He'll die as soon as his skin is exposed!"

"Relax," Duncan said. "Vern? Can you move anything?"

McIntyre wasn't very responsive. I could barely see his breath coming from his nose and mouth.

Tallor tossed another piece of kindling on the fire before kneeling by McIntyre. "Come on, old friend. I went through this last year. You'll be alright. Stay with us."

McIntyre opened his mouth, trying to respond. The most he could do was wrap his hand around Tallor's.

I tossed a set of McIntyre's clothes to Duncan and picked up a heavy bearskin blanket. "I'll keep this over him," I said.

From the corner of my eye, I saw Tallor had paled. "Don't bother," he murmured.

"What?"

"Don't bother. His hand... just went limp. I-I can't feel his pulse."

"That doesn't mean anything!" Duncan shouted. "Rub his body! Keep trying to get him warm! Do anything!"

Tallor looked defeated. I've never seen him give up on anything, nor have I seen him panic. All of a sudden, he looked torn over what to feel. He was talking partly to himself and partly to McIntyre as he rubbed his friend's arms and chest after we redressed him. "Stay with us! Stay with us, damn you!" Tallor slapped him, then grabbed McIntyre's head to shake him. "I'm not leaving you here! Wake up!"

I wasn't entirely sure what to feel, either. In the four years I had been with this team, we had never lost anyone. People have taken spills in the water, yes, but all were lucky enough to survive. Maybe I wasn't fast enough this time. Tallor could've easily been killed by me lowering the temperature of the water around him. Most people who hear the story even say that Tallor shouldn't have survived. I don't think I'll ever know why he got lucky but McIntyre didn't.

I had to step back from the scene when I stopped questioning what had happened and realized I wasn't going to see McIntyre ever again. I was in shock and disbelief, and everything I've heard about death being a part of life was banished from my mind. This wasn't old age. This was something that could have been prevented.

But could I have prevented it?

Tallor argued that we should turn back and go home, and I didn't blame him. Duncan wasn't sure what to do. Archie hadn't said a word since we buried McIntyre. I think it reawakened some of the trauma he felt from losing a team member in the Canadian Arctic. Things had been quiet aside from the wind after the makeshift funeral, and I needed to take a moment outside the tent. My strength was already sapped and all I could feel was a horrible knotting sensation in my stomach and a desire to cry. I thought of the little things about McIntyre, how he was quiet, thoughtful, very smart, and how he had welcomed me when I first joined the group. I was a little nervous around him and Tallor when I first met them, but beneath their strength was a sense of loyalty and gentleness.

"The South Pole isn't worth it now! Vern wanted to do this as much as any of us here. It's not right to continue without him," Tallor said.

Duncan was looking into the fire. "I think he'd want us to continue. At the very least, it'll honor his memory."

"What'll we do if something breaks down?" I asked.

"I'll take care of it," Duncan replied.

Tallor glared at both of us. "How can you seriously think about continuing?"

"It wouldn't be the first time. Remember Tilcott?"

"He wanted to continue after Avis died because all he cared about was getting to the Pole. Then he died along the way, and we never got to the Pole because you took command and ordered us to turn around. Tilcott brought his death upon himself!"

"I'm not Tilcott. What happened to McIntyre was an accident. Those are far too common down here." Duncan took a breath, looking at Tallor, Archie, and me. "If you all want to turn around, we will." His gaze settled on me. "Jay?"

"That depends on what the rest of you decide," I replied.

"Fine. Archie?"

Archie had been sitting in a corner of the tent, hugging his knees. He looked over at Duncan at the sound of his name. "What?" he said, nervously.

"Do you want to turn back, or keep going?"

"Doesn't matter."

Duncan glared at us. "I can't have two undecideds."

"Then I'm going back on my own." Tallor knelt to begin packing his sled.

"You're not going out there by yourself! Lyle, you knew from the start that this is a profession where people could die—"

"I know. I always felt I could keep that from happening. Now, I'm going back to the ship. If the rest of you want to continue, that's your call. I'll wait. If you're not back in three months, I'm going back to Argentina."

"I'll go with you. I don't want to stay." Archie sounded like he was going to cry.

"Have it your way, then." Duncan looked as though he didn't have any fight left in him. I knew he valued the opinions of his team members. Not once did he force anyone to do something they didn't want to do, unless it was a matter of life or death.

Given how dangerous it is down here, we weren't going to separate. We would turn back and go home. We gathered all of our supplies and belongings for the journey back to the ship and headed out once the winds lessened a bit.

It was truly heartbreaking how silent and distant we all became. I had never seen Tallor so distraught, but no one held it against him. He and McIntyre had been close. They worked together for years. They had a shared experience in World War I, though they served in different branches. They both knew how dangerous Antarctic exploration was, but it was something they both loved.

Duncan told us after we headed out that he would deliver the message to McIntyre's wife personally. I certainly didn't envy him taking on that task. It was something he had done many times before, and it never got easier. Mrs. McIntyre lived alone now that her two children were grown and on their own, but Duncan insisted on giving widows a decent sum of money to help them through.

I could tell Duncan felt responsible for McIntyre's death, as did I. I didn't understand why I had been able to save Tallor's life before but failed with McIntyre. Looking back on it, I think it was down to luck. Tallor got lucky. McIntyre didn't. Why? I don't know, but I've been racking my brain about it in the four years that have passed since.

None of us talked to each other in the days and weeks we spent walking through the hellish icy landscape. Eventually, Duncan spoke while we were hiking on a plateau. The sky was clear for once, and there were no clouds to be seen. It was quiet, and that made it all the more eerie.

"We should've waited until summer. This is my fault," Duncan said.

"This could have happened at any point in the year. You've mentioned that to me before," I replied. "This is nobody's fault."

Duncan fell silent again for a moment. "You saved Lyle last year. What happened?"

I was stunned at the question. "Sir?"

"I said, what happened, Jay? What changed this time around? You saved Lyle's life last year. Why couldn't you save Vern?"

"I don't know. I tried."

"Clearly, you didn't try hard enough."

I felt like I had been punched in the stomach with that statement. I understood Duncan was grieving, but to blame me? That I didn't understand. I looked over my shoulder at Tallor and Archie. Neither of them looked like they had heard, or they just didn't want to contribute. Suddenly, I wanted to hit my head against something. I wanted to go back in time and stop this from happening. I wanted to apologize to McIntyre. A tearing sensation overcame my chest and my eyes stung with tears.

I said nothing in defense of myself. To this day, I feel like it really was my fault he died.

"I'm sorry that happened."

I looked over at Halcomb after pulling myself out of my memories. A heavy feeling had filled my chest when I described McIntyre's death and the rift that formed between the team. As much as I wanted to continue the story, I knew I had to stop. It just... didn't feel healthy. "Don't be sorry," I said.

"It's hard not to feel sorry," Halcomb replied. "Even harder knowing McIntyre wasn't the only casualty."

I nodded, switching my gaze to the window. "Duncan died of hypothermia. He became... I guess you can say suicidal, and there was nothing I could do, no matter how many times I said it wasn't anybody's fault and that he needed to stop and rest with everyone else. I guess... I guess his loyalty and dedication to the people he was closest to was his downfall. Losing a friend was like losing a part of himself."

"You mentioned this wasn't the first time he had someone die on an expedition?"

"It wasn't. Sometimes I wonder if the guilt had been building up over the years and McIntyre was Duncan's breaking point. He also watched many people die in Europe. He did tell me once that he wondered why he survived." I found myself staring at the back of the seat in front of me, feeling sick. An intense cold feeling squeezed my insides. "Tallor froze to death in his sleep while I was on watch. I didn't know until I went back in the tent. The fire went out at some point. And Archie... Archie was swept under the ice when we crossed the Ross Sea. His grip went slack on the rope, and... I tried looking for him but I didn't find any trace of his body. There was no hope of me finding him alive."

Halcomb didn't say anything for a little while. He looked out the window as well, then looked back at me. "I can understand why you gave up exploration, then."

I nodded, feeling weak even though I was sitting. "All it took was one death to throw off everything and everyone. It was something to be expected, but our track record had given us all... a little too much confidence in our abilities. When I returned to the States, I immediately reported what happened. I was compensated financially and gave most of that away to the widows. Archie had no wife so I gave his share to his parents and sister. A few other explorers later told me that my team didn't make good choices that expedition, and I had to hold myself back from arguing. Outwardly I accepted it and moved on, but inside was a different story. One that I... don't want to go into right now."

"That's understandable. Honestly, I'm sorry for putting you through the memories, Mr. Loalin." Halcomb glanced out the window again. "We're approaching Washington anyway. If you feel up for it, perhaps we can continue this conversation at dinner."

Chapter 3

When we got off the plane in Washington, the first thing I noticed was the signs for recruitment and war bonds that adorned the airport. The last time I was there, the walls were covered in beautiful posters showing sights from around the world. Brochures had been replaced with military booklets and pamphlets on how to grow food at home and ads for scrap drives, carpooling, and saving gasoline for use overseas. The airport was empty save for soldiers and sailors. I've never seen an airport so quiet.

Halcomb and I left the airport to feel a gentle autumn breeze blowing through the city. I didn't say anything as I wasn't allowed to ask questions until we were in a more secure location. When we got in a taxicab to the hotel, I was glad that the sky was blue and only a few clouds dotted it. The sky had been a dull shade of gray on the day Duncan and I met Archie.

We arrived at a very grand-looking building stretching around the block, not too far from several of the government buildings. Chiseled into the concrete walkway above the stairs was "The Willard." As we headed into a space closed on three sides by the walls of the hotel, Halcomb guided me toward a covered lobby entrance. A pair of sailors walked out of the doors, and one of them was kind enough to hold the doors for us.

We didn't say another word to each other until we entered one of the rooms. As much as I didn't think Halcomb needed to spend the money on a suite, it was nice. The bed was enormous and covered with pillows. The carpet was patterned in red and gold. In the center of the room was a small round table with a large glass vase of white roses. I set my suitcase by the bed before approaching the table. Laurel had always liked roses—my ice roses in particular. It was tempting to make one and put it in the vase, but a part of me was worried about the cold meltwater killing the roses prematurely.

Halcomb was searching every crevice on the room, and I watched him in confusion until he finished. He gave me a nervous smile. "Looking for bugs. Listening devices and that sort of thing. Alright. As you recall, we're going to be training you to go into Europe and put an end to *Standartenführer* Wahler's experiments. That makes the mission twofold: stop the experiments by destroying his facilities, and assassinate Wahler himself."

"I take it you'll be training me with weapons, then?"

"Yes. Some hand-to-hand fighting, the use of rifles, handguns, and so on. Have you ever used a rifle or handgun before?"

"Never had the chance. Plus—" I held up my hands, "I... practically am a weapon. I'm not banned from using my powers, am I?"

"No, not at all. In fact, Colonel Stafford would like you to do a demonstration so we know what we're up against in case Wahler has been at all successful."

I nodded. "I'll do my best." When it grew quiet, I squeezed my hands together nervously. "I won't deny that this is very exciting, but terrifying at the same time."

"I've only been recruiting for a few months, but you're the first person I've recruited who really jumped at the opportunity. If you're in it for the adventure, I don't blame you, but don't let that go to your head. This is going to be extremely dangerous. That's why you're not going alone."

"I see. Who'll be going with me?"

"That'll be determined during training. We want someone you can work with easily."

I took that as I would be meeting and interacting with a lot of people over the next several days. Much like this mission, I was both excited and nervous, but mostly the latter.

Halcomb knocked on my door at around eight-thirty the next morning. We went to breakfast together and much like yesterday, we hardly said a word to each other for secrecy. At least I knew all my questions would be answered when we went to "school."

"School" was Halcomb's term for the spy training camp we'd be going to. We waited at a street corner for an unassuming black automobile. The driver was a young man in regular clothes and sunglasses, but, as Halcomb told me, he was the man who picked up recruits from anywhere in DC, Maryland, and Virginia to take them to "school." He had two handguns and a shotgun hidden in the car for his own protection.

The driver, whose name was Massey, took us out of the city and down a long, winding country road. Some trees had already started turning their vibrant autumn colors, but most were still holding onto their summer green. We passed by farm fields that were looking ready for harvest and eventually turned onto a road surrounded by pumpkin fields. At the beginning of the road was a sign reading "Warning: Trespassers Will Be Shot." Sitting on a hill was a massive manor, overlooking part of Washington in the distance. The manor had a wraparound porch with swings and Adirondack chairs and small tables. A pair of women sat at one of the tables drinking lemonade. Behind the manor was a long shooting range, and I saw three men standing at a table examining a rifle.

Massey drove us into a large garage at the end of the road. When he took off his sunglasses, I saw he had the burgundy eyes of a fire-variant. "Your stop, gentlemen," he said.

"Thank you," Halcomb replied, tipping his hat. After we stepped out of the vehicle, he turned to me. "All of your questions will be answered here. This is a completely secure location. First, I'll take you to meet the colonel."

We walked up the steps of the manor. Halcomb knocked on the door, and a young woman answered. "Lester Halcomb, yes?"

"Yes. With Mr. Jay Loalin."

The woman stepped aside for us. As I took off my coat, I looked around at the entryway. Above us was a winding staircase. In front of us was a doorway to the living room. On our right was a hallway to the kitchen and dining room. Everything was neat, clean, and at first glance no one would think the place was housing a training camp for spies. I wondered if it was really a farm or if that was just a disguise. Those pumpkins did look healthy and ready to be picked.

From the corner of my eye, I saw an older man in a blue-gray sweater and khaki pants walking up to us. He smiled and took Halcomb's hand in a firm grasp. "Good to see you, Lester, and I see you brought our newest agent." The man held out his hand to me. "Jay Loalin, welcome to the OSS."

"Thank you, sir," I said, taking his hand. "You are—"

"Colonel Dayton Stafford. I'm head of this operation."

"This is fascinating, to say the least. I though the Conjurus weren't going to be involved at all."

"Not all of you think so. This particular branch was started in cooperation with Conjurus who want to help fight. Come, we'll talk in the study."

Stafford led us up the stairs and down a hall to a room with a fireplace. In front of the fireplace were four chairs surrounding a small round table. On the table was a bottle of brandy, a tea kettle, and three glasses of pumpkin-chocolate milkshakes, a staple autumn treat among Conjurus. Once we were seated and took our beverage of choice, Stafford focused his gaze on me. "What all did Lester tell you about the Wahler mission?"

"He showed me those awful pictures from Poland, mentioned that this is largely due to the Nazis not being prepared for a lengthy stay in Russian winters without proper equipment and oil, and that the goal is for Wahler's facilities to be destroyed and him to be killed," I replied.

"So, the basics. Good." Stafford took a sip of his tea. "I think we'll start with what we know about Wahler. As you might know, he was present when your father killed an entire platoon of German soldiers in 1918. After the war he started studying the Conjurus and their abilities. That itself is harmless, but then he joined the SS. We have pictures-" Stafford opened an album on the table next to the tea kettle, "of him alongside Reinhard Heydrich and Heinrich Himmler, who has an obsession with pagan rituals and witchcraft."

"The Conjurus and witches have been fighting for years," I said. "I would've thought the Nazis would oppose his work."

"They did originally, but Himmler became interested in the fact that Conjurus are born with their abilities. Witches have to learn theirs. Imagine an army where you can spend less time training and more time fighting. It's efficient and terrifying, especially when that army controls elements of nature. That led to the creation of a new branch of the SS, called the *Zauberei-Abteilung*, or 'sorcery division'. Wahler's primary project, codenamed White Raven, wasn't given much attention until the Germans started experiencing massive defeats in the Soviet Union. With them pushed back from Moscow and being pounded outside Stalingrad, the Germans are frantically searching for a solution. That's where Wahler's work is coming in."

"Other than dissections, has he accomplished anything?"

"We don't know. Most intelligence we've gathered says he's created a lubricant out of ice-variant blood that keeps tank parts from freezing, but that hasn't been proven. I don't even know if that's possible."

"Witches have been harvesting the blood and organs of Conjurus for potions for over a thousand years. I wouldn't be surprised if—"

"Wahler's a warlock?"

"It's possible. It makes him a lot more dangerous."

"Why wouldn't he just create a spell that makes tanks and vehicles less susceptible to cold? Or—and this is horrifying to think about—something that makes *troops* less susceptible to the weather?"

"The effects of a spell typically aren't permanent and Wahler can't go around applying the spell to every tank in the German army. A lubricant or potion would be able to be distributed more efficiently. Using a potion on humans carries a lot more risk. Plus, we don't know if Wahler actually is a warlock."

"I think that's something we need to find out." Stafford set his cup down and unfurled a large map of Europe and North Africa that had been propped up against a table leg. "We'll be sending you to North Africa, where you'll meet up with a man who's been trying to escape from service in the German army for the last year or so. His name is Lieutenant Friedrich Altschul, but he's been going by the codename 'Winter' when in contact with us. He claims to have knowledge on Wahler that'll help you, but he won't give you that information unless he's guaranteed safe passage out of North Africa. A submarine will be waiting on the coast of North Africa to take you to Italy and bring Altschul back here to the States when he gives you the information you need. That sub won't stay in place, though. You'll have one week to make contact with Altschul and get him out of there. Once you're in Italy, there's a woman just outside of Genoa who'll help you get into Germany," Stafford pulled out a photograph of an unassuming-looking young woman with braided brown hair and chestnut eyes. She was holding a basket of tomatoes and her hands, face, and clothing were covered in dirt. "This is Elvira Cristaldi. Her family members are all contacts with us. We'll give you pictures to study so you can easily identify them. Her father is in Mussolini's inner circle and she has two brothers fighting in Libya. Her mother passed away several years ago, so she runs the farm almost entirely on her own. Her uncle helps out a few days a week, and I wouldn't advise you go while he's there. He only goes on Wednesdays and Fridays. She will ask you a question to determine who you are, and that question is 'Have you come to stay for dinner?' You have to answer, 'I'll have the schnitzel, please.' Memorize that."

I nodded. "What's our escape route?"

"Switzerland. There's an OSS office in Bern."

"Anything else I should know?"

"Not at the moment. In fact, there's something I'd like you to show us. "Lester told you we'd like to see a demonstration of what you're capable of, right?" Stafford queried.

I nodded. "Whenever you're ready."

Stafford took me to a different part of the range where he was joined by several other military officers and operatives, who sat in fold-out chairs in the grass. Several targets had been set up several yards away, crudely shaped like people. I turned to face the men and suddenly felt my words freeze. I've never done a presentation before.

"You alright, Jay?" asked Stafford.

"Yeah. Just... I have no idea where to start, sir." I bit my tongue, thinking hard. "Well, I guess I can start with the difference between the terms 'ice-variant' and 'cryomancer.' There is no difference in meaning, but if you hear someone exclusively use the word 'cryomancer,' it's almost a guarantee that person is a witch or warlock. There are many different types of Conjurus, the most common being ice, fire, and lightning. Less common types are water and wind. The easiest way to tell a Conjurus from a witch is that we don't use wands. We don't make potions. We can't cast spells, and we can't set curses on people. We also look a little different. Witches and warlocks look like ordinary people.

"Each variant has little things that make them stand out. Ice-variants, for example, are much, much paler than most Magicless. When exposed to the sun for long amounts of time, we become an almost translucent white color, like snow. The same can happen in extreme cold. Most of us have blue eyes, though silver and violet are a frequent occurrence."

A young captain raised his hand. "Someone mentioned to me yesterday that there are some Conjurus who use wands."

"There are. It's incredibly rare, though. Conjurus who have difficulties in honing their abilities are given specially-made wands to assist them. It's almost like a cane or a false limb for a Magicless." I looked over my shoulder at the targets. A gray blanket was beginning to encroach on the clear blue sky. "I think it goes without saying that our magic is dangerous. While I can do harmless things like this—" I opened my palm, feeling the cold mist before an ice rose appeared in my hand, "I can also do this." Holding the rose, I turned to the targets, and as soon as I raised my index finger, an icicle shot at one of the targets, fast as a bullet. The sharp end of the icicle was sticking out of the back. Bits of hay were jutting out with it. "I've just killed a man."

I also showed them hailstones, which can crack someone's skull, chips of ice that could embed in someone's skin, and how I can form a solid block of ice around someone's head, as well as defensive moves like walls and shields.

"Are you capable of doing what your father did in France?" someone asked.

I shook my head. "It's a move only done in death. It's an expulsion of all the magical energy a Conjurus possesses. No one's ever been recorded surviving doing this. I don't think it's possible. Is it something to expect? Yes. My best advice to counter it? Run. Run as far away as possible."

It began raining shortly after my demonstration ended, so everyone was ordered into the manor to wait out the weather. Halcomb was ready to take me back into Washington for the night, so I went into one of the downstairs studies while he went out to the garage with Massey to put the roof up on the automobile.

As I absentmindedly perused the books on the shelf, I heard someone whistling behind me and then a cheery voice called, "Well, look at this! Someone Colonel Stafford's failed to introduce me to?"

I turned to see a pale-blue, translucent figure standing in the doorway. He was dressed in a nice suit, with a pocket watch, hat, and a witch's staff transformed into a cane. The stone usually present at the top of the staff had been removed and replaced with a bronze pumpkin, but the engravings below remained. I smiled at the ghostly man. "My apologies. Jay Loalin, Stafford's newest recruit."

"And I—" the ghost tipped his hat, "am Phineas Calmont, guardian of this manor."

Guardian ghosts are, in simplest terms, dead Conjurus whose unfinished business is protecting a specific location, usually a home. By extent, they protect the occupants as well. Phineas went on to tell me that he had been guarding this manor for almost eighty years after he had been killed by a stray bullet during a Civil War battle while getting his horses into their stable.

"Since then, no one's moved in here. The claims that this place is haunted have kept many people away. Such a shame." Phineas looked down at the floor. "It has been terribly lonely here, but I keep my pumpkins tended to in the fall and people seem to love them."

"How do they know they can pick the pumpkins?" I asked.

"Why, I put up a 'free pumpkins' sign! And then they tell their friends and family and then they come back every single year. Only a few, though. Some have claimed the pumpkins are just as haunted as the house."

"I have to ask, how did you and Stafford meet?"

"Have you met the young lady who answers the door?"

I shook my head. "She greeted me when we arrived, but I wasn't formally introduced."

"That's Robyn Marrow. She's one of the few who comes here every year for pumpkins, and she knows about me. I don't know how she got involved with the OSS but I know Stafford values her encrypting and typing skills. Anyway, he was looking for a local place to train people, and she told him about my manor. For the first time in many years, I'm not so alone anymore."

"It was very kind of you to do this, sir. I just hope none of us ever seem like we're intruding."

"Oh, that's utter nonsense. Please, look around, read something, have a seat. I've been keeping everything in perfect condition in case someone dropped by, and I enjoy the company."

From the corner of my eye, I saw Halcomb peer into the room. "Mr. Loalin? We're ready."

Nodding, I turned back to Phineas. "Sorry. I have to leave for the night. It was nice meeting you, sir."

"And very nice meeting you, young man. Have a wonderful evening."

I walked over to Halcomb when Phineas vanished. "I certainly wasn't expecting any of this when I agreed to join," I said. "Our representatives don't want us involved in the war."

"Many of your people feel as you do. There've been meetings between Conjurus and the War Department since the day after Pearl Harbor, and now we have training camps being set up all across the country."

"I wish I had known about this sooner."

Rain was pouring down as we went out to the garage. Massey smiled at us as we got in the car, but I found myself unable to smile back. I haven't been around such supportive people since Antarctica. No one bombarded me with questions about my father. Hell, my father was the reason this had to be put together in secret. I just hoped this mission didn't end in disaster like Antarctica.

Every day over the course of the next several weeks was spent training me in learning how to cover my tracks, send coded messages, how the Germans thought and acted, the structure of the German military, what to look out for in Europe and North Africa, and so on and so forth.

It was exciting enough to where I didn't think of home much, but training wasn't twenty-four hours a day or seven days a week. Sundays were our days off, but we could still go to the manor to chat with Stafford or Phineas or any of the others who were permanently staffed there. It was my second Sunday there when a sense of homesickness hit me.

In hindsight, it was funny. I've been away from New York before, on my trips to Antarctica. My first trip was hard, but it became easier afterward. Why should I feel this way when I've traveled many times before?

I guess it was because I couldn't tell my family and Laurel the truth. Something could happen to me and they wouldn't know where I was. I could send letters as long as I was in the States, but I couldn't say anything about where I was or what I was doing. All I could say was that I was alright.

There was no sense in dwelling on it. It helped that I wasn't alone. Everyone at the manor was sworn to secrecy. Some had it more difficult than others. Stafford couldn't tell his wife what he was doing. Robyn knew everyone in the nearby town, and she told me it was almost painful not to talk to anyone whenever she went home.

I had assumed Halcomb had friends and family. He never spoke about home or loved ones in the weeks I had known him, and it made me curious what he had left behind. That Sunday, I found him behind the garage, sitting on one of the larger pumpkins and looking down the hill that offered a distant view of Washington. He was toying with his pocket watch while smoking a cigarette.

"Would you mind company?" I asked.

Startled, Halcomb turned to face me, then went back to looking down the hill. "Well... sure, you can join me."

Sitting on another pumpkin, I gazed at Washington for a few minutes before speaking again. "I know we've talked a lot over the last couple of weeks, but I don't think you've told me about who you've had to leave behind for this job."

Halcomb didn't make eye contact with me. "Considering you told me about what happened in Antarctica, I guess it's only fair I tell you about me."

I turned to face him, sensing he needed someone to listen to him.

"I guess you think I'm a very smart man, don't you?"

"I do."

"Would you believe me if I said I didn't learn to read until I was eighteen, or that I'd been homeless for a few years?"

"Just looking at you, no."

"Good. I don't want anyone getting that impression from me."

"What happened?"

"Like you, my father died in World War I. I wasn't even a year old. That left my mother with five children and a pig farm to take care of. She was an easily stressed woman and very crude. She drank a lot too. None of us were taught how to read at home. Doing poorly in school became commonplace. My oldest brother, Weldon, was sent to the Army. He only came home once after that. He's made friends and he met his wife when he was stationed in South Carolina. My sister, Millie, wound up being sent away to a school for girls. She didn't tell anyone where she came from because she was afraid of being made fun of, and now... now she's a secretary in Chicago and happily married. I was next." Halcomb suddenly looked lost. "When I went to be examined for the Army, I couldn't continue because I was underweight. My mother didn't even let me back in the house when I returned. She threw all my belongings onto the porch and told me to get lost."

"I'm sorry."

"Don't be. I figured leaving would be good for me. I hitchhiked on a train to Washington, and that was a journey I won't forget anytime soon. I didn't go right to Washington. The train stopped in several towns and cities along the way, and I just had to get off and see them all. That spring and summer were wonderful. I wasn't thinking about fall and winter when I got to Washington, and I hardly had the money for a hotel room." Halcomb's smile faded. "It was nice to see people and places for a few months, but reality hit me hard when the first leaves fell. I managed to get a job as a store clerk. The owner was nice to me, but I didn't want him to know I was living behind the store at night.

"I was embarrassed when he found out I was not only illiterate, but living behind the store as well. I was terrified of being fired, but instead he sent me to a private tutor. Long story short, I was taught how to read, write, and the tutor was kind enough to show me how to use a typewriter. Being in Washington, it was fairly easy to get a job in one of the government buildings. Granted, I can't tell you some of the papers I worked on when things started getting heated in Europe and Asia, but it did lead me here."

"What made you want to work with people like me, though?"

"That was purely chance. When Pearl Harbor was bombed, I was already working in the War Department so I volunteered to go over to the OSS when it was formed six months later. It's funny because when I walked into my new office, one of my superiors was in there with a fire-variant talking about the problems they've been having with their representatives and how he was sent on behalf of Conjurus who want to fight. I probably shouldn't have walked in on that conversation, but I don't regret doing so. Long story short, I was assigned to recruit Conjurus in major cities for various missions, including the one you're going on."

I nodded as Halcomb finished his story. "So I take it you don't have anyone you're missing or that you can't discuss your work with?"

"I'm in contact with my older brother and sister. Weldon has a vague idea, but there's only so much he can know due to his rank, and Millie can't know anything. Her husband's been drafted, though, I know that. I do miss them, but I don't see them often enough for it to be painful."

"And you don't have a wife?"

"No. Not yet, anyway." Halcomb took a draw on his cigarette and looked up at the clear sky where a couple of clouds could be seen in the distance. "I want someone I can be honest with, and unashamed to tell them about where I came from and what I had to do to get where I am now."

"I think the right person will come along when you're not looking," I said. "I probably should've told a friend back home how I feel before I came here, just in case... something happens to me and I don't come back."

"You could tell her in a letter."

I shook my head. "I'd rather tell her in person."

A slight grin crossed Halcomb's face. "I guess we'll have to make sure you come back alive, then."

I pondered writing to Laurel that night, but decided against it. It felt cheap to just tell her I'd like to pursue something greater than friendship in a letter, and the last thing I want is for something to happen and the only "I love you" Laurel ever got from me to be on a piece of paper.

Despite that, I still wrote something. I'd rather have her know than not, but I didn't want that letter delivered unless I died overseas. In the morning I gave the letter to Stafford, explaining my line of thinking and request. He smiled and told me he'd send it to the War Department to send along with any telegrams if I didn't make it back. I just hoped and prayed that letter would never have to be sent.

Along with weapons training, I was given a crash course on German and Italian by two native speakers who fled their countries before the war started. While I had a slim chance at passing as Italian, I was told by my tutor that I could certainly pass as German—most if not all ice-variants can.

"Has it been decided who'll be accompanying me?" I asked.

Stafford pointed in Halcomb's direction. He was sitting at a window facing one of the pumpkin fields with a drink. "I've noticed you and Lester bonding quite a bit over the last few weeks. He's already trained, speaks German almost fluently, and he can speak some conversational Arabic in case you need help from the locals in North Africa."

"I thought he was a recruiter."

"If we need him to be an agent, he can be one. Besides, he volunteered."

I glanced over at Halcomb. Frankly, I couldn't think of anyone else I'd want to accompany me to Europe. "I'm sure we'll work well together," I said. "Thank you."

When Stafford left the room, I walked over to Halcomb. "You volunteered? Why?"

"Why not? Do I have to have a specific reason?" asked Halcomb. "Truthfully, it's because I like you. Most Conjurus I've recruited don't speak to me after they've begun training. You're... different."

"Most of them probably haven't lost whole teams in Antarctica. Or have a parent that's responsible for getting us banned from the draft."

"No, but that's not what makes you different. It was your willingness to talk about it, and you got me to tell you what happened to me."

"All I did was ask. You didn't hesitate or fight me on it."

"I probably would have if you didn't trust me to tell me about Antarctica." Halcomb gave me a slight smile. "We both have things we don't want other people to know about, so it's nice to have someone to trust."

"That's true, I guess. But you know how dangerous this is, right? We're going into the heart of Hitler's Germany. Alone."

"I know, but no one else is going to volunteer to do this mission."

"And it's my father's fault Wahler's doing this."

Halcomb shook his head. "No, it's not. Don't ever say that."

"Well, would this have happened if my father hadn't killed every German soldier in front of him?"

"That's not something any of us will ever know, but you were two years old. You had nothing to do with what happened. It's not his fault and it's certainly not yours." Halcomb touched my shoulder. "Don't feel obliged to do this because of your father."

"That's not a feeling I can help. I'm sorry."

"It's not the only reason you're doing this, is it?"

"No."

"Good. I don't want you to feel guilty."

"I won't feel that way when we complete the mission." I looked Halcomb in the eye. "When are we heading out?"

Within a few days, Halcomb and I boarded a Navy destroyer guarding a convoy en route to Gibraltar. It would take some time to actually cross the Atlantic, and it was infested with U-boats, but nothing could stop me from feeling excited over the fact that I was achieving my dream of crossing the great Atlantic Ocean.

I watched the sea surround us as we left Chesapeake Bay and I found myself thinking back to when I was sailing down to South America with Duncan and the rest of the explorers. I would gaze at the Atlantic for hours, wondering about what lay across it. Of course, I knew what lay across it: Europe with its rich history, and Africa with its beautiful landscapes, but it's one thing to read about and see the paintings and photographs and another to see it for yourself. I couldn't believe I was finally going.

Halcomb wasn't used to sea travel. Several hours after we set sail, I found him throwing up over the side of the ship. I felt bad, especially since I had been the same way on my first voyage to Antarctica, and as I approached him, he slowly lowered himself to the deck. His face was a pale-green color and he was shivering from being so violently ill.

"I probably should have mentioned I've never been on a ship before," he said.

"It won't make a difference," I replied. "You'll get used to it in time."

We went below deck to our quarters so Halcomb could rest. It was a very small room, and the beds were only a few feet away from each other. Little compartments for our personal belongings were above and below the beds, and the captain firmly instructed us to lock our compartments so things didn't fly out if we hit a rough patch on the water. I became nervous we would every time I unlocked one of my compartments, and quickly closed and locked mine when I pulled a book out.

"You know, if I had known I'd react like this, I wouldn't have come." Halcomb stared up at the bottom of his compartment.

"No, I think you'd still come," I said.

"I'd bring a bottle of pills and some whiskey to put me out until we get there."

"I think that would just make you sicker. Besides, we probably shouldn't drink during this... little adventure."

"How about on the way back when it's over?"

"I'd rather not return to Stafford with you drunk out of your head."

Halcomb smiled. "I can appreciate you being the voice of sense."

"Well, that's the opposite of what my uncle thinks I am right now," I sighed.

"Ah. I remember you telling me what he said. I don't think your relationship with him is done for. I'd be willing to bet he probably misses you."

"He hasn't responded to any of my letters. Not sure what to make of that."

"I wouldn't jump to any conclusions until you see him again. From what you've told me about him, it sounds like he'll forgive you."

"If I survive. He accused me of striving too hard to be like my father, and maybe he's right."

"Why's that any of his concern, though?"

"I think it's mainly because my father died in the process of trying to be a hero. He doesn't want me throwing my life away."

"I don't think you're throwing your life away by doing this. There's a difference between throwing your life away for no reason and actually being a hero."

"Do you think that's what I'll become after this mission?"

"I don't know. That's up to you."

Chapter 4

I was so excited as we drew nearer to the Old World that it was hard to get any sleep. But sleep would have been difficult even if not for the excitement because of the constant threat of U-boats. In the light of a full moon, shadows and silhouettes of ships moved across the horizon. It would be easy to see something out of the ordinary breaking the light.

All was silent until a cargo ship exploded on our port side. I had been on the deck, far away from the action on the bridge. Racing over to the railing, I saw the ship tilting into the water, flames and black smoke billowing upward. I could see several dozen men in the water, along with several lifeboats. Our escorts were maneuvering into position to try to find the attacking U-boat and respond with depth charges. I was told to go below deck to my quarters, and Halcomb was lying awake when I came in. "What's going on?" he asked.

"Looks like a submarine torpedoed one of the cargo ships. They're getting the survivors onboard right now."

Halcomb was silent for a moment. "I'd hoped this trip would go without a hitch."

"Same here. I just hope everyone on that ship got out safely."

We had several more run-ins with U-boats over the next couple of nights, but none were as destructive as the night of the full moon, thankfully. They tended to flee once they realized the cargo ships weren't entirely defenseless. One morning, I awoke before Halcomb and went to the mess hall to grab a cup of coffee. I went onto the deck to watch the sunrise, and what I saw made me wish I had brought a camera.

Standing tall coming up in front of us, was an enormous rock, jutting up from the land. I've seen many pictures of the Rock of Gibraltar, but to see it in person was a completely new experience. It was like the first time I saw the ice sheets of Antarctica. Below the Rock, I could see Royal Navy vessels and British soldiers and sailors going about their duties, and again I found myself curious as to how the British Conjurus were faring.

I had plenty of time to take the sights in as the convoy pulled into the harbor, but when the ship stopped completely, I knew that was when Halcomb and I had to get to work.

We had to stay in Gibraltar for a few days while German *Afrika Korps* uniforms and fake assignment papers were procured for us. We couldn't discuss too much of our mission with the British, despite our alliance, but that didn't mean we couldn't interact with them. I was curious about them, and in the afternoon I joined a squad for lunch in the mess hall. They looked up at me when I walked over. Their sergeant, a skinny man with short, messily combed blond hair and bright green eyes, lit his cigarette while looking me in the eye. "Do you need something, Yank?"

I shook my head. "Not particularly. Not much I can talk about, if you want me to be honest."

"I see. You're ice Conjurus, right?"

"Yes. How did you know?"

"You're not exactly hard to spot."

I shrugged, figuring he was correct. My Magicless coworkers had never said anything about me being a Conjurus.

The sergeant took a draw on his cigarette. "What's your name, mate?"

I glanced at him. "It's Jay." I hesitated on my last name, not sure if the sergeant would be familiar with who my father was. He was Magicless. There was no way he knew. "Jay Loalin."

"Name's Josiah Prisk." He pulled out his carton of cigarettes. "You smoke?"

"No, thank you."

Nodding, Prisk put the carton back in his pocket. "Now, I know I'm not allowed to ask what you and your companion are doing here, but can I give you some advice about trekking through North Africa if that's where you're headed?"

I nodded. "Anything."

"The desert, not Jerry, is your number one enemy. I imagine someone like you is particularly sensitive to the heat."

I gave him another nod, and another question came to mind. "Have you fought the *Afrika Korps*?"

"Several times over the last several months. We'll be going back in a week or so."

"What can you tell me about how they operate?"

Prisk snorted. "All I can tell you is that they're led by a very crafty bastard with a knack for surprise attacks and poor sense of self-preservation." He gestured to the soldier next to him. "Amerton's nearly shot him. Hey—"

Prisk nudged Amerton's shoulder, "tell Mr. Loalin about how you almost shot Rommel."

Amerton took a sip of his tea, turning to face me and Prisk. "Do I have to tell this story every time you meet someone new? It's bad enough Wraight makes me tell that story to every woman he picks up on leave."

"I'm genuinely curious to hear what happened now," I said.

Amerton rolled his eyes. "Alright." He took a large bite from his bread. "I was camped with my spotter by a rock during a skirmish near the Egypt-Libya border. Late in the afternoon, it was very hot, hazy, and with the tank and artillery fire, it was very smoky and hard to get a shot off. Suddenly, this open-top vehicle came flying toward our lines. I thought it was one of ours—"

"It may have been one of ours originally," one of the other soldiers said. "The Germans keep picking our stuff up off the battlefield afterwards, bloody scavengers."

"Right. Anyway, I looked through the scope of my rifle, thinking I was going to see one of our officers inside. Instead, my sights were centered on the head of Rommel himself. I thought, 'This is perfect. We can end this campaign right here.' I don't know what he was thinking getting so close to the frontlines. He was either insane or really fucking lost. Anyway, I had the perfect shot lined up, but Rommel's driver must've realized what was going on and swerved the vehicle to go back behind their own lines. My bullet was probably several centimeters away from Rommel's head and I swear he looked in my direction as they were driving away."

"And you didn't take another shot at him?" I asked.

"I emptied the magazine trying to hit him. Hit the car, though." Amerton shook his head. "Spent the rest of the day cursing myself because I could've taken out one of Germany's best generals and I fucking missed."

"That's quite a story," I said.

"You're magic. You might have better luck killing him."

I shook my head. "That's not my mission, unfortunately."

"Think of it as a little detour. I'm sure Churchill will shake your hand over it."

"If such a mission comes up in the future, perhaps I'll take it. For now, I have to stick to the task at hand."

"Whatever it is you're doing, I wish you luck."

"Thank you."

Halcomb and I were basically guests in the base that night. We had some privileges that many of the troops there didn't have, but neither of us wanted to flaunt them in front of the British.

I did go up onto the Rock around sunset. It was hard to resist, to be honest. The colors of the sky reflecting on the sea, the astounding view of Morocco, and the ships on the water made a view I knew I would never forget. I couldn't believe I was there, sitting on a famous landmark, and gazing at another continent. It reminded me of seeing Antarctica for the first time. The wonder and excitement were light and heavy feelings at the same time. There was nothing else I could think of other than wanting to see every piece of it.

But back in Antarctica, I still had Duncan. I wasn't expecting to lose the people I was closest to because of an expedition gone wrong, and that's what I was afraid of now. It's why I had wanted to go on this mission alone in the first place.

I had thought I was alone on the Rock until I heard the soft *click* of a lighter. Turning around, I saw Prisk standing behind me. He made eye contact with me and smiled faintly. "Mr. Loalin."

"Sergeant," I replied.

"Mind if I join you?"

I shook my head.

Sitting next to me, Prisk looked around. "Lovely view, isn't it?"

I nodded.

"Not very talkative tonight, are you?" Prisk studied my face. "You seem troubled."

"Just thinking." I sighed. "I'm a former explorer. Antarctica-"

"I know."

I raised an eyebrow. "You know? Did Halcomb tell you?"

"No. Your name. I remember an article from a newspaper a few years ago about what happened in Antarctica. Your team was trying to get to the South Pole, correct?"

I nodded.

"You were the only survivor."

I didn't respond. I found myself squeezing my fists and trying not to cry.

"I didn't want to say anything in front of the others. Even now, I can see it upsets you." Prisk looked ahead, putting his cigarette back in his mouth.

A second later, he took a breath, taking the cigarette out and blowing smoke into the breeze. "I take it you were close to your team?"

Again, I didn't respond. Unclenching my fists, I said, "I was the only one who could survive in those conditions, but I couldn't save any of them."

"Why blame yourself, Loalin?"

"Duncan told me when we tried returning to our ship that I didn't try hard enough, and for the last several years, I've believed that. I know he was grieving for McIntyre, but... it still felt true. I've saved them from disaster before, why couldn't I do it then?"

"Do you think if Duncan survived, he would still mean what he told you?"

"I don't know."

"I don't think he would." Prisk took on a distant look. "I've yelled at my men whenever we experience a loss in combat, especially if someone gets killed. Loss sets off a powder keg of emotions that... shouldn't be unleashed on anyone." He drew up his knees, looking at the ground. "I've said and done things I regret whenever I grieve. When it blows over, I realize what I've done, apologize, and go back to my day."

"It can't be that easy. It took me almost a year to get over what happened."

"When you're a soldier, you have to get over things quickly, or else more people will be killed by your mistakes. The task at hand is your first priority. Your emotions shouldn't even be a factor. That's what makes it hard. You can't just turn off how you feel. Some people can, but... for others, it's impossible." Prisk glanced at me. "Kinda surprises me that you wound up in the military. Being a soldier isn't exactly a job that accommodates your emotions."

"My reasons for being here would make a lot of sense if I could tell you."

"I see. I won't force you to say anything else. We could both get in trouble."

Darkness shrouded the Mediterranean not too long after the conversation ended. It didn't come as a surprise that the entire territory was under a blackout curfew, save for the tunnels inside the Rock. Prisk stood up after finishing his cigarette, and offered me his hand. "I'm heading back in. Maybe you'd like to join us for a few rounds of Oh Hell before we hit the hay?"

"Sure." I followed Prisk back down into the base. My thoughts still dwelled on Antarctica and my fears of losing Halcomb on the mission, and although I was glad Prisk and his unit weren't accompanying us, I was still worried that this could be the last time I would ever see them. With that in mind, I treasured my time in Gibraltar—despite being utterly destroyed in Oh Hell. Then again, I was better than Halcomb, who spent most of his time sabotaging everyone else and nearly got punched in the jaw by Amerton.

When we finally got the uniforms and papers, our plan was simply to board a cargo vessel and sail to Tripoli with papers stating we were replacement troops for men who had been sent back to Germany while sick. Admittedly, it was hard saying goodbye to Prisk and his soldiers. I wasn't even sure if I wanted to say that we would see each other again soon, because that wasn't a given in war.

Somehow, Prisk could sense that was my reason for hesitation. "You'll see us again, mate," he said.

I bit my lip. "That's no guarantee, though."

"Oh, I know, but why go through life not making any friends just because you're afraid we could all be gone the next day? Seeing your friends again is something worth fighting for."

He had a point, there. "Thanks," I said. "Hopefully, we'll see each other again soon."

"I think we will." Prisk turned to head back inside the base, then paused to look over his shoulder. "One more thing, Loalin, if you see Rommel, tell him we said 'hello' and we'll get him next time we meet."

I highly doubted I was actually going to see Rommel in person. "I'll try," I replied.

Halcomb was adjusting the collar of his new uniform next to me. He waited until the British left before saying, "You didn't tell them everything we're doing, did you?"

"No. I'm not allowed to."

"Good." Halcomb was quiet for a moment. "They seem like nice people. I'm glad you made friends with them."

"I'm surprised you didn't even try."

"In all honesty, I have nothing to say, and I don't want to risk anything about our mission slipping out."

I raised an eyebrow. "They're our allies."

"Yeah? That doesn't mean there aren't Germans hiding among them. Plus, you were told not to tell your family, even though you trust them."

"I know that, but that doesn't mean we can't talk to them."

"In case you haven't noticed, Jay, I'm not going to go around trusting everyone I meet. You should keep that in mind."

I opened my mouth to argue, but stopped. It wasn't worth it.

We boarded the ship, and Halcomb admitted to having not eaten breakfast to avoid throwing up over the side. The Mediterranean was calm that day, but that still didn't stop Halcomb from feeling ill if he started thinking about it too hard. He also had to swap out his cigarettes for a German brand, and he told me they didn't taste the greatest as we continued along.

As we approached Libya, there was nothing but a sea of sand stretching out beyond the oasis of the coast. It was like Antarctica, but hot, and with sand instead of snow and ice.

"What's the name you got on your papers?" Halcomb asked, breaking the silence.

"Christoph Janke," I replied. "A private. You?"

"Private Max Theiner."

"We should probably get used to using them."

"Agreed." Halcomb glanced at me. "I still think this is a bad idea."

"Why?"

"Because I don't have a good feeling about this."

"About what we're doing right now, or the mission in general?"

"What we're doing right now. I know every way we could've gone is a plunge into enemy territory, but this... something feels off."

"How?"

"I don't know. It's not a feeling I can explain, but it's about more than just the fact that we have to meet up with a German claiming to be a defector."

My mind turned to Archie Marsden before my last trip to Antarctica. He had been nervous for no apparent reason about the voyage, and I thought it was because of his bad experience in Greenland. Now I know to take feelings like that seriously, because he had been right to be afraid, and he paid for it. "If we run into trouble, we'll figure it out," I said.

"Be happy I have faith in you, Jay."

Upon landing in Tripoli, we were greeted with the sound of Arabic chatter. It was the first time I had ever heard the language spoken by a native speaker, and it was quite entrancing and beautiful to listen to. I had to stop myself from getting distracted with memories from pulling books down from Tallor's shelves with the lovely illustrations of desert cities and oasis villages.

We could also hear the much harsher German among the crowds of people. The tan uniforms of German soldiers and officers stood out like sore thumbs against the white robes of the Arabs. I whispered to Halcomb, "This is it."

Halcomb shook his head. "I'm still not sure about this."

"Stafford wouldn't have sent us if he thought this was a bad idea."

Halcomb sighed, looking down. "Alright. I trust Stafford."

"Same. Let's go."

We headed down the ramp, deliberately seeking out German officers. One, a captain, was standing by a fruit stand, conversing with the vendor. Nervously, I approached him, saying, "Excuse me, sir?"

The captain turned around, and raised an eyebrow. "Fresh troops? I was not aware we were getting any."

I took out my papers, and Halcomb took out his. "From Berlin. We were ordered to replace a couple of men who are sick."

The captain took a long hard look at the papers. "I see. You're for Colonel Lehning's regiment. There's a plane taking water and food to his location in about an hour. You can board that." He grinned at us, then gestured for us to follow him. "Come, I'll show you."

I glanced at Halcomb. We were both impressed at how the captain bought our disguise, and I think even Halcomb was starting to think this whole trip might not be so bad. This was just the beginning, though. Who knows how the rest will go?

The flight took a little under an hour to reach the encampment, which was a sloppy mess of tents scattered about, tanks and trucks everywhere, and several scouting planes parked near each other. From the air, we could see soldiers going about their day, marching, exercises, cleaning their rifles, and playing games with each other. When we landed, we were approached by a stern-looking stocky man with a thin silver mustache and a slightly crooked officer's cap. The pilot was first to address him before going about unloading supplies, then we hopped off the plane, saluting the officer.

"Privates Janke and Theiner reporting for duty, sir," I said.

The officer wore a colonel's emblems. I assumed he was Lehning, but I didn't say anything yet to be sure. He looked both of us up and down. "When I put in a request for replacements, I was told they were sending everyone to fucking Russia. Guess Berlin actually had a speck of pity to send me two fresh-faced recruits." He jerked his thumb toward the tents. "Go get checked out by the medics. Don't need you spontaneously developing dysentery on my watch." Before we marched off, he glanced at me. "You especially. Never seen a man that pale before."

I was starting to feel tired and sick from being out in the sun and heat for the last several hours. The last thing I wanted was for the Germans to find out what I really was, especially if everything I had been told about their treatment of Conjurus was true. In the back of my mind, I had a feeling that if they found out I'm a Conjurus, they would send me right to Wahler. On the other hand, where would that leave Halcomb? I didn't want him to be abandoned and found to be an American spy. We volunteered for this together. We were going to complete this together.

Tanks and vehicles kicked up sand everywhere they went, and the fine particles swirled around tents of all sizes. The heat was unbearable. Halcomb's uniform was soaked in sweat, and I was feeling dizzy and nauseated. Something deep inside was screaming at me to crawl under a shady spot and throw up at the same time. If I needed to use my powers in that moment, I would certainly struggle.

In the hospital tent, most of the beds were occupied by soldiers recovering from injuries. Others were being looked at for heatstroke, and there were a few that looked ill and in pain. Medics with white armbands and helmets bearing large red crosses were tending to each of the men. Some of them sounded tired, while others were smiling and asking their patients what they needed. Others were going in and out of a room wearing blood-spattered smocks, and I could hear the hissing of a machine pressure valve, followed by panicked German shouts.

A short medic with messy blond hair and unusually bright blue eyes had me sit on a bed next to a soldier who was staring up at the ceiling and holding his right side. The medic looked at the soldier and said, "I take it you haven't passed the stone yet?"

The soldier shook his head, and the medic turned back to me. "How do you feel? You're quite pale."

"Been out in the sun ever since we arrived," I said.

"Ah." The medic smiled a little. "Anything else?"

"No," I replied. "I just need to lie down."

Nodding, the medic let me lay on my back. He did continue to look over me, and said, "Well, if all you need is some rest, you are my easiest patient of the day, then. Please, call if you need anything."

It was a great relief to rest, but something about that medic was nagging at the back of my mind. I closed my eyes and listened to everything around me. The sound of tanks and vehicles rumbling by the tent was the dominant sound, followed by the occasional grunt and moan from the poor man suffering from kidney stones next to me.

As I lay, I felt better gradually, but the tent was still absurdly hot, and everything seemed to spin above me. I wasn't sure how much time had passed, but I eventually sat up, unable to deal with the nausea anymore. Not wanting to wait for the medic, I wound up throwing up in the sand.

Halcomb was in the cot across from me. He sat up abruptly, saying, "Are you alright?"

"I'll be fine," I said, still leaning over the side of the cot. I now felt light and hollow inside, and I was starting to wonder if coming here really was a good idea. Prisk was right; the desert really was the bigger enemy here. All we could do was pray.

The sudden cooldown of the desert when night fell was a great relief to me. Halcomb and I were sent to a tent with three other soldiers, and although it was tempting to talk, we both knew anyone could hear us. It wasn't comforting to know there were men patrolling the camp every hour.

We found an excuse to get out when Halcomb needed a smoke. We walked out to a secluded spot, away from the tents, but close enough to the patrols so they didn't think we were sneaking off. Once they were out of earshot, Halcomb whispered, "I haven't seen this Winter fellow at all. I still think this is insanity."

"These are our orders. We get that information and we help Winter escape."

"If he turns out to be nothing but a rat, I'll shove him out of the submarine and let him drown."

"That is needlessly cruel."

Halcomb rolled his eyes. He nearly jumped when he looked over his shoulder and saw a patrolling German approaching us, but the soldier only asked, "Could I have a cigarette, Private?"

"Yeah... sure." Halcomb pulled one from his carton. "I suppose you want a light, too?"

"Yes, thank you," the soldier replied. Once he had the cigarette lit, he asked, "Is there anything I can get for you in return? Chocolate? Magazines?"

"Chocolate would be nice," Halcomb said. "Take your time, though. No rush."

The soldier walked away, a trail of smoke following him. Halcomb released his breath and looked at me. "We only have one week before that submarine leaves the coast. Let's find Winter and get the hell out of here."

"They don't suspect anything about us so far. As long as we keep up the charade and our heads low, we'll be fine," I said.

"Yeah, but how long are we going to have to keep this up? Surely not a whole week."

"I'm a patient man, and I can manage my time. I've waited my whole life to see these parts of the world. I can wait some more."

In the morning, we joined the rest of our new unit for breakfast. It was already hot, and sweat was rolling off the men in waves. Some had already taken their shirts off, including myself. A private named Heisig asked where we were from, and how we got here. Halcomb repeated what we told the captain in Tripoli, then Heisig said, "I meant, what part of Germany?"

Halcomb glanced at me. "I'm from a little town outside of Stuttgart. Very small. Mainly farming. I... helped raise pigs for slaughter."

"Munich," I said. "My family were furniture-makers. Quite comfortable furniture, too. I've heard Hitler has one of our couches."

Grinning, Heisig started telling us about growing up in Düsseldorf and how he didn't think he would ever go too far from home. He had already seen action in France, the Netherlands, and now North Africa. As he was about to start telling us about his first battle in Egypt, someone barked at us all to stand.

Dropping everything, we stood, and faced the tent flap. Four officers entered, followed by a couple of medics, including the one who looked over Halcomb and me the day before and a short man with thinning blond hair and tired-looking blue eyes. The pins and emblems on his cap were obscured by a pair of goggles, and a pair of binoculars was around his neck. His uniform was certainly different from the others with its off-white color, and it seemed to say to everyone that he was the most important man in the room. The other officers were wearing shorts and their sleeves were cut down. It was baffling that this man was wearing clothing typical of a more temperate climate. The silence was unbearably heavy as he stepped in, then he spoke. "Please, sit down."

Everyone sat, almost in unison. My stomach was tightening as I feared he was going to call out me and Halcomb.

"This is not a happy occasion. Last night, one of our own brave men, Private Johann Kunst, passed away due to complications from kidney stones. I'm telling you all this because one of your medics, Corporal Lexis, informed me that Kunst went to him a little too late. I don't think I have to emphasize how badly we need everyone to be fighting fit. Please, don't wait until the pain is unbearable to get checked out. That's an order."

Halcomb glanced at me, visibly confused. "Kidney stones? I've never heard of anyone dying from them."

"My uncle had to pass one a few years ago. He said he wished he could've died because it's excruciating," I replied.

"Even so. That's unfortunate."

"Unfortunately, and highly unusual."

Heisig next to us suddenly looked withdrawn. "I was with Kunst since we were both sent here last year."

The officer speaking glanced in our direction, and waited until we stopped talking. "On a slightly lighter note, two soldiers were sent to us to replace some who've already went home to recover from illness. Privates Janke and Theiner."

Halcomb wasn't at all thrilled with the attention being placed on us. I maintained a stoic expression, despite my anxiety.

"They're brand-new from training. They won't last a day out here," Colonel Lehning said.

The man addressing us turned to glare at him. "We were all fresh out of training once. I know you wanted experienced soldiers, but those two are all Berlin could spare."

"I just hope they don't run at the first sign of battle, Field-Marshal."

"I don't think they will. Give them confidence, treat them well, make sure they partake in training like everyone else, and they'll be model soldiers."

The colonel didn't say another word.

When the announcements were over, Halcomb gave me a stunned look. "That was Field-Marshal Rommel himself."

My thoughts turned to Sergeant Prisk and his men. They would be jealous right now, and probably yelling at me to put him down.

"Why are you surprised?" Heisig asked.

"Well... I wasn't expecting him to deliver that in person."

"Oh, he goes out of his way to. Very personable. Chivalrous, too. I'm glad to be under his command, and much happier that I'm not on the Eastern Front."

Frankly, the last thing I would expect from any German officer is chivalry, given what I knew about *Standartenführer* Wahler. Regardless, we still had to be cautious.

When we finally saw Altschul in person, we spent that day observing him. He was a tall, well-built man with short and neatly done blond hair. He was very loud when it came to directing us in exercise, and it was interesting to see Rommel stepping up and guiding him in how to speak, how to stand, and how to project himself. After that session, I whispered to Halcomb that we needed to study Altschul's routine in order to catch him alone.

Over the course of the day, another soldier died because of kidney stones, and that's when things began to feel suspicious, especially since this soldier had gone to the hospital tent as soon as he realized what was going on.

Long hours were spent on training exercises. Sometimes Altschul led us, sometimes it was someone else. I would frequently catch Rommel observing from a short distance, often with a camera, and I would hear Colonel Lehning muttering about how we seemed "out of practice." He seemed prone to complaining about everything, not just me and Halcomb. Frequently, I caught Rommel's chief-of-staff, Colonel Bayerlein, rolling his eyes at whatever comment Lehning was making. Several other officers had an overall numbness to Lehning's behavior. They were clearly used to this.

It seemed like Lehning had a comment on everything, from the weather to a private's cap being crooked to the fact that Rommel occasionally slept in his staff car and especially anything about me or Halcomb. It's worth noting that I learned Lehning would perform his own patrols at night, and I heard rumors not just from enlisted but also officers that it was because Lehning had no one to write home to and nothing to really keep his mind occupied. It didn't surprise me that he was a lonely man. Frankly, his behavior is probably the reason he has no one to talk to about personal matters.

I didn't think it excused his behavior. Fed up with his griping about how I looked like I was trying to "dance instead of fight," I stared down my opponent, sweat dripping from our hair and faces. We both understood this was a friendly, practice spar, but we treated it like a real fight. Grunting, I lunged at my opponent, a lanky *obergefreiter*, and barreled him into the sand. I heard his breath rush from his lungs, and someone blew a whistle. Standing, I extended my hand to the corporal, who was struggling to breathe as he got up. He was escorted off the field.

"'Out of practice,'" I heard Rommel say with a snort. "Absolute nonsense."

Lehning looked down at the sand, embarrassed. "Janke is capable, Field-Marshal, I will admit, but what about Theiner?"

Needless to say, Halcomb thoroughly embarrassed Lehning by taking down his opponent in the first few seconds. We both hoped that would be the end of him questioning us, but he continued to watch us like a hawk, making it difficult for us to have time alone or find Altschul. No one except Rommel could really have alone-time with Lehning around. At the same time, there were some parts of the day where Lehning would either vanish or stop complaining altogether, but those were entirely unpredictable.

It was odd, but it seemed like this happened so often that the rest of the officers and enlisted men didn't even notice.

"You'll get used to Lehning's behavior," Heisig told me and Halcomb one evening. "He's all talk, no action."

"Why exactly is he such an ass?" Halcomb asked.

Heisig put his finger to his lips. "Don't let him hear you say that. Frankly, I have no idea why he's so angry all the time. All I know is that he was transferred here from the Eastern Front after an attack didn't go so well. I've heard him in his tent a few times, breathing heavily from nightmares. I wouldn't be surprised if that's the real reason he rarely sleeps."

"That's all you know?" I asked.

Heisig nodded. "Lehning is harsh and bitter for reasons only he knows. Everything else is just rumors and speculation. I've heard he was only sent here so he can be watched. There's a big rumor around that he was involved with the death of an officer during an advance to the Caucasus, but there's no evidence to back it up. I think he's angry because he was blamed."

"That's no reason to take it out on everyone else."

"I know, but good luck trying to talk to him about it."

Knowing that, it didn't come as a surprise that Lehning hated anyone bringing up Russia. There was definitely more to his story, but I wasn't sure I wanted to know more. He wasn't exactly someone who liked making conversation, and he seemed to have a problem with myself and Halcomb being in the camp, simply because we were new in his eyes.

When Rommel wasn't around, Lehning singled us out, pulling us away from whatever we were doing and giving us strenuous and impossible tasks as "tests." He mainly picked mealtimes as the chance to take us and make us clean the inside of a tank, which is unbearably hot after baking in the desert sun for several hours. Touching the metal was nothing short of excruciating.

"I hope that British sniper you met in Gibraltar gets Lehning," Halcomb whispered to me. "He's a fucking menace. This whole ordeal had better be worth it."

I wasn't sure if Halcomb was going to blame me for this or not. I had no idea any of this was going to happen. Instead of assuming he was upset with me, I said, "It'll be worth it when we kill Wahler."

Halcomb nodded. "Still. We need a plan to get out of here. We don't have a lot of time."

Being an ice-variant in a tank that had turned into an oven, I agreed with him.

Chapter 5

There were multiple times throughout our stay in North Africa when I was worried my heat sensitivity would expose me as a Conjurus, and I did nearly pass out a few times. However, there was a point where it wasn't my sensitivity but my compassion that nearly got me in trouble, and Halcomb hasn't let me forget about it.

What I saw of Rommel there was vastly different to the newsreels. German propaganda did its best to hide his ill health, and the longer we stayed in North Africa, the more I realized that his strength was held together by mere shreds, and he was forcing himself to work despite that. From what I knew about my father, even he didn't push himself this hard.

Halcomb and I were field-stripping and cleaning our rifles when Rommel and another officer passed by, discussing logistics. Quite abruptly, the officer changed the topic. "Why don't you go lie down, sir? Your eyes glazed over and you haven't had a drop of water all day."

"I will drink when I have the chance," Rommel replied.

"Rest is important, sir. Lie down for at least ten minutes, please. We can't get anything done if you don't have your strength."

I've never seen anyone resist the idea of resting. Rommel agreed reluctantly. The two parted ways, and I watched Rommel head to his tent. A second later I heard the sound of something heavy hitting the sand and glanced over to see the field-marshal's boots sticking out of the tent. For a moment I wondered if he really had just laid down in the sand, but that didn't make any sense.

"Jay, what are you doing?" Halcomb hissed when I stood up.

"Something's wrong," I said.

"It's none of our business!"

Ignoring him, I walked over to the tent. Rommel was laying on the ground, completely unconscious. Kneeling by him, I put a finger on his neck. His pulse was rapid but shallow. I stood up to go outside, calling, "Theiner! Get a medic!"

Halcomb dashed off to the hospital tent, and I went back to kneeling by Rommel. There wasn't a trace of sweat anywhere on his skin, and he was very warm to the touch. Without thinking about it, I put my hand over his forehead, slowly lowering the temperature of my skin. It required conscious effort to keep my hand from getting too cold, or else I would accidentally kill him through shock.

"Shit, what happened?" a voice behind me said.

I looked over my shoulder to see Altschul's tall figure standing in the entrance to the tent. "He passed out," I replied.

"I see that." Altschul stepped over Rommel to kneel on his other side. "This is not the first time, unfortunately."

Meltwater was running down the sides of Rommel's head, and I became nervous Altschul would notice. Pulling my hand away when Altschul got up to look for something, I prayed he wouldn't see it at all.

Altschul knelt back down with a canteen. "Make him sit up. We should get some water in him."

As I started to prop up the field-marshal, I heard Lehning shouting, "Make way! Step aside!"

I whirled around to see Lehning, Lexis, and a few other men at the entrance of the tent. Lehning didn't hesitate to grab me by the front of my tunic and yank me upright. "And just what the *hell* are you doing in here?!"

"I'm the one who found him like this!" I shouted. "I called for a medic!"

"Then why are you still here?!"

I couldn't figure out why Lehning was so infuriated by the fact that I was in Rommel's tent. "I was trying to help bring him around."

"And clearly you didn't. Get out so the medics can do their job." Lehning shoved me out of the tent. "None of you should be seeing the field-marshal in this state."

Altschul stood up. "Colonel, stop! We both had this situation under control!"

"I'll believe that when I see it, Lieutenant," Lehning replied. "And don't you ever speak to your superior like that!"

I resisted the urge to ask if Lehning would have tried to help if he was the one who found Rommel. Instead, I left the scene, wishing I could just walk out of the camp with Halcomb and Altschul right then and there.

The only time Halcomb and I had time to talk was later that night, and even that was risky. Despite that, we found a secluded spot where we could at least talk quietly to each other.

"What exactly did you do when you found Rommel?" Halcomb asked. "After you told me to go get the medic?"

"I tried cooling him with my magic," I said.

Halcomb gave me a dirty look. "Even though you know how much trouble you could get in?"

"I had to do something—"

"No, you didn't. We don't have time for shit like this. Our job is getting out of here, getting on that sub with Winter, and getting to Italy, so we can meet up with Elvira, get to Germany, and assassinate Wahler. You can't let any emotions you have get in the way of this."

That sounded similar to what Prisk had told me about grief, and how letting my emotions take over could result in people getting killed. Perhaps I just did lengthen the North African campaign by alerting the medics and preventing Rommel from developing sunstroke. He was already suffering from dehydration. Perhaps I should have let him go, but from what I've heard, dying that way is incredibly painful.

"Just don't do it again, alright?" Halcomb lit up a cigarette. "I don't think we'll get a chance to talk to Winter anytime soon. It's impossible to find him alone at any point of the day."

I was just about to open my mouth and talk about what happened in the tent when I heard someone walking up in the sand behind us. Much to our surprise, it was Altschul.

"There you are," he said, pointing to me. "I've been looking all over camp for you. Private Janke, right?"

"Not exactly, Winter."

Blood drained from Altschul's face. "No. No, there is no way you are-"

"We're OSS," Halcomb said. "Sent to get the information you claim to have and get you out of here."

Altschul looked as if he was about to collapse "I cannot believe it! You actually came! I thought no one was ever going to get me out of here!"

"Everything will be alright," I promised. "You will be out of here before you know it."

"Thank you. I-I... I never thought it would actually happen."

"I just hope, for your sake, that you are who you say you are," Halcomb said.

Altschul gave him a confused look. "You think I am a spy?"

"I do not know. I just know that I do not trust you."

"I understand. After all, for all I know you two are Germans looking to arrest me, but... somehow, I don't feel like you are." Altschul switched his gaze between us. "Do you have a plan for safe passage?"

"There is a submarine waiting for us just off the coast. It will not be there for very long, so we need to get out of here as soon as possible."

"How much time do we have?"

"Four days."

"Plenty of time, then. However, you do realize I will only tell you what you want to know when I am on that submarine, correct?"

Halcomb glared at him. "We are the ones guaranteeing your ass will be on that submarine, so I suggest you cooperate."

I nudged him. "You need to cooperate too."

Altschul held up his hands, gesturing for us to stop. "I will have my personal things ready to go by tomorrow night and we can go then."

"Tomorrow?" Halcomb gave him a look. "Why not now?"

"I want to draw as little suspicion as possible. I am sorry. Please, trust me." He gave Halcomb a pleading and desperate look.

Halcomb sighed. "Fine. Tomorrow night." He pitched his cigarette butt away. "I am going back to bed." He walked away, leaving me alone with Altschul.

"Is he... always like this?" Altschul asked.

"Only when dealing with Germans, I guess."

"I see. Look, I wanted to talk about earlier, when we found Rommel in his tent. I know Lehning shouted at you, but you should not feel bad for trying to help."

"Don't worry about it." I gave him a confused look. "I'm a little surprised you care when you're trying to defect."

"He has been tutoring me in leadership. I am grateful for it, but... I cannot stay here. Not with what I know. Not with Wahler still out there."

"You've met Wahler personally?"

"I will tell you my story when we're on the sub."

Halcomb and I agreed that we needed to scout around so we could narrow down a potential escape route to the coast. In order for us to scout, though, we needed to be put on patrol. I certainly didn't want to go to Lehning to discuss that, so I went with the next best thing.

Getting an opportunity to speak with Rommel wasn't as easy as it looked. "Free time" didn't seem to be in his vocabulary, except at night. He didn't even stop to eat some days. I waited until after morning exercise that day to approach the field-marshal, mustering as much boldness as I could. It was now or never.

Of course, Lehning stepped in front of me without hesitation. "And where are you going, Private?"

"I would like a word with the Field-Marshal, Colonel," I said.

"Why? What could possibly be so important that you couldn't go to me, your own regimental commander?"

Nerves suddenly gripped my throat. It was hard to swallow, much less speak.

A vein throbbed on the side of Lehning's head, and he was turning red with anger. "You are not a guest at some fancy party. I could care less how new you are. There's no room for sympathy here. You came here to fight, and that is what you're going to do. And for the record," Lehning grabbed my collar, "if you try this again without authorization, I'll have you shot and your head mounted on my-"

A stern voice spoke up. "Colonel."

Lehning whirled around to face Rommel.

"Let him go. If he needs to speak to me, he can."

"Sir, you are just letting him undermine the chain of command-"

"Like you undermined your superiors in Russia?"

"I did that out of necessity." Lehning pushed me in Rommel's direction. "Take him and coddle him all you want, *sir*."

I didn't say anything, even after Lehning stormed off. Rommel had to look up just to make eye contact with me, and gave me a weak smile. "I am sorry if he has been an annoyance since you and Theiner arrived."

"Nothing we cannot handle," I replied. A part of me expected him to say something about what happened yesterday. I hoped he didn't; the last thing I needed to was him suspecting that I am a Conjurus.

"I respect your courage. Now, what do you need?"

"Theiner and I... would like to request to be put on patrol today."

"Why?"

I had hoped he wouldn't ask that. "Experience in, um, situational awareness, sir. All Lehning's been doing is making us clean tanks when it's too hot to do so. I... I do not believe that will make us better soldiers."

"I have noticed Lehning has been unnecessarily hard on you and Theiner." Rommel paused to think for a moment. "Alright. Permission granted. Go get Theiner. You two will be on the next rotation this afternoon."

I struggled to hide my glee. "Thank you, sir," I said, saluting and turning around. I didn't get far, though.

"One more thing, Private."

I paused.

"I vaguely remember your face above me when I fainted yesterday. Am I correct?"

"Yes, sir. I was the one who called for a medic."

"I should thank you, then. Next time, though, please do not overreact. I have fainted before."

I gave him a confused look. "Fainting can be serious, sir."

Rommel shook his head a little, wearing almost no expression. "I am too busy to be laid up in a hospital bed. I would have to be physically dragged out of here before I rest. Go back to work, Private."

I saluted again, but before I could march off, we both saw Lehning running up to us. He was deathly pale with fright. I didn't think it was possible for a cold-hearted man to look so scared. "Field-Marshal! Field-Marshal Rommel, you need to come see this quickly!"

A massive group of German soldiers was gathered around an area. I heard someone sobbing, and found Halcomb and Altschul consoling Heisig. At the center of the commotion was a half-buried, sandy corpse next to a Panzer III.

"We nearly ran over this body," the tank's commander said once Rommel appeared. "It... looks like Private Kunst, sir."

Kunst had been stripped naked. Every orifice was filled with sand and his skin was shriveled and leathery. A hole had been cut in his right side, and his kidney, which now looked like a large raisin from its time in the dry, desert heat, had been slashed from the tendons holding it in place. The tube running from the kidney to the bladder had also been cut, and was lying outside the mummifying corpse.

"What in the hell did this?" Lehning asked.

"Not an animal," Rommel replied. "These cuts are too neat, and it doesn't look like any part of Kunst was eaten."

I felt sick when I came to a conclusion as to what did this to Kunst's body. Or rather, *who* did this to Kunst's body, and it all began to make sense. This was the work of a witch.

Up until that point, I didn't think I would encounter the handiwork of a witch or warlock before getting to Wahler's White Raven project. Living in the city where witches are less common, and also given that I'm not a witch-hunter, I didn't think I would ever encounter a witch at all. My mind flashed to the photographs of the horrid dissections Halcomb had shown me in my apartment. This was less of a dissection and more of a harvesting for ingredients. In fact, it was definitely a harvesting.

I should've put things together when more than one soldier died due to kidney stones. They are an ingredient in many different potions, as are most other body parts. The harvesting of human organs is what leads to most Conjurus-witch conflicts, and it never ends well.

This wasn't something I wanted to stay silent on. I couldn't stay silent on this, not when lives were at stake. "Is there anything else missing?" I asked.

Lehning gave me a shocked look. "What kind of a sick question is that?"

"I am being serious, Colonel. A witch or warlock killed Kunst for his kidney stones. That's the only logical conclusion I can come to."

"A witch." Lehning looked at Rommel, then back at me. "Really? You think there are witches out here in the damned desert? In case you have not noticed, we are in the middle of nowhere! It is impossible for there to be any witches here! That is a ridiculous conclusion to come to!"

My face reddened and heated with anger at Lehning's disbelief. "Excuse me, Colonel, but where is the body of the other soldier? If his stones are missing, then we definitely have a witch here." It was extremely risky, but I glared at Lehning. "Do you have any idea how dangerous witches are?"

"I know how dangerous witches can be! They are menaces! But we are in the middle of nowhere, and to the best of my knowledge, there are no witches in the *Afrika Korps*!"

Rommel looked indecisive, his gaze switching between me and Lehning depending on who was speaking. I quietly took a breath, figuring being patient would win over the field-marshal. Finally, Rommel spoke. "If it is not a witch, then what do you think did this, Colonel?"

Lehning had no response. It took a few moments for him to calm down. "We are out here in the middle of nowhere. If there is a witch, it is among our own ranks."

Rommel gave him a confused look. "I thought you said there were no witches in the *Afrika Korps*."

"I am probably wrong. I hope I am not, but I am probably wrong."

I was terrified that Lehning was going to accuse Halcomb or me of being the warlock, but not one soldier could place either of us in the hospital tent around the time of Kunst's death. Even Lehning himself admitted to seeing us nowhere near the tent or the makeshift grave.

All of the medics seemed surprised that someone had taken Kunst's corpse from the morgue. When we searched for the second soldier, we couldn't find the body, and there was visible confusion, disappointment, and sadness among the medics. The only one who didn't wear much of an expression was Lexis, and I initially suspected that was due to shock.

Training was put off for the day, which meant Halcomb and I couldn't scout for an escape route like we originally intended. That made both Halcomb and me anxious, as we didn't have much time left before the submarine left. Everyone was given a shovel and ordered to search around the camp perimeter for the other body. Sure enough, it was found just south of the camp.

Just like Kunst, the body was naked and nearly mummified. However, this one had both kidneys cut out and split open like shelled nuts. He also had a massive, sand-filled incision just above his stomach, which, upon examination, revealed his liver and gallbladder were missing.

There was an air of tension and fear around the camp, and between myself and Halcomb. We couldn't spend a lot of time worrying about this, but a warlock in the camp was equally pressing. It was just as big a threat to us as it was to the Germans. That afternoon, I was lying in my cot trying to think of a plan when I heard someone walking up to the tent and the flap parted to reveal Lehning.

"Rommel wants to see you in his tent," he whispered.

I gestured to myself.

"Yes, you. Come on."

The sun was low in the western horizon as we walked, painting the sand and sky a rich, red-orange color. Lehning looked over his shoulder at me as we made our way through the maze of the camp. "How did you figure out a witch is killing our men?"

I shrugged. "It makes sense."

Lehning didn't respond at first, but then he said, "You must be from an area where they're everywhere. I know I was. They are animals. Mindless, bloodthirsty animals."

"I take it that is why you don't think a witch could be among our ranks."

"Exactly. Surely if we did have any they would have revealed themselves already. They're impulsive. The minute they find someone willing to buy one of their potions, they will kill the person standing next to them in order to get a heart or lung or something." Lehning shook his head and laughed a little. "But the SS wants witches for some reason."

I gave him a look of confusion, eager to hear what he knew. "I haven't heard about this."

"It is natural a lowly private like yourself would have no idea what the SS is doing. I only know because I had to work alongside them in Russia." Lehning paused and looked down at the sand, falling silent.

I didn't say anything more as we headed to the field-marshal's tent. Lehning looked tired and acted a lot less condescending toward me when we paused in front of the entrance flaps. In fact, he held them open for me. Once I entered the tent, Lehning sighed and turned to leave. I was completely alone with Rommel, who was sitting at his desk with a cup of tea. Papers were strewn all over his desk, and I noticed photographs among them. One featured a woman with dark hair standing next to Rommel in civilian clothes, and a very tall young man in glasses on Rommel's other side. I guessed they were his wife and son.

For a moment, standing alone in front of the most powerful man in the camp, I was terrified, knowing just how vulnerable I was, despite having positive earlier interactions with him. The smell of the tea was, strangely enough, a comfort. I was reminded of home. Suddenly, I was homesick. I was anxious and scared.

My last conversation with my uncle still rang in my ears. I could still hear him telling me how quick I was to put myself in danger. Well, here I was, in danger of being discovered as a spy, and I really wanted to go home. Frankly, I wanted to burst into tears like a child.

"Private. Have a seat." Rommel gestured to the chair across from his desk. His exhaustion was palpable, and about as heavy as humid air. I just hoped he didn't pass out again.

Nervously, I sat down, my thoughts still echoing in my mind. "You wanted to see me, sir?"

"Yes. You were the only one who spoke up when we found Kunst's body, and you seem to know a thing or two about witches."

"Yes, sir."

"The last thing I want to find is that there is a warlock in my own army, but I am afraid that is what has happened here. I want to know what you know."

That came dangerously close to revealing my identity. Although I'm not a witch-hunter by trade, all Conjurus are taught how to identify witchcraft to protect the Magicless they live near. It's dangerous to engage a witch or warlock because of their unpredictability, but there's hope in the fact that they're not indestructible. They're not the worst magical adversary out there.

Rommel and I weren't on the same side, but we had a common enemy in this warlock. At the same time, I could easily have left this warlock alone and let him decimate Rommel's forces, but then what would have stopped him from infiltrating any Allied forces that came along? The Americans and British might not be able to stop it before it threw them off course.

"One easy test for witches and warlocks is to ask them about the Conjurus," I explained. "From what I've been told, Conjurus and the Magicless refer to them as 'variants' of whatever element they use, such as ice or fire, but witches use the terms 'cryomancer', 'pyromancer', etcetera. Some are smart enough not to use these terms, but others do use them simply because it's been engrained into them."

"Alright. So, what if we have a smart warlock on our hands?"

"Search them for a wand or staff. They cannot do anything without them. I know I am not in the place to give orders, but... my suggestion would be to do a surprise search of everyone's tent. Wands are usually the length of your baton here, made of varying woods and polished neatly. Staffs are easy to identify because they have stones at the top."

"Do you have any idea as to what... potion they could be making?"

"The fact that this warlock took the liver and gallbladder suggests an acid potion. I am not sure what he could be using it for. A potion like that cannot be brewed in the camp; everyone will smell it. The easiest thing to do is find his wand. They cannot make potions without them."

"I can't believe you had a private audience with that man," Halcomb whispered to me when I returned to our tent.

We watched Rommel, Lehning, and several other officers standing around in a cluster outside one of the tents. I was just as surprised as Halcomb, but I also wasn't. I was the key to finding a warlock hidden within the camp. I didn't want to be, knowing how important our mission was, but this was equally serious.

When I explained discussion with Rommel, Halcomb pulled me aside, and looked like he wanted to strangle me. "We can't stay here! We don't have time!"

"I'm not letting this warlock wreak havoc here! If and when the British attack, we do not need him doing the same thing to them if he gets captured! Now, look, I told Rommel most of what I know. He can take that knowledge and do whatever he damn well pleases. We can grab Winter and leave when the opportunity arises."

"Yeah? And when is that going to be?"

I opened my mouth to argue when Lehning started shouting at a group of soldiers to get out of their tent. The rest of the officers, save for Rommel, began searching other tents as well.

As night fell over the desert, not a single bed was left unturned—literally. Everything in every tent was searched. It only paused when Lehning berated a private for having a dirty magazine hidden under his mattress, but then it continued after that private was sentenced to night patrol for the next three days.

When nothing was found in the soldiers' tents, the officers turned to searching *each other's* tents, including Rommel's. Lehning suggested taking apart his ceremonial baton, but that idea was tossed when someone reminded him that the baton was solid.

Tanks were searched. Trucks were searched. The tents were searched. Not one wand was found. When everyone set about putting their tents back together, there was an air of confusion.

"This is a waste of time!" Lehning shouted. "We searched everywhere and found nothing." He glared at me. "If the British catch us unaware, it will be all your fault. I will personally execute you if we lose that battle."

"That is enough, Colonel," Rommel said, calmly. "Unless you have any knowledge on witches that could help us, your silence would be more helpful."

"You actually believe this? Field Marshal, I hate witches as much as anyone, but we looked everywhere and have found nothing. Either we're looking in all the wrong places, or we're not dealing with a witch at all."

Rommel's expression didn't change. "I said, do you have any knowledge on witches that could help us? You did mention that you know how dangerous they are yesterday."

"That does not mean I know any of the minor details about how they operate."

Nodding, Rommel turned to me. Uncomfortable with the pressure, I struggled to stand straight and say, "The only thing I can think of is to start digging. They might have buried it in the sand."

Rommel shook his head. "Not possible. I don't agree with everything Lehning says, but we cannot spend too much time on this. We won't be able to stay a step ahead of the British if we keep this up."

"But, sir—"

"Unless you have another way we can narrow down who this warlock is, I cannot let this continue, as much as it pains me to say this. Kunst and Redler were murdered, but we are not in a position to put everything down and investigate."

I backed down. It was hard, but I accepted that there was nothing more I could do. Perhaps it was a local witch making the journey out here. In that case, it was up to Rommel whether or not they would start interrogating the locals. However, I had the feeling that the war was a much greater priority despite the value he placed on his men.

I managed to approach Altschul the following morning, while he was sitting on a rock with a tin of food. Glancing around to make sure we were alone, I said, "I am definitely caught between a rock and a hard place. Halcomb thinks we should just make a run for it. I think we need to catch the warlock before we go. What do you think?"

"Catch the warlock," Altschul replied. "Catch it and kill it."

I nodded.

"You cannot send them back to Germany to be tried for their crimes. They will be released or be sent to Wahler to be put to work."

"Can you tell me now what you know?"

Altschul fell silent. He looked down at his tin, then made eye contact with me. He looked pained. Horrible memories seemed to be flashing across his eyes. "Not yet. Both because I am not on that submarine, and because I am not ready to talk about it yet."

I respected his wishes, but, out of curiosity, I asked, "Do you have any ideas on who the witch could be?"

Altschul shook his head. "Whoever it is, they are hiding themselves well."

Chapter 6

Towards the end of the morning, two Italian trucks pulled in, braking so hard that they nearly flipped. A tall man with thick dark hair and prominent five o'clock shadow stepped out of one of the trucks. He marched up to Rommel and Lehning, and growled, "I was promised six Panzer IIIs three days ago! Where the hell are they?"

I would later learn he was General Faraci, a terrifying man on his own, but utterly useless without the right number of troops and weaponry. In fact, he's incredibly impatient, and I also learned that he was more than willing to butt heads with Mussolini himself about the strength of his forces. Apparently, he's done the same with every *Afrika Korps* commander, too.

"I cannot send any," Rommel said. "Did you not get my message?"

"'Cannot send any?!' Do you want the British to roll us over, like they did before you arrived?!" Faraci shouted.

"No, I do not, but our forces are spread thin as it is. We cannot afford to send anything, not even a drop of oil."

As Faraci continued trying to argue, Halcomb, Altschul, and I calmly walked over to listen to the conversation, though a part of me was sure that there was nothing really worth paying attention to.

"So, this is a normal occurrence?" Halcomb asked.

Altschul nodded. "It would be strange if Faraci was not haranguing us every few days for supplies."

Halcomb folded his arms over his chest and started pacing. He rubbed his chin, thinking, then looked at both of us. "If he comes every few days, what if the warlock is among the Italians? Someone could have easily snuck in the last time he was here."

"That is possible. He was here just a few hours before you two arrived."

The three of us turned when we heard Lehning start shouting at Faraci, along with Rommel trying to push them apart before it came to blows.

"Alright, well, who wants to go into a hornets' nest?" Halcomb asked.

I sighed before leaving the group and walked up to the chaos that was Faraci and Lehning arguing. It ended when Rommel finally got between them and shoved them apart. "Alright, that is enough! I am not continuing this discussion about transferring a Panzer unit. I do not want the British forcing us out any more than you, General, but your area is close enough to mine. If there is trouble, you can call me on the radio. That is final. Go home."

Panic surfaced in my chest. I couldn't let Faraci leave now. "Field-Marshal!" I called. "What if the warlock is among the Italians?"

"What the hell is he talking about?" Faraci asked, raising a thick eyebrow.

"A warlock has been killing my men," said Rommel. "We were trying to find it this morning, but—" he glanced at me, "we have not had much luck."

"And this man is accusing *us* of harboring one?!" Faraci pointed at me.

"You might not even know he is there," I said. "Any one of you could be hiding it."

Faraci didn't hesitate to go off on me. "Private, you are full of shit, and shame on you for talking out of turn, in front of your own superior!"

"That is nothing new with this one." Lehning rolled his eyes. "He thinks this whole thing is a fucking tea party."

Rommel turned to face him. "Colonel, show at least a little respect. If it wasn't for Janke, we wouldn't have known what happened to Kunst and Redler."

"Who the hell does Janke think he is? A damn Conjurus?"

I tried not to react. All three of them were looking at me. Lehning with annoyance. Faraci with contempt. Rommel with curiosity. Finally, I said, "No, I am not a Conjurus. I... did read their books, years ago. My family knew some."

"That does not make you the *Afrika Korps*'s dedicated witch-hunter," Lehning said. "We have not found any wands, or signs that someone among us is a warlock. I already said this morning that we are wasting time. Wasting time while the British gather up their forces in Egypt. How do we know you are not an infiltrator, distracting us so the British can catch us with our trousers down?"

I looked him in the eye. "Colonel, that is not true and you know it."

Without hesitation, Lehning slapped me across the face hard. "How dare you accuse me of being a liar?! You have been nothing but trouble since you came here! More and more, I think you're a spy."

"That is a strong accusation, Colonel," Rommel said in a low voice. "What makes you think he is a spy?"

"More than once, I have heard his friend talking about how they need to 'get out of here,' talking about something in Italy."

My heart was pounding, and I felt a sickening knot forming in my stomach, but I kept a stoic expression. I was silently begging for Rommel not to believe him.

"And how do you think 'Janke' knows so much about witches? Because he *is* a fucking Conjurus. Tell me, do people turn this white in the sun? No. Only Conjurus do that." Lehning gave Rommel a hard stare. "I know you think I am unbearable, but you know damn well I'm not a liar. I came from a part of Germany where his people and witches were everywhere. I know what they look like."

When Rommel looked me in the eye, I suddenly felt as though he could see right through me as he pondered all this. "You are Conjurus, aren't you? Lehning's right; human beings turn red in the sun. You turn whiter than snow the longer you are out here. I've yet to see anyone *not* develop sunburn during my entire stay here in North Africa. You've been here almost a week and not once have I seen you being treated for sunburn."

Lehning was in my ear. There was a strong tension about him, and suddenly I was afraid he was going to get physically violent with me. "Now who is the liar?" He turned to Rommel. "Do I have permission to execute him and his friend for being spies?"

"You will do no such thing," Rommel said, calmly. "Your orders are to find Theiner and put them in a tent. Tie them to a chair and put them under guard. I'll deal with them later."

Halcomb had been swearing ever since we were placed in the center of a tent, bound to two chairs with their backs to each other. "We should have left sooner!" he snarled. "Do you have any idea what they're going to do to us now? We're going to be tortured, and possibly shot!"

"We can still get out of here," I said, trying to remain calm. "We also have Winter to worry about."

"Oh, right, because now that Rommel and Lehning know that we're spies, Winter is going to want to be associated with us."

No one came to question us over the rest of the day. When the camp went to sleep, I was thinking about how grateful I was that Altschul hadn't been brought up. Lehning certainly didn't hear all of our conversations. As the hours began to drag on, the only sounds were the crunching of sand beneath boots as the Germans patrolled around us, and the wind against the tent.

I was partly asleep when I heard a voice say, "You are dismissed. I will be fine," and I straightened a little when Rommel entered the tent, holding a chair.

Halcomb glared at him. "Have you come to execute us personally?"

"On the contrary. I've come to talk to you. I want to know exactly who you are." Rommel sat in the chair with its back to us.

"Why should we say anything if you are going to kill us in the end?"

"Because I am not. You will be sent to a prisoner-of-war camp. And trust me when I say I am a lot more pleasant than Lehning when it comes to interrogation."

Halcomb looked at me, then spoke in English. "We can't tell him anything."

"I won't tell him what we're doing, but I do have an idea," I said. "You just need to trust me." I switched back to German, making eye contact with Rommel. "We are spies, but our mission has nothing to do with you. The only thing I will say is that the warlock we have been trying to find is real, and it is not a ruse we're using to make you unprepared for an Allied attack."

Resting his arms on the back of the chair, Rommel looked deep in thought before turning his gaze to me. "So, you are actually a Conjurus."

"I am," I said. "Ice-variant."

"That certainly explains why your hand was so cold on my head when I fainted a couple of days ago."

I didn't respond. "Did you know then?"

"No. I was only partly conscious, but I remember something cold and wet. I thought you were using a wet rag." A slight grin crossed Rommel's face. "I can respect a man who goes out of his way to assist his opponent. Spies tend to be a ruthless breed." He was quiet for a moment, and I wondered if he was expecting me to respond. When I didn't, he continued, "I take it 'Christoph Janke' is not your real name?"

"No. It is actually Jay Loalin."

"Loalin. Are you related to a—"

"Morgan Loalin is my father, yes. I hear that all the time." I had gone for so long without anyone bringing up my father. The most naïve parts of me had thought going halfway around the world would take me away from everyone who would always bring up my father, how reckless he was in the war, and blame him for how Germany responded. That couldn't be possible. The Germans themselves probably remembered the incident best.

Over the last week, I had been so focused on developing the persona of "Christoph Janke" that I didn't think about home. The pain of missing and longing surfaced rapidly, like a cork after being held underwater. Laurel's face came to mind first, and all I could see were the two of us dancing at every Christmas party we attended in the last three years. Then I saw Uncle Redvar. Not the angered and disappointed frown from when we last saw each other, but the look of pride when we were up in the Adirondacks for my training.

I can only hope he looks that way again when I return. *If* I return.

"Your father is something of a legend, but it does not seem like he is held in high regard where you come from," Rommel said.

"No. My family did, but the others... not so much. He died when I was two, so I grew up idolizing him. He was a bit of an outcast, and... so am I, in some ways."

I couldn't tell if this was an elaborate means of interrogation, or if Rommel was genuinely interested. What surprised Halcomb and I was that he untied us from the chairs, and let us stand and walk around while he talked. "I have done a lot in terms of battle tactics—well, tactics for humans. I did not exactly feature a chapter on facing Conjurus in my book because I never had the chance to. I do remember the... discussions about Morgan Loalin after the war. At first I thought it was a hoax, some shell-shocked nightmare or hallucination, and then I met a young man in a restaurant in late 1919. Everyone was pushing me in his direction, saying, 'This is the soldier who saw that ice-variant's last stand!' and I still did not believe it. But not only was he the last survivor, but he had kept all the pictures taken after another battalion arrived.

"I know what the Conjurus are. I had just never met one in real-life until about two years ago, in France. There was a town several kilometers outside of Cherbourg that had a sizable Conjurus population, and although I ordered my troops to leave them alone, the citizens attacked in the dead of night with power I cannot even begin to imagine. It makes dealing with the British here easy."

"Even if we were on the same side," I said, "I could not tell you how to battle Conjurus. Our unpredictability is what has kept us alive, especially when dealing with witches."

"If the Allies ever tried to get into Europe, I do not envy them the headache they would have to endure. Unless, of course, the Americans and the British decide to bring their own armies of Conjurus."

I kept my mouth shut. I had no idea what the British were doing with their Conjurus, but I already knew about the OSS's collaboration with ours. The last thing I needed was any one of Germany's commanders to know. "I would rather not think about it," I replied.

All Rommel offered me was a smirk and a headshake. Underneath, I could sense there was more to the story about what happened in France. I could sense it was a nightmare for everyone involved.

"What else do you want from us?" Halcomb asked.

"I would like this warlock out of my camp," Rommel said. "In exchange for your help, I will send you to a much more comfortable prisoner-of-war camp in Italy. After all, you did want to go there, Jay Loalin."

"That's fair," I replied.

"Good. Now, my terms are as follows: you will have free roam of the camp to do your work, but you cannot leave the perimeter, or I will be forced to take harsh measures against both you and your companion. You will be under my protection, and whatever tools you need to catch the warlock, I will give you. If you are still insistent on digging for this warlock's wand, you will have to do it yourself. Whatever you do, do not even *think* about abusing my trust and kindness. You are a special circumstance, but the second this investigation is over, all your privileges will be revoked, and you will spend the remainder of your time in my camp here, in this tent."

"What about Halcomb?"

"Halcomb will stay here for the day, but he will get three meals, water, and half a pack of cigarettes per day." Rommel made eye contact with Halcomb. "I have seen how you smoke."

From the corner of my eye, I saw Halcomb shrug and heard him mutter, "Fair enough." Facing Rommel, I held out my hand. "We have a deal, then."

You can imagine the look on Lehning's face when he found out he was exactly right about me. After we sat down to breakfast, he was red in the face and shouting at Rommel for not doing anything about me and Halcomb sooner.

"How is it that you knew something was wrong with 'Janke' and you did nothing about it! *You knew*, and yet you are treating them like guests instead of spies?! They do not deserve this kind of treatment!"

"We could keep an eye on them so long as they did not leave the camp, and I would take action if they tried to escape," Rommel said.

"Just because he's a Conjurus does not mean he should get any special privileges! He snuck in wearing a German uniform, therefore he's a spy and should be treated as such!"

"That is enough, Colonel! He and his companion will be sent to a prison camp once this is over. Is that too complicated for you to understand?"

Lehning left the tent without a sound. I wasn't sure if I was in a position to talk about the relationships between high-ranking officers, but I asked, "Is he usually like this? I have heard rumors, but I can't really be sure if any of them are true. That, and he came close to telling me what happened in Russia."

Rommel thought about that for a moment. "Without going into too much detail, Lehning... has certainly had a tumultuous past. We served together in France and then he was sent to the Soviet Union. He is a combative individual, headstrong, likes leading from the front, has no tolerance for cowardice, and arguing with him typically goes nowhere. Sometimes he does it just because he can, which is why I have had to learn how to silence him. He is a former boxer, after all. Aggression and strength are more his style."

"He is not the first person I've met who is like that," I said, taking a sip of my coffee. "That is why it was so easy to just stand there and take it."

"Having observed your conduct, Mr. Loalin, I was impressed. You would have made a fine German soldier."

I didn't want to press for details, but I still asked, "Do you know exactly what happened in Russia?"

"Why do you want to know?"

"I would like the truth. It might provide some answers as to why he behaves the way he does."

"I certainly wish I had the truth as well, but what occurred in southern Russia is, according to some in Hitler's inner circle, 'not for my ears'."

I wasn't sure if he was telling the truth, or trying to avoid giving me too much information. Rommel's smile faded slowly when it was clear I wasn't going to continue the conversation. "Finish your breakfast quickly so we can get to work."

I was always escorted by two guards now. They both seemed a little terrified of me, and it didn't help that their instructions on taking me down if I got out of hand were so specific in avoiding an expulsion of power akin to what my father had done—they had to knock me unconscious first, then shoot.

I was the most powerful man in the camp, and yet I felt completely helpless. I knew I could singlehandedly get myself and Halcomb out of here, and I probably should, but I couldn't explain what was holding me back. Was it because ending up here wasn't part of the mission? Was it because the risk of us getting recaptured and executed was too high? Was it because I felt obligated to help these people—the enemy, of all things—with a problem my people were traditionally charged with solving? Was I caught up in the thrill of being in a strange place? Or was I scared?

Halcomb had been scared from the moment we set foot in Morocco, and I couldn't blame him. He had never been in a situation like this before. Then again, neither have I. Previously, the most hostile thing I had faced was Antarctica itself. Nature was the enemy, and it was nature that killed my team. Now my enemy was a group of people. I was determined not to let them hurt or kill Halcomb, and I felt cooperation was the best way.

I know cooperation with a nation we're at war with can have serious consequences, but what exactly was the definition of cooperation? I wasn't giving Rommel sensitive information about the whereabouts of Allied soldiers. I didn't tell him my mission was to kill one of his fellow countrymen. I'm not entirely sure what I'm doing counts as "giving aid and comfort." This felt more like a situation where "the enemy of my enemy is my friend," at least temporarily. It felt like a necessary step to take to prevent unnecessary casualties.

I spent that morning on my hands and knees in the sand, digging with a spade under the tents to search for any traces of wands or staffs or really anything related to witchcraft. By ten in the morning, it was already scorching out, and I no longer had the protection of my disguise as a German soldier. I was afraid to ask the men guarding me for water and shade.

I lost count of how many tents I dug under when I felt like my body was ready to give out. The sand and sweat all over my hands made generating ice nearly impossible, and when I saw my reflection in glass, I was so pale that I didn't think I looked human anymore.

Lehning came by to see how progress was coming. "Well? Have you found anything yet?"

After putting up with him for the last few days, I was tired of answering to him. Never in my life have I had to deal with someone this cruel and angry. Whatever happened in his past didn't excuse his behavior. Then again, perhaps what I did next wasn't excusable, either. At the time, I decided that since I wasn't under his command anymore, I took full confidence in saying, "Fuck you. No. I will let Rommel know if I find anything."

Before the guards could move, Lehning shoved them aside to lift me up by the collar of my tunic and drag me out of the tent. For a man of his age, he had no problems with trying to beat me senseless. I knew I could be shot for hitting him, but as soon as I forced myself back up, I swung at his jaw. He ducked, and tried doing the same to me.

"Stop immediately!" one of the guards shouted.

Lehning wasn't listening. "Pestilence," he hissed at me before punching me in the stomach. My breath rushed from my lungs and I keeled over, stumbling away and clutching my abdomen. "Use your magic, Loalin!" he taunted.

I stood straight, despite an intense soreness pulsing in my stomach. Without hesitation, I struck him in the cheek. Lehning was still standing, but he was spitting blood from biting the inside of his mouth.

Breathing hard and glaring at me, Lehning held up his fists again. "Come on, Conjurus, is that the limit of your strength?!"

Well, Rommel wasn't wrong when he said Lehning had previously been a boxer. I wasn't sure I wanted to keep fighting him. He certainly didn't like settling his disputes peacefully. He eyed each movement I made the way a big cat stalks its prey. I couldn't use magic, though. For one, I was weak from the heat, and two, I could accidentally kill him. Then I'd really be in trouble.

A thought crossed my mind when I made eye contact with Lehning. Perhaps this was a means of gaining his respect, the way being patient and chivalrous earned Rommel's. Swallowing what little saliva I had left in my mouth, I held up my fists.

Lehning charged forward to punch up and into my ribs. Blinding pain seared through me and the next thing I knew I was lying in the sand staring up at the cloudless blue sky. I couldn't get a full breath in with the raging epicenter of pain in the right side of my ribcage.

As I was trying to brace myself for whatever Lehning was going to do next, I heard Rommel shouting, "*That is enough!* I want to see both of you in my tent at this instant!" Turning around, I heard him mutter, "Animals," under his breath.

I had to be helped up to follow him and Lehning to the tent, clutching my chest as I went. Lehning didn't say a word, and I could sense he knew he was in just as much trouble as I was. That didn't mean he wasn't giving me dirty looks along the way. At the same time, he knew he started it. It was a childish thing to think, but even the guards said that Lehning went too far in reprimanding me for my language.

Rommel dismissed the guards and closed the flaps of his tent before getting in front of both of us and having us stand at attention. His expression was a mix of sheer rage and disappointment. He had to take a few deep breaths before saying anything. Despite his anger, he was as calm as he could possibly be when he spoke. "Both of you should be ashamed of yourselves."

I didn't say anything. Neither did Lehning.

"Aldrich Lehning, what is your rank?" Rommel asked.

Lehning raised an eyebrow. "Sir?"

"I said, what is your rank?"

"Colonel, sir."

"And how are colonels supposed to act? Are they supposed to start fights with prisoners?"

Lehning bit his lip, looking down at the ground. "No, sir."

"Officers are supposed to set examples for their men. Do I have to demote you in order to get that through your thick head?"

"I would not like that at all, sir."

"Honestly, I do not care what you want. You were the one moaning about how the search for the warlock is wasting precious time, and yet here you are starting fights with a prisoner. Your regiment is composed of capable men, and yet you insist on resorting to thuggish tactics in order to get them to listen to you. You and you alone are holding them back. Do not think for one second that the complaints lodged against you have not reached my desk. What goes on in your personal life should not be bleeding out into your command. This is not how you solve personal problems with other people. Is that the example you want to set?"

"I do not want to set an example of cowardice."

"If anything, you have been displaying cowardice by acting like this. I have problems with you, but do I start punching you over it? No. Do I make you clean the inside of a hot tank whenever I am angry with you? No. I talk to you about it, like I am doing now. Frankly, I have lost count of how many of these chats we have had since I arrived to check on your regiment. I am appalled by your behavior, and I feel I should not give you another chance. The fact that you struck a prisoner, which is a violation of the Geneva Convention—"

"He is a spy! He is not covered by the damn Geneva Convention!"

"He will be treated with the same respect we show every prisoner! That is final! As I was saying, the fact that you struck a prisoner is grounds for punishment. As for your personal conduct, I will decide tonight what will become of you. Go to your tent and stay there until I call for you."

My heart was beating faster and harder when Lehning left the tent. Rommel gave a heavy sigh and paced a bit before stopping in front of me. "Tell me the truth, Mr. Loalin, did he strike you first?"

I nodded.

"But, you did say, if your guard is recounting this correctly, 'Fuck you' to Lehning?"

"I did, sir."

"So, you are both in the wrong. You both decided to act like children."

I said nothing.

"If I did not have a warlock to worry about, I'd put you in your tent for the rest of the day. I know you Americans have very rough mannerisms, but you should know better than to mouth off to an officer."

"I am sorry, sir. I guess it was built up from how he treated us while we were in disguise. I felt like it was going to come to blows sooner or later. It was all a matter of time."

"Like I said, you should have handled yourself better. However, I will applaud you on your restraint with your... magical powers."

"I did not have the strength for it, and I knew using them could kill him."

"You would not use them if you had the strength?"

"No, sir."

"I just wish you had shown the same restraint when responding to Lehning."

"That is not always easy."

"It is not supposed to be easy, but it is what sets good leaders apart from others."

"I am no leader." My mind wandered to Antarctica. If I was a good leader, I wouldn't have let the South Pole journey end in disaster.

"You have the potential to be one if you set your heart and mind to it." Rommel glanced at his watch, and sighed. "Get back to searching for that wand. I will tell your guards that no one except myself is allowed to bother you."

I didn't rest until that night. Much to the disappointment of myself and everyone in the camp, my digging came up empty. I didn't say this to anyone, but I suspected the frequent arguing and pausing had given the warlock time to put his wand or staff in a new place.

Altschul approached me shortly before I was escorted to my tent. "I am sorry I have not talked to you sooner, but I have an idea. When you and Halcomb are taken to Tripoli, I will sneak onto the truck with you."

"You are prepared to do this? It will be obvious you've deserted."

Altschul nodded. "I am ready. I know I will be leaving a lot of friends behind, but this is more important."

"You will see your friends again. Are you leaving any family behind?"

"Just my parents. I fear what could happen to them after I am reported missing. I have not told them anything, but... that will not stop the Nazis from punishing them for my desertion."

"Perhaps there is something we can do."

"Do not concern yourself with that. It will be my problem, not yours." Glancing around, Altschul leaned in to whisper. "I also heard what happened today with Lehning. Frankly, if he gets demoted, it will be well earned."

"I tried my best to punch him hard," I said, grinning a little.

"Thank you. Now, you should get to bed." Altschul turned to head to his own tent.

I went to find the two guards assigned to me. They seemed a bit surprised I was so cooperative with them, but simply shrugged and led me to the tent where Halcomb and I were kept for the night.

"Anything?" Halcomb asked when I entered.

I shook my head before pulling my shirt off. Sure enough, there was a large bruise forming on my ribs where Lehning struck me.

"What happened?"

"Lehning happened," I said. "He asked if I had found anything and I told him to fuck off. He pulled me out of the tent I was digging under and we had a fistfight. Rommel broke it up and yelled at both of us in his tent."

Halcomb shook his head. "Can't believe the son of a bitch hit you."

I nodded as I sat on my cot, leaning over with my arms on my knees. Heat was pulsing through my body, and I felt like I was going to throw up.

"Did you hit him back?"

"I did."

"Hard?"

"As hard as I could." I rubbed my face. My hair was plastered to my forehead with sweat. "I need water."

Halcomb handed me his canteen. "Are you alright?"

"I'll be alright as the night goes on," I said. "Just need cold and rest."

A German soldier peered inside the tent. "Lamps out," he said.

Halcomb blew out the flame in the lamp in the center of the tent and laid back down on his cot. "We have to get out of here soon."

"I know."

"I'm not just referring to the mission anymore. The desert isn't healthy for you."

"The desert isn't healthy for anyone."

"And especially not for you. We need to just get up, grab Winter, and run."

"And what will happen when we're recaptured? I gave Rommel my trust and he gave me his. Following through on his word is the only way we're going to get out of this alive."

"I think you're taking a big risk by trusting a German field-marshal."

"It's been paying off so far."

"What about trusting me?"

"I am trusting you!"

"Not if you're trusting Rommel. I don't trust him."

"We both lose if we don't trust each other. I think he knows that. I'm the only one who can find the warlock, and he doesn't want it hanging around here anymore."

Halcomb shook his head. "I still don't trust him."

Sighing, I closed my eyes. Being stuck with two hard decisions wasn't a position I wanted to be in, despite knowing this was part of life. Then again, how many people will be stuck in a warzone and faced with having to trust their enemy to get out of it? Not many, I think. At the same time, did I have to agree to help the Germans? Honestly, I didn't. I was thinking long-term. I didn't want this warlock sneaking into the British or American ranks, but my other concern was just getting out of this alive.

Chapter 7

In the morning, I was roused by one of the German guards, who marched me to the mess tent. Private Heisig was inside, and he looked up at me before going back to his meal. I got the impression that he was sad or disappointed. He picked at his food and kept glancing at me. It was tempting to go over and talk to him, but I didn't see any way I would have a chance.

I was seated with Rommel, a few members of his staff, and some of the Italian liaisons, as well as General Faraci. They all looked at me when I sat down, and my face flushed red in embarrassment.

"We cannot dig up the whole of the Sahara to find this warlock," Rommel said. "What else do you know about witches? What else do they use or possess?"

I paused to think, staring down at my cup of watery coffee. "Cauldrons, crystal balls, Ouija boards, amulets. They fly on broomsticks."

"Any ordinary broomstick?"

"No. As far as I know, witch brooms are thicker. They are also highly polished to prevent splinters, and they are known to have a grip near the top."

Nodding, Rommel reached into his coat pocket. "Can you tell me what these are?" He pulled out a small empty glass bottle closed with a cork, and a flat wooden charm shaped like a bear.

The ornateness of the bottle told me it was likely a potion bottle. At the same time, it could be a woman's perfume bottle, but perfume usually isn't covered with a cork. The bear charm could just be someone's private memento, or it could very well be a witch's cursed charm. Given that Rommel was holding it with no ill effects, I didn't think it was cursed.

"They could belong to a witch, but they look ordinary enough to belong to anyone," I said. I took the cork out of the bottle. It smelled clean. "This could have had alcohol in it, but it is too small. Some highly potent potions are sold in bottles this size. Where did you find this?"

"Just outside the entrance of Lehning's tent. I went to speak to him last night and when I left, these were on the ground, half-buried in the sand."

The fact that the bear charm had been buried suggested it was indeed connected to a witch. "Do you think Lehning is the warlock?"

Rommel shrugged. "I highly doubt it, but is there a way to figure that out?"

"He would have sensed I'm a Conjurus from the beginning, and I do not think he murdered Kunst and Redler. He is crude, but I do not think he is a murderer or a warlock."

"I imagine all of that can be hidden."

"It can, but... no. I do not believe it is him." My curiosity got the best of me. "What is going to become of him?"

"He will not be demoted. Unfortunately, I need all of the officers I have. He will be punished, but what that will be is still to be decided."

Faraci leaned over to say, "I cannot believe you let a spy sit at this table and talk to him as an equal. This goes against all the rules. Are you not worried about him escaping?"

"Not particularly." Rommel glanced at me. "That does beg the question of why you have not attempted to flee."

"I want to find this warlock as much as you do," I said.

Faraci shook his head. "You cannot trust spies, even your own. They are too independent."

"This is a unique circumstance and must be treated as such. You have not run into witches in your ranks, have you?" asked Rommel.

"The witches and Conjurus back in Italy are fiercely independent and too dangerous to be brought into the fold of Italian life. We leave them alone and they leave us alone. We have never had problems with them."

"I guess our witches are a bit different, then."

"Most witches are barbarians," I said. "That is not to say they are not smart, though."

Rommel was silent for moment, deep in thought as he closely examined the bear charm. "Is it possible that there are some... I guess you could say, 'good' or 'passive' witches?"

"I've heard of some witch communities that are passive, but I still would not trust them. Witches are driven mainly by greed and lust for control. They have no rules, other than their own. They kill indiscriminately when they need something for a potion, which is exactly what happened here."

"What exactly does that make you, then?" an officer down the table spoke up. "Magical law enforcement?"

"No. I did not train to become a witch-hunter. Conjurus do not need anything to possess magic. We are born with it."

"It must make life interesting for you," Rommel said. "I imagine you are better suited to service in the harsh northern climates or mountaineering."

The conversation inched closer to Antarctica. I wasn't sure I wanted it to go there. "I am, but such opportunities have not presented themselves yet." I bit my tongue, hoping my attempts to dodge the topic weren't too obvious. I toyed with the bear charm a little. "We should get back to finding this warlock."

I started to wonder if I was going about this investigation the wrong way. After all, most start right at the scene of the crime. The problem was that no one had any idea where the murders could have taken place. They most likely occurred in the hospital tent, but there hadn't been any evidence of foul play when it was searched two days ago.

"It is entirely possible the warlock either suffocated Kunst and Redler or gave them poison in their food or water," I suggested a few hours after the breakfast talk I had with Rommel and his officers.

"According to the hospital paperwork, Lexis was primarily working with Kunst and Redler. I am surprised he did not find that when he last checked on them," Rommel said.

"He might not have found that necessary." I paused, holding the charm by its string. "Or Lexis is our warlock."

"Impossible. Lexis has served with me since the Battle of France. He saved many lives then."

"Remember what I said this morning. Witches will do anything to maximize their power. Being a medic or healer is a common ruse for them."

"In this case, I do not think so. Lexis proved his loyalty and worth in France."

"Sir, it is worth a check. We could be overlooking the clues we need."

"It would be a waste of time."

"Do you realize what could happen if we—"

Rommel silenced me with a glare. "I said, it would be a waste of time. I know Lexis well. His performance is why I brought him here."

"You need to trust me. I'm not saying this to belittle Lexis—I hardly know him—but it is possible that he is the warlock and he's been hiding it all this time."

"To trust you in this matter would be going against my own judgement."

"This is not an accusation against Lexis. If you let me examine his tent, perhaps I will be proven wrong."

The silence that filled the tent was heavy and tense. Rommel was looking down at his desk. The map that lay across it had been flipped to keep me from seeing any of his writing on it. He let out a sigh. "The bear is on the coat of arms for Berlin. Lexis is from a village just outside Berlin. That is the only connection I can see."

"If he is a warlock, his familiar might be a bear."

"What is a familiar?"

"A magical animal companion, one of the few things a witch can conjure without a wand. They have a somewhat ghostly appearance and they are more than capable of hurting living people."

"I have not seen any bear tracks around here."

"Well, I do not think anyone could summon a bear without being noticed."

"True." Rommel rubbed his face, sighing again. "I will let you check the hospital tent."

"Thank you. I really am sorry about—"

"Do not apologize. You have every right to suspect Lexis. I just pray you're wrong."

I hoped I was wrong as well, but much of the evidence was now pointing to Lexis. Leaving Rommel alone in his tent, I made my way over to the field hospital. None of the cots were occupied at the time. One of the medics was checking drip bags and sanitizing instruments. Corporal Lexis was coming out of the morgue just as I entered. "Good morning," he said. "What can I do for you?"

"I think I might be able to find clues of our warlock here," I replied.

Lexis shook his head. "I looked. No wands, no staffs, and no signs of warlocks. He just took the body and ran. No trace."

"Perhaps you missed something. I am just making sure."

Lexis sighed. "Fine." He eyed me as I headed to the back of the tent, looking displeased.

There were a couple of bodies awaiting burial in the small space. Something about that little room was... unsettling, and a sense of unease passed through me. Fighting it, I looked under the tables and in the cabinets. Nothing. Standing straight, I looked over at Lexis, who was standing in the doorway. "Did you see anything suspicious at all when this happened?"

Lexis shook his head. "No."

The two corpses on the tables were starting to look like McIntyre and Duncan. I could see frost spreading over their faces, their lips and extremities turning a dark purple. The soft sound of sand moving in the wind outside suddenly turned into a howling blizzard. "No, get me out of here!" I covered my face, a gasping cry escaping me.

I backed out of the room unsteadily. Suddenly the howling blizzard stopped, replaced by the sound of sand again.

Lexis walked over to me. In his hand was a black, wood wand. He gave me a slight smile. "Have you had enough, Conjurus?"

I backed away from him, anxiously switching my gaze between Lexis and the wand. It was no different from staring down the barrel of a gun.

"Did you think I did not know what you are when you came here?" Lexis placed his wand close to my face.

"What is it that you want?"

"Originally, I wanted nothing. Now that you are here, my orders are to make you disappear and send you up to Germany. Wahler will be proud of this one."

"What are you talking about?"

"What do you think I'm talking about? You might not be a German soldier, but you are good enough for White Raven, a Conjurus all the same, and you are the son of Morgan Loalin, the one who inspired this project. You, and the powerless humans you claim to protect, are nothing more than cattle. Every part of you and them is harvestable."

"So, you are a spy for Wahler?" I was stunned that a soldier would spy on his fellow soldiers. "Why? These are your own people."

"Not the Conjurus, and certainly not the useless non-magicals. Nobody here is 'my people.' My job is to weed you out and send you to Wahler, and I am not the only one. We are on the Eastern Front as well, and in France, the Netherlands, Belgium, Norway, and Denmark. Everywhere the Germans have occupied, Wahler has sent spies to collect any cryomancers who might be hiding."

"In return for what? I knew witches and warlocks were cruel, but this is a step above what you normally do."

"In return for being left alone when the war is over, when we no longer have to live in the shadows, afraid of you." Lexis grinned, poking his wand into my neck. "I am honestly insulted the Allies sent someone with no experience in handling us. What, do you think I'm only capable of pulling a rabbit out of a hat?" He lowered his wand to my chest and flicked it. An invisible force sent me flying out of the morgue, tearing through the tent fabric and rolling into the sand. The air had been sucked from my lungs, and I gasped for breath as I struggled to get back up.

Lexis appeared in the doorway, brandishing his wand. Frost and mist formed around my hands. A blue dome appeared around Lexis as he pushed a bed onto its side and ducked for cover after I threw an icicle at him. The dome disappeared and Lexis's wand popped up, shooting a bolt of energy at me.

Still trying to breathe, I crossed my wrists, grunting with the effort as a shield of ice formed swiftly in front of myself. The magic bolt gouged a hole in the surface of the ice.

The shield wasn't going to hold up for long in the desert heat. Finding my breath, I broke cover to throw a hailstone. It knocked Lexis's bed back and smashed into large chunks. Another magic bolt hit the shield, creating a massive crack across it, and water ran down and darkened the sand beneath as it melted. I clenched my fist and flicked my fingers forward, sending small shards of ice toward Lexis. The shards cut through parts of the bed, and I heard Lexis grunt in pain.

The noise hadn't gone unnoticed. Altschul and several soldiers and medics ran in, and were shocked at what was going on. One of the soldiers grabbed the back of my shirt, demanding what I was doing when Altschul shouted, "Lexis has a wand! He's a fucking witch!"

"So you murdered Kunst and Redler!" the soldier yelled at Lexis, aiming an MP40 at him. "One of our own fucking medics!"

I managed to stand and slowly walked over to the bed. Lexis was lying on his side, blood running from jagged wounds all over his body. I reached down to take his wand, and his hand lashed out to grab my right wrist. Blood dripped from his mouth as he pulled himself up to tackle me over the bed. I tried to cross my wrists and put up an ice shield before he could punch me, but he kept wrestling with my hand. Then he turned my wrist hard and I howled in pain. He was trying to break it.

There was a loud thump and Lexis's grip went slack. I opened my eyes to see Lexis off to the side, and Altschul standing over us, gripping his pistol by the barrel. Holding my arm, I scrambled away from Lexis's unconscious form.

"Are you alright?" Altschul held out his hand.

"I think so." I took his hand, letting him help me up. My wrist was sore and throbbing. It hurt to move. "Thank you."

"No, I should thank you. I... cannot believe Lexis... was a warlock."

"It is not easy to spot if you don't know what to look for," I said.

"I knew witches cannot be trusted, and I've seen them do horrible things, but I just cannot believe he was hiding in plain sight."

"He deliberately chose that position to do as much damage as he could." I picked up Lexis's wand and snapped it in half. There was a puff of smoke and sparks from the two halves. "These need to be burned," I said.

"What do you propose we do with him?" Altschul asked.

"Usually witch-hunters kill them with a stake through their heart and then burn the body to prevent necromancers from getting ahold of it."

As I discussed the procedure with Altschul, Rommel stepped in the tent, trailed by more soldiers. "What's going on in here?" he asked.

I looked down at Lexis, unsure of what to say. "I was right. Lexis was the warlock."

"I still want to know what happened."

"I came in looking for clues. He attacked me with his wand." I held up the wand pieces. "I had no choice. I had to defend myself."

"He is telling the truth, sir," Altschul said. "Lexis got on top of him and tried to break his wrist when we arrived."

"So, all this time, it was Lexis." Rommel looked conflicted. He folded his arms over his chest and began to pace, staring down at the ground. "I thought I knew him. I trusted him. Somehow, I still see the boy who enlisted from the outskirts of Berlin. I cannot believe it was all a lie. He seemed so innocent and genuine when I met him in France, and he was a good medic, too. He saved an innumerable amount of infantrymen and tank crew members. That is why I requested he be moved to the *Afrika Korps*. That is not something I would do for just anyone, only someone who really proves their worth."

"Witches and warlocks are master manipulators, never to be trusted." I could tell this betrayal was hitting Rommel hard. "Anyone could have been taken in by it."

"I cannot just kill him. It's not right."

"I'll do it."

"No. We will send him back to Germany and put him on trial for this. He can sit in prison."

I wasn't sure if it was right for me to tell Rommel the truth about what would actually happen. Lexis wouldn't be put on trial. He would just get sent somewhere else. That, and Rommel could get in serious trouble for letting an

Allied spy help him. Part of me even wondered if he could get in trouble for disrupting Lexis's mission, but then again, this was none of my business anymore.

Lexis was given treatment, but several hours after the fight, he died from internal bleeding. He was buried unceremoniously and quietly—those were Rommel's terms. I wasn't allowed to destroy Lexis's heart, but he wouldn't be given any honors upon burial.

I found it fair, and, frankly, I didn't think I would be able to put a stake through a man's chest anyway. It was quite horrible listening to the other medics in camp talking in shocked and hushed tones about how they couldn't believe Lexis had been faking and using them all this time.

That night, I knew our adventures in North Africa had to come to a close before midnight, or else the submarine would be gone. As I headed back to my tent, I was just hoping we could get Altschul out along with us.

Halcomb was surprised that Lexis turned out to be the warlock when I told him. "He was the last person in this entire sandpit that I thought would be one. I actually thought it would be Lehning."

"I knew it wasn't Lehning," I said. "He seemed in shock when he found Kunst's body."

"I'm just glad we're leaving soon." Halcomb made sure he had everything packed in his knapsack, then whispered, "Where's Winter?"

I didn't want to say anything more with the guards outside. Escaping probably won't be easy, and a part of me felt horrible that after being as cooperative as possible, we were now going to break the trust of the Germans by fleeing into the night with one of their own.

At least with the warlock out of the picture, all we had to worry about now was getting Altschul. Shortly before lights-out, Rommel entered the tent with Altschul close behind, holding a chocolate bar. "I believe one of my men promised this for a cigarette." He handed it to Halcomb.

"That is alright," Halcomb said. "I had forgotten about it anyway. Keep it."

"No, no, I insist. Take it."

Halcomb gave him a mistrustful look, before plucking the bar from Rommel's hand. "Fine."

Rommel looked at me, not paying much attention to Halcomb's behavior. "If we were not on opposing sides of a war, I would reward you handsomely. I suppose the best I can do is offer you tea. You might have saved all of our lives by exposing Lexis." Rommel didn't sound at all happy. The fact that Lexis wasn't who he had made himself out to be was still hitting him hard, and I suspected Rommel was going to have a much harder time trusting people. "This is probably going to be the only time in my life I am going to interact with a Conjurus."

I glanced at Halcomb, who sighed and shrugged. "Go if you want." I could feel he wanted to tell me not to take too long.

I followed Rommel out. Altschul nodded to me before disappearing into our tent to talk with Halcomb. It felt strange that this was our last day here. In a way, I would miss it. Perhaps not the abuse and the weather, but the people and the experience.

I don't think many people throughout the course of the war would be able to say they had tea with one of Germany's most prolific field-marshals. It felt more like two ordinary men, which was probably the best part of it. Rommel was also highly curious about the Conjurus in general, and I didn't mind the questions. Frankly, it was nice not having someone pity me because I lost my father so young, or look at me strangely because my father was the one who got Conjurus banned from the draft back in the States. I guess this was where I started to feel that I was more than my last name.

When the tea was finished, I was escorted back to my tent. Along the way, we spotted Lehning pacing outside his, smoking a cigarette. He looked as sour as ever. Rommel stood in front of me when he approached us, but he held up his hands.

"I am not here to fight, sir," he said. "I want to say something to Loalin."

Rommel let out a sigh. "Just remember what we discussed last night." He stepped off the side, observing us closely.

Lehning looked at me. His sourness had turned into something a bit more somber. "Lexis was the warlock?"

I nodded.

"I cannot believe it." Lehning swore aloud. "He was the last person in the entire army I would have suspected of being a warlock."

"His disguise was almost perfect," I said.

"Rommel trusted him since France." Lehning bit his lip. "I know what it is like."

"What exactly do you want?" I asked.

"I know I gave you a hard time when you came, but are you willing to accept an apology?"

I shifted my weight, folding my arms over my chest. "I guess. Why do you want to apologize now? Is it because we're leaving tomorrow and you will never see us again?"

"Partly, if you want me to be completely honest."

"Did Rommel make you do this?"

"He said it would be a good idea, but, again, that is only part of the reason."

"Then spit it out."

Lehning sighed, clearly unsure of whether or not he wanted to do this, but he finally said, "I owe you my respect, Loalin. I did not expect you to actually fight back when I struck you. I honestly thought you were just going to curl up in the sand and cry, but you managed to hold your own. I was impressed. That, and I am glad you didn't give up looking for the warlock."

"This has something to do with Russia, doesn't it?"

"It does. The officer who died, Colonel Seydel, was a warlock, and I am telling the truth when I say I did not kill him. Somebody else did. He did not kill any of our troops like Lexis did, but he went after civilians. I was one of a few who tried to stop it, and I suppose that is how the blame fell on me."

"Convenience," I said.

"That is what it looked like. Much like Lexis, no one suspected there was anything off about Seydel. It was only when civilians started disappearing and corpses turned up with pieces missing that we realized something was terribly wrong. I knew right away it was a witch. The cuts were too neat to have been left by an animal."

"And yet you did not want to believe me when I said there was a warlock in this camp."

"I did not want it to be true, because I did not want to go through Russia again." Lehning stepped closer, whispering, "I am sure that's something you in particular would understand."

I looked down at the sand, nodding.

"I thought so." Lehning stepped back. "I will see you at the end of the war, Loalin." He held out his hand.

I figured it was best to not hold a grudge anymore, so I took it. "As long as the British do not capture you before then."

As Lehning walked away, I began wondering if I could ever really trust him, but I had to be careful in thinking that, because there might be a day where I might wind up in a situation where I have to depend on him to survive. I prayed I never did.

Rommel walked back over to me. "Lehning still has a lot to learn, but apologizing and admitting his mistakes was the first step."

"I am surprised you convinced him to apologize," I replied.

"I have my ways." As we headed back to my tent, Rommel looked at me from the corner of his eye. "I would like to end this with saying that I hope we meet again under better circumstances. You are a fascinating individual, Mr. Loalin."

"As are you, Field-Marshal."

Stopping at the tent, Rommel offered his hand. I took it, and he gripped mine firmly before letting go and going back to his own tent for the night. To this day, I'm still surprised that I was able to interact so closely with a man who had become quite a legendary figure, and as much as I hoped I would see him again—under better circumstances—I didn't think I ever would. Such things were a once-in-a-lifetime occurrence.

"I'll never understand how you did it," Halcomb muttered as I came in.

"Did what?" I asked.

"Well, you clearly impressed him."

"I impressed you, didn't I?"

"You did."

"I seem to have that effect on people. Even though I don't feel that impressive."

"Could you at least take pride in the fact that you persuaded one of Germany's best commanders to spare us?"

"That wasn't me. He chose to spare us when it was within his right to execute both of us for being spies. I had nothing to do with it."

"I doubt that. If we were ordinary spies or if you hadn't said anything, we would've been shot."

I shrugged. "I don't think we'll ever be sure. I just hope we don't get in trouble for this."

"'We?' Oh, no, Jay, you deciding to catch a warlock and help the Germans was all you. I was the one trying to convince you that we needed to get out as soon as possible."

"I probably saved a lot of people, both Allied and Axis, by doing this. If Stafford can't understand that then that's on him."

Altschul breathed a sigh of relief when Rommel left. "Do you think he saw me?"

"I do not think so," I said.

Halcomb looked at his watch. "We have four hours to get to the coast. We need to move now."

"Right." Altschul glanced outside. "We should make it look like we're just going out for a smoke."

"It cannot be that easy."

"You said we don't have a lot of time. It's worth a try. The moon is not full, so we have the cover of darkness. Just follow my lead until we are out of camp. Wait here."

Altschul left the tent, saying good night to the guards on the way out. A moment later, we heard a soft tapping on the fabric at the back of the tent. Halcomb slipped under the bottom edge first, and I followed him. We walked out to the base perimeter, occasionally glancing over our shoulders to make sure we weren't being watched. Altschul wasn't comfortable with using the fact that most of the men in camp trusted him in order to break their trust. When we were a good distance away, we waited until a patrol passed by and then Altschul pulled out a compass.

We began heading north, breaking into a run at first, but slowing as we got farther and farther away from the camp. I frantically kept looking over my shoulder, afraid the Germans were coming after us, but there were no signs of pursuit. They had no idea we were gone yet.

It took us well over an hour to get to the coast. Once we could see the Mediterranean Sea, we began looking for the rock outcropping where we had been told one of the submarine's crew would be stationed at all times to keep watch for us. After several minutes, we saw what looked like the right place in the distance, and began jogging towards it. As we closed in, a solitary figure stood up from one of the top rocks, partially silhouetted against the starlit sky. "It's a warm night," the figure called in English.

"But the winter is cold where we're going," Halcomb replied with the countersign.

The man jumped down from the rocks and approached us, and I saw he was about my age and wore a sailor's uniform with a crooked cap covering thick, dark hair. "I was starting to think you weren't going to show up. I'll radio the submarine and we'll row out to it."

Altschul, Halcomb, and I dragged the small inflatable raft out from its hiding place down to the water while the sailor used a hand radio to contact the submarine. As all four of us got into the raft and began rowing into deeper water, we saw the submarine breach the surface of the water a short distance away.

Once we were on board the submarine, the sailor, Petty Officer Norman, showed us to a room and told us to get comfortable for the trip to Italy. Altschul was quiet until Norman left, and then sighed before saying, "I did say I would give you the information once I knew I was getting out of here."

"You did," Halcomb said.

"Well, it is a long story. I was a platoon leader in Poland when the war started. Not long after the occupation started, Wahler and his personnel came looking for ice-variant Conjurus. There are Conjurus serving in all branches of the German military. It is how they hide, to avoid suspicion and protect their families. Wahler was trying to find if there were any among the regular military. He made it look like he just needed guards for his facilities, because Himmler supposedly was not giving him anymore than he was already assigned."

"You were among them?" I asked.

Altschul nodded. "I saw things no man should ever see, and I have seen horrible things here and in Poland."

"We have pictures from Poland."

"Those were from me. I passed them on to a Polish Conjurus who said he had a way of getting them out of the country. I knew it was a risk, but who else could I trust?" Altschul looked down at the deck. "The experiments they performed were... unspeakable."

"On living people?"

"On living people. Not just on Polish soldiers, but on our own men as well. And we were all threatened into silence. The only thing I knew was that there was no one to trust. Himmler sanctioned this. There was no way I could go to any of my commanding officers, because they would probably be told the same thing. This is all for the betterment of Germany, so I heard, and there are going to be sacrifices." Altschul's face reddened as he held back his anger. "I cannot let them get away with it."

"That is our mission," I said. "We are going to get you out of here and then we will kill Wahler. We just need to know exactly where he is."

"I cannot be sure if he is still there, but his primary headquarters is a castle in town just south of Munich. I have heard rumors that he has necromancers assisting him, but I left before I could verify them, so I would go into this very carefully."

I nodded. "We will do what we can."

"I wish I knew how to thank you, Loalin, and the OSS for actually trusting me." Altschul looked at Halcomb. "We are not all crazy monsters."

"I can look at you differently because you did keep your word and told us," Halcomb replied. "The rest of your people—" he shook his head. "Lehning did not help your image."

"Lehning actually apologized to me before we left," I said. "I figured I would accept it so there is no more ill will between us."

Halcomb snorted. "I would happily punch him myself if we ever run into him again."

"I served with Lehning ever since being transferred to North Africa," Altschul said. "There is more to him than you might suspect."

"I am curious how his career as a boxer went," I said.

"He does not talk much about it, but one of the other lieutenants said he remembered going to a match with his father and seeing Lehning fight about fifteen years ago. He asked the colonel about it, and that was the first time I saw something more to him than just the military officer. He spoke calmly and told the lieutenant about his career. He was well-known in his home city of Mannheim, but never had any fights outside of Germany."

"How did he end up in the military?" Halcomb asked.

"He needed to pay his bills somehow. He made some money boxing, but not enough, especially since he was not the best of the best. With the restrictions from the Treaty of Versailles, he wasn't given much to do after training, but he at least had something coming in while boxing on the side. Anyway, when the Nazis came to power, Lehning had less time to box. He was never well-liked by the old Prussian officers because of how stubborn and impulsive he was. That caught the attention of officers like Rommel, though. He thought he could take Lehning under his wing and help him channel his energy into command."

"We have already seen that did not work."

"According to Rommel, Lehning was showing promise during the Battle of France. Yes, he was brutish and needed to stop terrorizing his men whenever they so much as flinched, but he had no problems with being right up in the action with them. One more than one occasion he took control of a machine gun when the gunner was injured and provided cover while the medics took the gunner away. There was an incident where a gunner died before the medics could reach him, and Lehning did not realize it until the medics arrived. I heard later he admitted he had been talking to the kid the whole time."

"He certainly did not act like he cares for those under him while we were there."

"That was before Operation Barbarossa. I only know some of what happened there-"

"Lehning did tell me about the murder of Colonel Seydel," I interrupted. "He was a warlock who started killing civilians in southern Russia. Lehning wanted to put a stop to it, but someone else got to Seydel first. He was blamed simply because he was there, but there was no actual evidence."

"How did he know Seydel was a warlock?"

"The condition the bodies were in when they were found."

Altschul nodded. "Lehning was moved to North Africa back at the end of July. Rommel was happy to see him again, but Lehning was… not quite the same. He was a more withdrawn. I have a feeling he saw things in the Soviet Union that no one should see."

"He did mention to me that he had to work with the SS."

Altschul fell silent for a moment. "I do not want to imagine the things he saw."

Halcomb glanced at me, then back at Altschul. "We might not be able to end the war, but at least we will try to prevent more horrible things from being witnessed."

Chapter 8

The journey from the coast of Libya to Genoa was incredibly long and risky. The submarine had to navigate around the Italian Navy's ships, and we were all nervous despite Norman assuring us that this particular submarine was no stranger to spy operations.

When Norman came to announce we were approaching the European mainland, I looked at Halcomb, and somehow, I could sense that we were thinking the same thing. *Was this a dream?* No, it can't have been a dream. I could still feel the aching in my wrist from when Lexis tried to break it and the hot dryness of the desert, hear the rumbling of tanks passing by the tents Lehning's shouting whenever he grew irritated with the slightest thing, and smell gasoline and cleaning solutions, Rommel's tea and the watery coffee of the mess tent. It wasn't a dream.

Altschul was asleep on a small bunk nearby. I couldn't imagine what was going through his mind. He was leaving everything and everyone he knew and loved just to give us some information. Then again, I left my home and family so I could have this adventure. The only difference was that my family was safe. If the Nazis wanted, they would execute Altschul's if they suspected they had a hand in turning him against the Reich. When I asked him if there was a chance we could rescue his parents, Altschul's reply was, "They're all the way up in Essen. That's a bit too much of a detour from Munich."

Norman's voice pulled me from my thoughts. "Good morning, gentlemen. Everyone up and ready to go?"

Halcomb reached over to gently shake Altschul, who jumped and recoiled. When he saw it was only Halcomb, he released his breath and sat up. "What is going on?"

"We are almost at Genoa."

"We're down the coast from Genoa," Norman said. "We'll be dropping you off in a secluded area, as close to the city as we can, but not so close that we attract attention."

"How close are we talking?" Halcomb asked.

"A few miles. There are naval vessels in the area and we don't need them seeing us."

"Fair enough. When will we be landing?"

"About half-an-hour." Norman turned to Altschul. "You'll be riding with us back to the States. That's what you wanted, correct?"

After I translated, Altschul nodded. At the same time, he looked conflicted. "I want to go with you, but I'm also terrified of what could happen if we were to be captured. By now, everyone in North Africa probably knows I'm missing."

I nodded. "We'll be alright. You gave us what we need, and we appreciate you for that."

"I don't know how to thank you for believing me and getting me out of there."

"All I ask is that you take care of yourself. The United States is a big country, so there will be plenty to keep you occupied while you are there. Personally, I recommend New York, but you might feel more at home in Pennsylvania. There are lot of historic German communities there."

Altschul gave me a weak smile. "I cannot imagine what everyone's thinking in North Africa, especially the people I was close to. Getting up and running without saying a word to them feels... heartless."

"You had a good reason to run."

"I know, but I trusted them. I should have said something to prevent them from worrying."

"You think they could be trusted with the knowledge that you were going to defect?" Halcomb raised an eyebrow.

"I think they could, but I did not tell them because I know if they knew, they would say something if interrogated. Keeping this information from them will keep them safe."

The next half-hour went by rather slowly, as the crew tried to surface somewhere secluded. Once we stopped, Norman came to get me and Halcomb. Before leaving the submarine, I turned to Altschul, taking his hand in a firm grip. "It was a pleasure working with you."

Altschul managed a more genuine smile. "It was a pleasure working with you as well. Hopefully, we will work together again someday. I am sure the OSS will find my inside knowledge useful."

"They probably will." I looked over at Halcomb. "You are not going to say goodbye?"

Altschul shook his head, whispering, "He does not have to if he doesn't want to."

Halcomb sighed before holding out his hand. "At least you proved to me that some Germans can be trusted."

"There are a good number of Germans that can be trusted," Altschul replied. "The trick is finding them, and separating them out from the ones who will happily do you harm." He glanced at me. "I wish you both the best of luck out there. Please, come find me when the mission is over. I would like to hear everything you are allowed to tell me about it."

"We will," I said.

With that, Halcomb and I climbed up the ladder out of the submarine. We had to swim from the sub, which disappeared below the waves as soon as we were away. It was fairly late in the morning, as the sun wasn't yet directly over us. All was quiet aside from the seabirds and low horns from civilian ships in the harbors of Genoa. Climbing up the hill that guarded the beach, Halcomb and I could see that we were indeed several miles away from the city.

"Right." Halcomb looked around. "The Cristaldi farm is about fifteen miles directly east of the city. We have some walking to do."

Early autumn in Italy is truly a sight to see. The landscape was probably the most beautiful thing about our circumstances. I couldn't believe I was there, although, to quote Rommel, I wish it were under better circumstances.

We started walking, and eventually Halcomb broke the silence. "I'd like to apologize for how I acted in North Africa. I should have just trusted you."

"You had a right to be upset. What happened was something I could have easily ignored and saved us a lot of time."

"No, I think you were right. If we let Lexis go, we could have created a lot of unnecessary casualties."

"Which is exactly what I told you."

"I had to think about it for a little bit. For that, I'm sorry, and... if we're going to be partners on this mission, we have to trust each other. I'm honestly surprised you didn't seem offended by how I was acting."

I shook my head. "I could understand your frustration. That, and I'm used to arguing from my time in Antarctica. You weren't nearly as bad as some of those instances."

"Well, I appreciate you putting up with me and being so calm."

"No problem." I rested my head against a tree trunk, and looked at my watch. "It's nearly four. Should we keep going, or should we rest for the night?"

"I think we should keep going. The sooner we get to the farm, the better. We already spent more time than necessary in North Africa."

"Agreed. What are we doing about food? I know there's a stream nearby that we can drink from, but we can't go into any towns nearby. We have no money and it would be too much of a detour."

"I already ate that chocolate bar."

"For heaven's sake, Lester, that thing had to be over a foot long and several inches wide."

"Possibly, but I'll give the Germans this; they make good chocolate."

I resisted a smirk. "Have you ever hunted before? I've seen rabbits around here."

"No, but I know how to butcher an animal."

"Good. We'll do that."

"We also have no weapons."

"We're not entirely unarmed," I said. "You have me."

"True. Please forgive me if I forget sometimes."

We managed to catch one rabbit, so our dinner was small, but it would be enough for the next few hours. We buried everything afterward, not wanting to leave any traces of our presence.

We were reliant on the sun and road signs to point us in the right direction, though we had to switch to the moon once the sun began going down. Admittedly, it didn't take long for us to start feeling hungry, but we pressed on, even as the countryside grew darker. As we walked along a dirt path, we both froze when we heard the clopping of horse hooves and the creaking of wooden wheels, and ran into the bushes along the side of the path. A cart drawn by a single horse came along. The cart itself was full of crates and hay bales, and it was driven by a little old man in a patchy brown cloak.

The cart stopped, and the old man got off. "I am not blind yet! Come out of there!"

We both emerged from the bushes with our hands over our heads. Halcomb was looking at me, and hissed, "If he figures out who we are—"

"I don't think he will," I said, then I switched to Italian. "Who are you? Can you help us?"

"Help with what? I have to get this cart to market. I am already extremely late after a whole herd of sheep escaped and blocked a road earlier."

"We need a ride. We are going to see a friend, and… our horse was spooked by a plane and ran off."

The old man rubbed his beard, and shrugged. "I do not like helping strangers I meet in the middle of nowhere, but…" He stepped closer, and squinted at me. "You are an ice-variant, are you not, boy?"

I nodded.

"I have never seen you around before. I am Marsilio." He held out a shaky arthritic hand.

"Pleased to meet you, sir," I said. "Will you help us?"

"No. Not until I know who you are. If you were Italian soldiers—which you do not look like—I would, because they would have my head mounted on *Il Duce's* mantelpiece if I did not. Are you German, then? Italian resistance?"

"How can we trust you if we tell you who we are?"

"I am a fire-variant. We are not involved with the war. It does not matter to me who you're fighting for, just leave me and my family out of it." Marsilio jerked his thumb toward his cart. "Get in. I will take you to my village. Just watch your mouths when we get there. Some of my people have killed or chased out both Axis and resistance soldiers for trying to persuade us to join them."

Isolated Conjurus villages exist in just about every country. They don't mind outsiders, but don't wish to be dragged into any outsiders' business. When we arrived in the village, it was fairly easy to see that Faraci was right about their Conjurus being fiercely independent from the rest of Italy. The village Marsilio took us to was a large cluster of medieval-style houses and some Victorian houses lining cobblestone streets. Conjurus are picky about what new technologies and styles they adopt, and only do so if it benefits them. We have no common language, though attempts have been made to form one. Marsilio's village, thankfully, spoke Italian. He dropped us off in the village square, which was packed with merchant stands. Some were closing up for the night, while others were still open. There was a fountain in the center, and some children were tossing coins and pebbles into it. Men and women walked the streets in heavy cloaks and cowls.

"Where are you going?" Marsilio asked after unloading his product from the back of his cart.

"A farm owned by the Cristaldi family," I replied.

"I do not know that family. Talk to the town librarian. He knows everyone from here to Genoa."

I was a little disheartened, but accepted it anyway. "Thank you. How can we repay you?"

"Do you have any money? Buy some apples."

"Unfortunately, we do not have any."

"Then leave the village as soon as you can without starting trouble."

Nodding, I glanced at Halcomb. "We won't be eating here, not unless you want to do favors for some of the vendors."

"What?" Halcomb gave me a look.

"Charity is not a concept among these villages. If you want something you can't pay for, you must work."

"Whatever. We don't have time to eat anyway. Let's find that librarian."

I could hear Halcomb's stomach grumbling behind me, and all I could do was pray his crankiness didn't get us in a heap of trouble. Sighing, I looked down the streets stretching out before us. Several looked like they led to residential sections. Not wanting to wonder the village all day, I approached a vendor packing up her candles for the night. "Excuse me, ma'am? We are looking for the library. Could you-"

"You see the fruit stand in front of the bakery? Go down the street on its left," the woman said, pointing.

"Thank you."

"You are welcome. Get out of here."

Halcomb leaned in to whisper when we left the stand. "Why are they so hostile?"

"We're outsiders," I said. "I imagine they haven't had much positive contact with people outside of this village lately."

We turned and headed down a street lined with shops and trees and glowing streetlamps. A couple was taking a leisurely stroll, holding hands. They didn't pay us a second glance when they passed us.

It didn't take us long to find the library. We walked up the steps of a brick mansion with a library sign by the sidewalk. The doors were unlocked, but when we entered, we couldn't see anyone. The check-out desk had books scattered over it, and there were stacks and stacks of books behind it. If we weren't on a mission, I would have gladly done some exploring.

A black cat was asleep in a box by the stairway. It looked at us lazily with icy blue eyes, then sat up to meow up the stairs. A second later, a skinny older man in a suit with a pocket watch came jogging down. "Hello, hello!" he said, holding out his hand. "Lyco Amadeo. And you?"

"Jay Loalin, and this is Lester Halcomb," I replied.

"A Conjurus? You are not from around here, then. I know just about everyone here."

"No. We are trying to get to the Cristaldi farm, and we were told you knew how to get there."

"Are you friends of theirs?" Amadeo looked suspicious of us.

"Yes."

Amadeo paused to think for a moment. "I can lend you a horse and cart, and you can stay here for the night. It will rain soon."

I was grateful for Amadeo's kindness, but I had to remind myself that he might give us away to the Italians if they came along, as unlikely as that might be. Frankly, I wouldn't blame him if giving us up meant the village wouldn't get razed to the ground.

The rain had started falling and was drumming the roof and clacking against the window by the time the three of us sat down to dinner.

"I would assume you both would like a hot beverage this evening?" Amadeo asked.

"Yes, please," I said. "Thank you."

Amadeo disappeared into the kitchen and returned with a box of teabags and a steaming kettle of water. "You are not Italian, and you are not German, so who are you?"

Halcomb and I exchanged glances. "Why would we tell you if we were not? And what makes you think we are not?"

"It is my job to be observant and to see things others do not. Might your presence have something to do with a raven, perhaps? One with an unusual color?"

"You are with the Italian Resistance," I said, leaning forward in my chair.

"The Conjurus side, yes. Along with Vivaldo, Elvira's father." Amadeo waited until we had filled our plates and glasses before serving himself. "I received word over a month ago that someone would be attempting to go into Germany to deal with the experiments being conducted on our people and that I might need to help them. You're going right into the heart of enemy territory. You would have to be extremely brave or extremely suicidal to pull this off."

"I think extremely insane might be the better term," Halcomb said. "Jay is certainly that."

I wasn't sure whether to smirk or roll my eyes. "We volunteered for this task, and we will see it through to the end."

"I certainly hope you do," Amadeo replied. "My only wish is to take Italy out of this war. Nothing more, nothing less. The Italian Conjurus have lived in peace for centuries, and we would like it to stay that way. However, too many of us think that just ignoring the conflict will make it go away. German soldiers, Italian soldiers, and Magicless resistance fighters have been murdered because of this. Almost none of our people have stopped to think about helping others beyond the walls of our village, to help end the war."

"That's how they will be until the war comes to them," Halcomb replied. "Many Conjurus in Poland were the same way until the Germans ripped them from their homes. Now they are collaborating with witches to assist the Home Army, or so I have heard."

Amadeo nodded a little. "Truly a strange sight to see, given our history with witches."

"But no more unusual than the fact that we are allied with the Soviet Union. They persecute Conjurus and witches, and yet here we are."

"That persecution has been a driving force in changing the relations between Conjurus and witches all across Europe. My village even took in several witches who fled Russia shortly after the fall of the czar, which is certainly a first."

"I never thought that could be possible," I said. "I had been taught witches cannot be trusted, and after having an encounter with a witch in North Africa... I'd be hard-pressed to trust one."

"While relations in general may change, I think it is safe to say not all witches will become trustworthy. Many of the ones who came here only did so because we promised protection in exchange for them not hunting us or the local Magicless farmers. Several of them were not thrilled with that, but the majority of them complied. Now, they still live here, and they have assimilated well. You might have seen them and not even known it." Amadeo glanced at me and Halcomb, smiling a little. "I cannot force everyone in this village to assist me. That is why I am very grateful for your help. When you return home, send my thanks to Colonel Stafford."

In the morning, Amadeo gave us a cart and a horse with black and white splotches. "Follow the northwest road, through the forest. You will come out to a large vineyard. Follow the vineyard north until you see a sign for the farm at a fork in the road. You will see the house and the fields once you are on that road." Amadeo patted the horse on its neck. "And take care of Marietta, please? The Cristaldi family will ensure she is returned to me."

"We will take good care of her," I said, adjusting my cloak.

"Good. That is the only payment I want for this. Be careful in the forest if you get stuck there overnight. Witches and werewolves have always made travel through there difficult."

"We can handle ourselves," I replied.

Halcomb looked at me once we were away. "Witches *and* werewolves?"

"They hate each other, but they hate the Conjurus more," I explained. "Same with vampires."

"Are they as awful in reality as they are in the stories?"

"They're both a lot more complicated than in the stories, but they're still dangerous and should be left to the professionals to deal with."

"And you're not a professional."

"No, but I can defend us if it comes down to it. Just do what I say if we run into trouble."

The forest was quite pretty and peaceful, especially since the weather was decent. It was calm, and I was grateful for that after the last several weeks of feeling tense and on edge. It was nice not feeling like someone was looking over my shoulder. It was nice feeling alone.

We came out of the forest just before noon, though we still had several hours of travel ahead of us. After resting and having something to eat, we continued traveling, as the western horizon turned a deep red hue and darkness began shrouding the sky.

Halcomb broke the silence. "You know, if I told myself a month ago that I would be going over to Europe in the middle of a war, I wouldn't believe myself. I know I volunteered, but I can't get over how... how surreal this mission has been, and we haven't even reached our main destination yet." He glanced at me. "What I don't understand is how you've been so calm this whole time. You persuaded Field-Marshal Rommel himself to let you help him deal with Lexis. You stood up to Lehning the psychopath—"

"I'd hardly call what I did 'standing up' to him, save for punching him in the jaw."

"And you managed to get us not one, but two rides to get us closer to the farm. All without losing your temper."

I shrugged. "Never had much of a reason to get angry. Being calm and patient seemed to appeal to Rommel. Lehning... I did lose my temper with him, but it seems like actually fighting back showed him I wasn't as useless as he originally thought I was. I didn't pressure Marsilio or Amadeo into giving us what we needed. It was just... easier to be calm and state my point without being too forceful. I've always been that way."

"I have noticed you're... I guess 'passive' is the right word. You like to please."

"Honestly, I'd like to not get either of us killed. Fighting our way out of North Africa just wasn't a good option. I might be a magical being, but I'm not all-powerful. I could never fight that many soldiers at once. With Marsilio, I already know pressuring a Conjurus from an isolated village is a bad idea, so it wasn't worth it."

Halcomb was quiet for a moment. "I thought we would have to fight everyone we came across once we were in North Africa. I was wrong. I also thought I'd be fighting the war from a desk, so... I haven't been doing a good job with predictions."

"This is more exciting, isn't it?"

"Yes, I'll admit that." Halcomb looked around, somewhat anxiously. "Didn't you tell me that your uncle wasn't too happy about you seeking excitement in danger?"

"I did." I let out a sigh, unsure if I wanted to be thinking about that. "I don't think he'd care if it wasn't similar to how my father was. He would've taken up this mission in a heartbeat."

"But do you think he would be as successful as you? I mean, in terms of what we've done so far. Would he be calm with Rommel and Lehning? Would he have gotten us into that Conjurus village?"

"That, I can't be sure of."

"I know you don't like talking about what happened, but I can't help but think about when we go home. I don't want you to be alone and ashamed of what you've done here, especially if it's from your own family."

"We can save that talk for when we actually go home. It all depends on my success."

"I'd say you're successful just for getting us out of North Africa alive."

"Again, I don't think that was entirely my doing."

"I think you're underestimating yourself, Jay."

I was grateful we didn't encounter anyone or anything during our ride. From certain high points, we could see the city of Genoa in all its beauty. Though I longed to walk its streets and take in the sights, I kept my mind on our task.

The Cristaldi farm was on a hilltop overlooking the road. It was a perfect and peaceful location. The only sounds were chirping birds and clucking chickens. A field of various grains and vegetables stretched out around the farm. I expected to see someone out there, but there was no one.

As we got closer to the house, I saw a ruddy face peering out through the window curtains. She disappeared, then reappeared at the door, looking nervous.

I got off the cart, and pulled down my hood. "Good evening, ma'am. I am Jay Loalin. Might we stay for dinner?"

"You will have the schnitzel, yes?" Elvira asked.

I nodded. "We are not late, are we?"

"Oh, no, no, I wasn't sure when to expect you. Come in, come in." She looked very relieved as Halcomb and I entered the house. It smelled wonderful and cozy. There was bread baking in the oven and clove upon clove of freshly cut garlic sitting on a board by a pan. Big blocks of cheese of all kinds sat nearby. "Has it been long since you have had a meal?" she asked.

"A few hours, actually," Halcomb replied.

"Good gracious, you must be starving! Wait here, I will go grab a chicken."

We both sat at the dining room table. I could tell Halcomb was eager to discuss the mission, but he also looked a little lightheaded from not having a full meal in a while. I was a bit dizzy as well, and wouldn't have any energy until I had eaten something.

Elvira was a little whirlwind in the kitchen as she prepared us a rich and creamy chicken alfredo, seemingly cutting up the chicken, shredding cheese, and chopping more garlic all at the same time. She remained highly focused on cooking until we were both served, and only when we began eating did she say a word to us. "I hope the trip here was not too difficult." She set a plate of butter and a knife next to the bread.

"No, but it could have been easier," I said.

"And you assisted Friedrich Altschul?"

"Hopefully, he is on his way to the States right now. How did you know about him?"

"You would be surprised if you knew how big our 'little' network is here. If something had happened and Friedrich made his way to Italy, I was to be his safehouse."

"Ah, I see. He did make it out safely, so we no longer have to worry."

"We were stuck in North Africa for longer than we really needed because of a warlock in one of Rommel's camps," Halcomb explained. He jerked his thumb at me. "Jay got to meet the field-marshal face-to-face."

"Well, that sounds like quite the adventure!" Elvira sat across from us, eager to hear our story.

"We were going to be sent to a POW camp, but we escaped the camp with Altschul the night before," I replied. "We caught the submarine in time, managed to get a ride to a Conjurus village, and their librarian, a Lyco Amadeo, lent us his horse and cart to get here."

"Bless him, then. He has been a big help these past few years. After all, this is the brainchild of him and Father."

"We were told your father is something of a spy in Mussolini's government."

"That is correct. It did not exactly make the Conjurus population happy."

I raised an eyebrow. "Why?"

"He is a fire-variant. Everyone was terrified of him dragging them into something they wanted no part in, but he never told anyone in the government what he actually is. When word spread around the villages that he is a spy, things quieted down, but there were still some who did not want to be involved, spy or not."

"So, that makes you a—"

"Half-Conjurus. My mother was a Magicless. I am..." Elvira suddenly looked embarrassed, "not capable of using any powers. I was never trained. Neither were my brothers. Father wanted us to blend in. Even his use of fire has become limited from years of disuse. He was a witch-hunter before meeting Mother, but something... something made him change. That is why we are farmers." A look of longing manifested in Elvira's eyes. "His stories about witch-hunting were always so exciting, but without any powers or training, it is just a dream for me."

"With training, I think you could achieve that," I replied. "If you decide to come with us to America, I know someone who could help you."

"That would be nice, Mr. Loalin, but I could never abandon the farm, or Father, or my brothers. I will go with you to Germany, but when that is over, I want to come back here."

"If that is what you want."

"How exactly did you get involved with this mission in particular?" Halcomb asked.

"Amadeo needed someone to give a copy of German plans to, and for someone to be a safehouse in case Friedrich needed a place to hide." Elvira stood up, jogging into another room. She came back with a worn folder full of documents. "He took them from a sleeping SS officer, copied them, and put the originals back. If something ever happened, he did not want them, so he sent them where no one would ever suspect."

I skimmed the documents. Halcomb was mumbling to himself as he tried translating them in his head, then he looked up at Elvira. "These are directives from Wahler himself for the ZA to abduct ice-variants in Italy, Romania, Greece, Yugoslavia... everywhere the Germans have troops stationed."

"They mention the use of witches and warlocks as spies, just like we encountered in Libya," I added.

"I do not know who the officer Amadeo took these from was, but I do know that there have been disappearances of ice-variants over the last several months. They increased after the Germans were pushed out of Moscow." Elvira pointed to a paragraph on one of the pages. "This mentions that several *Wehrmacht* officers on the Eastern Front were not in favor of this plan because of the volatile nature of witches and warlocks. They wreak havoc on the troops and cause unnecessary losses on a front that has already decimated entire divisions. Many openly stated they will execute anyone suspected of being a warlock, so Wahler sent this document out saying that they will proceed with the plan, without letting anyone outside the SS know where they will plant these spies.”

“I doubt many within the German army know how to hunt warlocks,” I said. “As much as I think leaving them is a bad idea because of the risk they pose to the Soviets, it’s too far out. Plus, who knows how many have been planted.”

“None of these documents say, but I think getting rid of Wahler will put an end to this. Without direction, his warlocks will scatter.”

I nodded. “Altschul told us Wahler is performing sick and twisted experiments on these people. It has to end.”

“That does remind me, did Friedrich tell you what you needed to know?”

“Yes. Wahler is set up in a castle outside of Munich. That’s where we have to go.”

Chapter 9

Elvira sent a message to her father in Rome that "two friends arrived and want to go up to a mountain retreat in Munich." His response was that he would have plane tickets procured within a day or two, so we were stuck at the farm until then.

With nothing much to do, we decided to help Elvira out with some of the daily chores around the farm. Despite being the only person in the house most of the time, Elvira was quite energetic and thoroughly enjoyed what she did. Only Halcomb had some experience with running a farm, but it had been several years since he last touched any farming equipment, and his parents' farm dealt solely with pigs. He also wasn't too keen on helping at first, and although he wouldn't say, I had a pretty good idea as to why. Eventually, though, he forced himself to come out into the wheat field one afternoon and said flatly to Elvira, "Just do not beat me like my mother did if I do something wrong."

Having grown up with a happy and tight-knit family, Elvira didn't fully understand, so I explained to her in private what happened to Halcomb. A sympathetic look crossing her face, Elvira went over to where Halcomb was inspecting the wheat stalks. I could hear them talking to each other in low voices, and they were inseparable for the rest of the day, chatting endlessly about how vastly different their childhoods and experiences growing up were.

We tended to the crops, fed the chickens, collected eggs, and cleaned up the house. When we settled down for the evening, Elvira took me aside to show me some of the trophies her father collected as a witch-hunter.

She pulled a large trunk out from under the bed in the master bedroom. The latch was starting to rust, and the wood was splintering. Inside were broken wands, staffs, cracked crystal balls, and Ouija boards broken in half.

"This is very impressive," I said. "I have never even seen most of these items for myself before."

Elvira raised an eyebrow. "You are not a witch-hunter?"

"No. I had to deal with the warlock in North Africa out of necessity." Sighing, I added, "I am sorry if I gave you the wrong impression. Where I come from, I am... no one important. I took part in Antarctic exploration until my whole team died trying to reach the South Pole. After that, I wanted nothing more to do with Antarctica, and became a laborer."

"That does not make you unimportant. You have a story to tell—everyone does. That makes you important in a unique way."

Nodding a little, I gestured to the box. "May I hold some of these?"

"Of course." Elvira pulled the trunk further out.

I picked up one of the crystal ball pieces. It was heavy and translucent, and looked more like a broken decoration than a magical item. "I take it you look up to your father?"

"When I was younger, I wanted to be just like him. I asked for story after story about when he was a witch-hunter. Then, one day, he said that when we turn thirteen, he was not going to teach us how to use our powers. He said we needed to blend in with the Magicless, for the protection of other Conjurus. He grew up in the village you came from—he and Amadeo are childhood friends—and when he suggested becoming part of Mussolini's government to be a spy, everyone thought he was mad. None of the village Conjurus wanted to be part of this idea, but there were plenty of Magicless who did, so he continued. In order to protect the village if he was ever found out, my father decided not to train us."

"I cannot imagine your disappointment."

"I was old enough to understand, but young enough to still fantasize about what could have been, and I still do at times."

"When this is over, I think you can achieve that dream. The war will not last forever, and you are doing your best."

"Thank you, Mr. Loalin. To be honest, I have not done much."

"It may seem that way now, but what you are doing now could make a difference down the line." I slowly closed the trunk. "We should get some sleep. Be ready for whatever is thrown at us tomorrow."

We were given the plane tickets by another contact who showed up at the house a little after eleven the following morning. Within an hour we were packed up and ready to go.

It didn't hit me until we were on the road to the airport that we were going right into the heart of Nazi Germany. One false move could be the end of all three of us. Worse yet, we were going into an SS nest: a castle in southern Germany, possibly full of necromancers. We would have no allies except ourselves.

Our flight was short, but the weather past the mountainous border was vastly different. The sky was dark and threatening precipitation, and the air was cold enough to make me wonder if it would snow. We were greeted with the gray, blue, and forest green of German uniforms from every branch when we stepped off the plane in Munich. The black SS uniforms stood out like sore thumbs, and the only thing I kept whispering to myself was to avoid making eye contact with them. I noticed they had *Zauberei-Abteilung* armbands near the ends of their left sleeves.

I at least had some confidence in getting out of North Africa alive. Here, I wasn't even sure we would get out of the airport alive. Closing my eyes, I released my breath, and told myself I needed to stop being so paranoid.

The castle was in a town several miles outside of Munich. We boarded a train to get there, and I felt Halcomb tense up next me when we came to a stop halfway there, and four SS-ZA men entered. I elbowed him. "Don't look nervous," I hissed.

The men were simply looking for identification. Thankfully, Elvira had us covered. Her being the daughter of a member of the Italian government carried some weight. When the group was about to leave the train, I noticed one of them still staring at us. A pale scar ran across his left cheek. He looked thin, almost malnourished. Though he only stared at us for a moment, it felt much longer with how uncomfortable it was, like he was studying us for some purpose only he knew about.

"This is not going to be easy," Halcomb muttered after the SS-ZA left. "They all look like brutes."

"Brutes they may be, but they are not to be underestimated," Elvira whispered. "You do not climb the ranks of the SS by being stupid. That is what makes them scary."

"And yet we only know about some of Wahler's plans because one of them fell asleep and did not lock up his documents."

"Contrary to what they might think, they are not supermen. They are human, like us, and they make the same mistakes as we do," I said. "Still, we need to proceed with caution."

"Caution can only get us so far. We are going to have to take some risks if we want to succeed," Elvira replied.

"Just approaching that castle is going to be a risk," Halcomb said.

"There must be an unguarded spot we can get into. A window, most likely," I suggested.

"Before we do that, we can try the main gate." Elvira grinned a little. "I can distract the guards while you two slip inside."

"Then what will you do once we are in?"

"I will think of something."

I looked at Halcomb. "It is worth a try."

Halcomb looked like he wanted to argue, but then sighed and rubbed his face. "Alright. We will try it that way."

The castle in question was an old vampire lair, built almost two hundred years ago, and from there, the master vampire terrorized the village inhabitants, Magicless and Conjurus alike. It ended around the turn of the century when the people had enough and stormed the lair. It was a rare event where Conjurus and witches worked together, and it was an extremely bloody event, too. The vampire was killed as was everyone in his harem. Since then the castle has been empty, inhabited only by mice and rats and spiders.

The taking back of the village is commemorated each year with a festival, which usually takes place in the castle courtyard. However, as of a year ago, the ZA took over the castle for reasons they wouldn't explain to the townspeople.

We spent several hours listening to the conversations between citizens. Several people mentioned ice-variants had gone missing without a trace, and no one could figure out why. The only thing they noticed was that the disappearances started about a month after the ZA took over the castle.

From our place at a table outside a small restaurant, we could see the castle overlooking the town from the east. A steep tree-covered hill guarded the side we were facing. There were five spires, with one spire taller and thicker than the rest on the southern part of the castle. As the sun continued to set, we could see lights in some of the windows.

"Well, at least we know somebody is home," Halcomb said, taking a sip of his tea. "Going at night would be preferable."

"Actually," I said, "I was thinking we go during the day, if we are going to use Elvira's plan. It will look less suspicious."

"True." Halcomb kept staring up at the castle, then abruptly turned when the quiet of the town was shattered by two staff cars and three trucks roaring down the road, red Nazi flags flapping in the cold breeze. "Staying over for the night?"

"I heard someone mention that the officers have been staying at hotels. The owners are not exactly fond of them," Elvira whispered.

We would have to stay at a hotel ourselves that night. Since this mission began, I haven't had much time to myself, and that night was the first. As soon as I closed the door, I heard deafening silence and then everything came flooding back. Uncle Redvar. Laurel. Antarctica. Father. I realized how much I missed New York. I missed the sounds of automobiles going down every street, going to Central Park and the charming shops, and seeing the Brooklyn Bridge every morning on the way to work. The pain of homesickness felt like a blade being slowly driven into me, and I spent over an hour just sitting on the bed and trying not to sink into a depressive fit. I've already done that. Sighing and looking up at the ceiling, I told myself that the only way I would be able to go back was to succeed with the mission.

I tossed and turned for part of the night. I could still see the ZA man from the train, the one with the scar who was staring at us. I didn't think I would ever know why he stared so long. My thoughts were going backward. I could still see Italy. I could still see the sands of North Africa, Rommel, and Altschul. A smile crossed my face when I pictured Lehning still complaining about us, but it faded when I saw Lexis and his wicked grin as he blasted me through the tent wall of the morgue with his wand. Most Conjurus face a witch at some point in their lives, but I didn't think I ever would until a little over a month ago.

In an attempt to turn my thoughts into something more positive, I thought about Laurel. I thought about the Christmas dances. I thought about how different this mission might be if I had found a way to take her along. I certainly hope she and Elvira meet. Maybe after the war, Laurel can teach her how to use her powers. I can't imagine knowing I have magic but being incapable of using it. In some ways, I felt blessed to have been taught. It's certainly come in handy, especially during this mission.

One memory stuck with me as I tried to fall asleep. Last year's Christmas dance. Laurel was wearing a necklace with a poinsettia charm. At some point during the dance, I made a poinsettia from ice, and we both held it, even as it melted. I finally drifted off while daydreaming about telling Laurel about my adventures here in the Old World.

The three of us had to share a restaurant space with about six SS-ZA officers the following morning. We tried to keep the conversation mundane, but the castle came up at some point. Granted, we didn't talk about going inside— just hiking up to the woods around it—but one of the officers looked in our direction. To my horror, it was the scarred one from the day before. He gestured to his companions as he stood up and walked over to us. Up close, he was quite tall, and him looking down at us only made him more intimidating. I resisted the urge to look away, knowing that would tell him I was weaker than I appeared.

"Ah, Miss Cristaldi," the officer said, smiling a little. "It is a pleasure to see you again."

Elvira grinned at him. "I know I wasn't expecting to see you again. Small world."

"Well, I could not help but overhear your conversation with these two gentlemen about the castle, and I think I should warn you that the castle is off-limits to tourists."

"I see. We were just thinking about hiking near—"

"Strictly forbidden until further notice. Once you see the two guards behind the gates at the base of the hill, you have gone too far. They have orders to shoot anyone getting too close. What we are working on is top secret, for the benefit of the Reich."

"I understand. We will keep away. Could you recommend anywhere we could hike? We have been looking forward to this place for quite a while."

"Behind the hill is the lake; just take the path leading out to the east and follow it into the forest."

"Alright. Thank you, sir."

The officer gave a more genuine smile. "My pleasure."

Elvira faced us after he left. "I do not think he suspects anything."

"I would hope not," Halcomb muttered. "I do not like the look of him."

"He is not a warlock, that's for sure."

"How can you tell? I thought they were hard to find."

"I might not be trained, but my father did show me how to sense a witch. It is the only extent of my powers that I have."

"I did not feel anything strange about him, either," I said. "Regardless, I did not like how he was staring at us in the bus yesterday, and I kept seeing his face before I went to sleep last night."

"He's probably one of Wahler's minions," Halcomb said. "Nobody important. Nobody worth worrying about. Probably someone we will have to kill once we are inside the castle."

Elvira and I nodded and we resumed our breakfast.

The ZA disappeared from the town shortly after we left the restaurant. We could see their trucks and staff cars going up to the castle. Within a minute of them leaving, a sense of relief came over me, but the last thing I wanted was to be lulled into a false sense of security.

As much as I didn't want us to split up for anything, we agreed it would be best to seek out ways of getting into the castle without being spotted. Once we hiked up to the woods between the castle and the lake, we spread out. Halcomb went back to into town to scout the hill. Elvira went to the northwest edge of the woods. I went right through the woods, right up to the road leading into the castle grounds.

I managed to get a good view of the castle while hidden in the bushes by the road. Moss and vines covered much of the old gray stone that made up the castle itself. Clearly, the Germans had no interest in renovating the place. The black ZA uniforms stood out against the green of the moss and vines as the men paced around the castle grounds just past the enormous metal gates.

Something was telling me that I would have a better idea of the layout from a higher place, so I climbed up a tree. It was tough not to make a lot of ruckus. Frankly, I hoped the guards would dismiss it as squirrels running around the branches.

From my new vantage point, I could see the walls that surrounded the front grounds. There was one doorway, but lots of windows. Many of the first-floor windows were barred, and it didn't look like there was anything to grab onto in order to get into any windows on the floors above.

We were going to have to get creative if we wanted to get in. After a moment of thinking, I decided to watch the patterns of the pacing guards to see if there were any gaps we could exploit. Unfortunately, I saw none.

With this area out of the question, I climbed down from the tree, thinking I should meet up with Halcomb. Almost as soon as I touched the ground, I heard a German shout, and whirled around to see the scarred man from earlier pointing at me and yelling, "You do not belong here!"

Cursing to myself, I bolted into the woods. I had no idea if the officer recognized me, and I prayed he didn't. Although I could hear shouting, I refused to look over my shoulder, especially when I heard gunshots. Bullets whizzed by my head. One of them struck a tree, sending splinters flying.

At the rate my pursuer was firing, I assumed it was only one person, likely the officer, using a semi-automatic handgun. I quickly broke his line of sight by ducking behind a tree, and began forming a hailstone with my hands. Bushes rustled as the scarred man came running toward me, and I first spotted the blood-red color of his armband. He was shouting for me to come out and explain myself.

Drawing in and releasing a breath, I popped out from behind the tree, whipping the ice at the officer. His eyes widened to the size of plates as the ice hurtled toward him and smashed into the lower part of his chest. He flew backward, landing in the grass and dropping his handgun. He was struggling to breathe and was staring at the hailstone lying near him. He was wheezing hard and tried crawling away from me as I walked toward him.

"You... You are one of the men Miss Cristaldi brought..." The officer broke off coughing. "I told you not to come here!"

Spotting an opportunity, I grabbed him by the front of his uniform, and pinned him against a tree. "How do we get into the castle?" I growled.

The man was struggling to breathe, and feebly tried pushing me off. "I will not telling you anything! Once the guards hear me screaming, they will—"

I wrapped one hand around the man's neck, and let frost come to my fingertips. He squirmed with the cold. "I will kill you before you scream. Now, tell me how to get in."

"No! Wahler will catch you! He will do horrible things to you!" Tears started streaming down the man's face. "You would beg for death. Just like the others. They beg and beg and still death does not come. The necromancers keep reviving them. You do not want to go in there." He squeezed his eyes shut. The skin on his neck around my fingertips was starting to redden.

"I already know what he is doing in there. That is why I am here."

"You have no idea what he is doing in there." The officer gave me a pleading look. "For your own sake, I cannot let you in!"

I held him for a few more seconds before letting him go. The officer slumped to the ground. Five frosty fingerprints covered his neck, and he rubbed at them furiously to warm up. I picked up his P38, leaving him defenseless and completely at my mercy. "Why are you so insistent on not letting me in?"

"Why do you want to go in anyway?" he asked. "No one except the ZA can leave. What you are doing is insane."

"Like I said, I already know what Wahler is doing. I am here to put an end to it."

The officer shook his head. "There is no putting an end to it. None. You want to put an end to this madness? Go to Berlin and kill Hitler. Kill every

Nazi Party member. Kill every member of the SS and the ZA. Then this will all end."

I couldn't tell if he was playing a trick on me in order to lure me into giving him information, or if he was being genuine. He sounded desperate, angry, even. "I am only one man," I said. "I cannot do any of that."

"Then do not bother trying to stop Wahler. It will not do anything. They will just kill you and keep working. No amount of resistance is going to help."

He wasn't desperate, he was hopeless. I couldn't let my guard down, though. "You are at my mercy here. You have no reason to hide who or what you are. Be honest and you might get out of this alive."

"This is not a game. Otherwise, why would I chase you alone? I can tell by your accent that you are not a native German speaker. You are a spy, aren't you?"

He had a point, but that could also be a trap. "Maybe, but how do I know you are not trying to trick me into giving you information? I know nothing about troop movements or ship movements, or where any Allied commander is right now. You already know everything about my mission; I am here to disrupt Wahler's experiments on ice-variants. If you hate them so much, why stop me?"

"Because I do not want to see anyone else be shackled up, tortured, dissected, disemboweled, and lobotomized! I do not know what you were told about Wahler, but it was probably the short version. He is a monster."

"Yes, but he is not unstoppable."

"It is not worth your effort. It is not worth the endless hours of pain and suffering you will go through. Please, if I can save one life from Wahler's torture, I will die happy."

"We are going to take a walk," I said, pointing the gun at him. "Move."

I didn't trust his behavior, but I didn't want to make any assumptions until I spent more time with him. With the P38's barrel in the officer's back, I led him through the forest, down to the lake. "What is your name?"

"Soren Kiefer. And yours?"

"Jay Loalin."

"Why are we walking?"

"I do not trust you. I do not know what your motives are."

"Motives? I have none. I do not even know if I am going to survive another day here even if I survive you."

"Unless I am given a good reason to kill you, I will not hurt you."

Kiefer glanced over his shoulder at me. "Very well. You want to know my motives? When I saw you and your companions on the bus yesterday, I could see clearly that you are an ice-variant. It is not difficult after being around so many the last year or so."

"So, that is why you were staring?"

"I did not mean to make you uncomfortable, but I could not act friendly in front of my superiors."

"Fair point."

"I had hoped that telling you at your breakfast that the castle is off-limits would be warning enough. I did not want anything to happen to another ice-variant." Kiefer shrugged. "That is all. I told the guards I would handle you myself, and now here we are."

"If you are so... caring, why are you in the SS? I thought there was no room for kindness."

"Do you have friends, Jay?"

"Very few. Why?"

"Because when you have none, and spend a lot of time with only yourself, people tend to look at you strangely. Where you come from, you take that ability to be comfortably alone for granted. You might be a bit of an outcast, but it does not completely ruin your life. Here? The whispers never end, and suddenly people start suspecting if something is truly wrong with you, and then they start saying that you cannot and will not provide anything that will better the German people as a whole."

"So, you joined the SS to prove you can provide for the German people as a whole."

"It is a long story, but I will say I did not join on my own accord. I have always been... odd. My ability to focus on certain tasks is not the greatest, but when I do focus, I get things done quickly and exceed expectations. You would think that would be perfect for the SS, but caring about people—complete strangers, actually—is what makes me an imperfect specimen. I was also confronted with things I did not think were real."

Kiefer went in detail about the SS's cozy relationship with witchcraft and the creation of the ZA branch. The most fanatical of members actually attempted to practice witchcraft, and from what I understand, it's a difficult process. The vast majority of witches and warlocks are born into their culture, and taught from the moment they can hold a wand. Wands are the key to a witch's success. No ordinary stick can be picked up and claimed to be a wand. It must be shaped, polished, and enchanted.

Himmler isn't exactly the patient type with witchcraft, having not been born into it or spent a lot of time around it. Many of the witches and warlocks "employed" by the SS attempted to explain the difficulties of mastering the craft at older ages, but they were simply told to just keep teaching. Even Reinhard Heydrich gave it a go. He was able to master the standard "bolt spell" fairly quickly, but that is the magical equivalent to mastering just the ABCs. Fortunately, he died before he could learn more. It's quite terrifying to think some of the more powerful Nazis have attempted actual magic.

I asked if Wahler was a warlock, and Kiefer replied, "In a limited sense. He has a wand. He has used it-" Here, Kiefer ran his index finger along the scar on his cheek, "and he has been spending a lot of time reading about potions and crystal balls and familiars, but he is not a true warlock."

"So, what is he doing in that castle? What is his goal?"

"I know his goal is to make the German forces in Russia more resistant to the cold. I have also heard rumors that he wants to create a being with the abilities of every Conjurus variant. He calls it '*Übermensch*'. 'Beyond human'."

"I wonder if he knows that will not be easy," I said, grinning a little. "Hybrid Conjurus are extremely rare."

"I do not think he cares. He will do what he thinks will get him that goal."

"And that is why I was sent to stop him."

Kiefer gave me a look. "You might be an ice-variant, but you will not be able to take on everyone in that castle."

"No, but that is why I have help." I made a gesture for Kiefer to sit when we reached the lake. The serenity was a sharp contrast to the creepy tension of the castle gates.

Kiefer's posture relaxed when he sat. His shoulders slumped and he took his cap off, his unkempt blond hair ruffling in the breeze. "How much help?"

"Two other people."

"Miss Cristaldi and the nervous-looking fellow with darker hair, yes?" I nodded.

"You are still heavily outnumbered, even if all three of you are Conjurus."

"If I offered you a chance to come aboard, and get out of Germany in the process, would you take it?"

"You still have not convinced me that you can win."

I sighed, wanting to tear my hair out. "You are only hopeless because you have no one around you to give you hope."

For once, Kiefer didn't shut me down. He looked over his shoulder at me, attentively.

"You have been alone for so long that you have no one else to turn to. If someone else felt as you do, you would feel differently. No situation, no matter how desperate, is hopeless. The French are sorely outnumbered, but they still fight to take their country back. The Polish are fighting to take their country back. The British haven't let the frequent bombings push them down. Even though everyone is faced with Germany's might, they are not giving up."

Kiefer nodded a little.

"We can get you out of here. We can put you somewhere you can start fighting back. Your inside knowledge of the SS-ZA would prove useful—"

"No. If I am going to get out of here, it's so I can live out the rest of my life in peace. That's all I want. If I was captured I would be sent to a death camp or hung. I just want to live out a simple life. Alone."

Something deep inside me was telling me to respect that, so I nodded. "Alright. If you help us, we will take you to the States. You can become a citizen and move wherever you like."

"Promise?"

"Promise."

A slight smile crossed Kiefer's face. "Alright, then. We have a deal."

If someone told me a few months ago that I would be traveling to Europe and giving hope to an SS officer who only signed up to avoid ridicule and having his life ruined, I would think they were completely insane. Then again, I never expected to shake hands with Erwin Rommel, either. It's funny how life plays out sometimes.

I wasn't really sure how we would go about this. The guards would probably send a team out soon to find Kiefer, and I realized sending him back meant trusting that this wasn't an elaborate trap. I don't know what we would do if we were found out, especially with Elvira involved. It would spell disaster for her and her family.

"If you are going to desert anyway, there is no point in going back," I said.

Kiefer looked undecided. "You do not trust me. I understand. I do not know what I can do to let you trust me. It is the uniform, is it not?"

"In some ways, yes."

"If I were in civilian clothes, you would not hesitate to trust me."

I shrugged. "Perhaps."

"Perhaps you might think I am lying when I tell you how I got the scar on my face."

"You said Wahler gave it to you."

Kiefer nodded. "I refused to shoot a crippled witch and her child over a mass grave dug in Poland, because she looked me in the eye. All of a sudden, I could feel her panic, her pleading, and... it felt like a wave rushing over me. My hands were shaking and I could not do it. Wahler and another officer were screaming at me to shoot, and I could not force myself to do it. The more they yelled, the more I wanted to put the gun down. I still have nightmares of the woman and child crying, giving me that pleading look. I was overcome with feelings of... 'what have I done?' I was disgusted with my own uniform. Wahler dragged me away while the other officer shot them. I was berated, beaten, and then Wahler hit me with energy from his wand. Obviously, he did not use full power or I would not be here right now, but... I was numb for a while. He did not even want to kill me. I was... to be an example."

His scar definitely had the characteristics of a wand blast. It's like a lightning strike, but the skin hit by the blast is much redder, and the skin surrounding the scar turns paper-white. Full-power blasts actually gouge through the skin and appear more like burns. Kiefer got lucky.

A part of me was wondering if the scar was merely from a training accident, but his story seemed too specific to be a lie unless he's a very talented liar.

I needed to make a decision soon. Kiefer didn't lose eye contact with me for a second. I could tell he didn't want to go back, but if he was willing to do this to help us put an end to Wahler's pet project, I felt I had to let him. Giving a nod, I said, "Return to the castle. Meet me back at this spot tonight at exactly midnight. Can you do that?"

"Yes."

"Alright. Good luck." I handed his pistol back to him, then he jogged back up the hill, occasionally looking back at me as he did.

Chapter 10

Halcomb looked like he wanted to strangle me when I told him and Elvira what happened after meeting up with them in the forest below the castle. "You did what? *You did what?!* Jay, are you fucking insane? Are you completely, absolutely fucking *insane?!*"

"There is no reason to yell," Elvira said.

"Oh, no, I have to yell, because this is too far. This is ridiculous. We were ordered to trust Altschul, and I know we were forced to trust Rommel, but that was a completely different situation, because at least only my life and Jay's life were at stake. Trusting a *fucking SS officer* is another animal, not only because they are murderous lunatics, but also because you are involved, ma'am. If word of this gets back to your father, your whole family could be exiled, or slaughtered, or—"

"I already thought of that," I said.

"Clearly, you did not think enough! If you were doing this alone, I would not care, but you are taking some pretty extreme risks and gambling with *our* lives!" Halcomb's face reddened the more he talked. "In all honesty, I am tired of this. You are going to get us killed, and by that, you are going to get Elvira's family killed, too."

"You knew how dangerous this would be when you volunteered!"

"There are many things we could have done to make it less dangerous! We could have left North Africa without getting friendly with Rommel! We could have left that warlock alone! We could have kept going on that road in Italy without stopping in a village full of aggressively neutral Conjurus! And we could have found our way into that damned castle without placing our lives in the hands of a damned SS officer!"

"You admitted I was right when we were on our way to the farm in Italy! What happened to that?"

"I did not know you were going to go and do something as insane and stupid as this! We are in Germany! We cannot trust anyone!"

"Oh, so, now you have no faith in me?"

"Not to make rational decisions." Halcomb looked at Elvira. "You cannot possibly think this was a good idea."

Elvira shook her head as she looked at the ground. "We will not know until we see Kiefer again. It is too late now."

My chest felt heavy with regret. "If this puts your family in danger, I am—"

"Do not apologize. Us being found out was bound to happen sooner or later."

"It should not have happened this way. Or at all."

"Regardless, we cannot afford to fight over this. We should go back to town and get some rest."

Halcomb glared at both of us. "What is the plan for if the SS start tearing apart the town looking for us?"

"We abort the mission and just head for Switzerland. Continuing would not be worth it at that point."

"And what about Elvira's family?"

"We already talked about refuge in Switzerland," Elvira said. "We could meet up there."

"What about your brothers? There is no way they'd get out of North Africa."

"They know what to do if something happens. Please, Lester, relax. You getting stressed about things that have not even happened is not helping the situation."

Halcomb took a deep breath. He sat on a rock, looking deflated, and didn't say another word.

"If we are going to get any rest, we had better go now," I said, ignoring the tension emanating from Halcomb. He stood up with a sigh, and walked ahead of us back down to the town.

I had more regrets over the fact that Halcomb no longer trusted me than over the risk I took with Kiefer. Was I trying too hard to be a hero? Was I even trying at all? Was I trying to help too many people at once? Was it all even worth it? Was I helping the wrong people? Was I being lied to, and was my kindness being taken advantage of? In that moment, I couldn't tell.

Even though I was supposed to be resting in my hotel room, I found it hard to get any sleep with my thoughts running wild. If we come out of this alive, I feared I was going to lose Halcomb as a friend, and I hadn't realized how much I cared until then. I felt like I hadn't been taking any of his thoughts and feelings into consideration. He wasn't wrong to be nervous in North Africa, or Italy, or here in Germany, but I just couldn't figure out the balance between too risky and too cautious. I guess I hadn't stopped to think about it.

It was bitterly cold that night. Frost had covered the grass in the forest, and small patches of ice were forming on the lake's surface. I felt bad for Elvira, being unable to warm herself. Her frustration was palpable, and she cursed to herself until we heard a soft, "Come here," from Halcomb.

Without hesitation, Elvira moved closer to him, letting him put his arms around her. She whispered a "thank you" to him, and they sat for the next several minutes huddled up to each other. While they kept each other warm, I kept a lookout for Kiefer, obsessively looking down at my watch. As we drew closer to midnight, I was becoming more and more anxious that he wouldn't come. I had to distract myself by making things from ice. That became the perfect distraction, as the first thing I set my mind to making was a rose.

As I stared into the rose, I tried to picture myself home. Clear as day, I could hear the ambience of New York. Every muscle in me relaxed. I could see myself in the Wendalines' brownstone home, looking out the window at falling snow, people walking by, bundled up and carrying Christmas packages. It was last year, when I offered to help set up for the party, though it was partly an excuse for me to spend more time with Laurel. Her mother was baking, her father was decorating the tree, and Laurel was running back and forth trying to help both parents at once.

I joked that everything looked under control, which prompted Laurel's father to toss me a bundle of tinsel and say, "If you want everything under control, son, come and help me hang this up."

Frankly, I think he wanted to keep a closer eye on me. Even though I've been nothing but a gentleman the last three years, Mr. Wendaline had seen my melancholy after the incident in Antarctica. I couldn't blame him for assuming I wouldn't be capable of starting a family if I was so lost in my misery. Even I didn't think I would be capable. Things have changed, but after what happened in the morgue, where I could see, vividly, Duncan and McIntyre's corpses on the beds, I wasn't sure how much of me had changed. What would it take for me to sink back into that depression? A mere mention of them? It really was no wonder no one wanted to talk about Antarctica with me.

It was nice not to think about it, but I knew burying it wouldn't resolve the guilt. Then again, why should I feel guilty for something beyond my control? I only survived because I'm capable of surviving in such environments. I was born with it.

When I looked over at Elvira and Halcomb, the same feelings I had felt watching McIntyre die resurfaced. I couldn't help them. The best I could do was get them inside a warm house when it became clear Kiefer won't show.

A minute past midnight, I refused to stay any longer, but as soon as I turned to look at Halcomb and Elvira, I heard bushes and leaves rustling and crunching, and whirled around to see Kiefer running through the forest. He nearly fell when he stopped in front of us. "I am sorry for being late," he panted. "Very sorry." He put his hands on his knees, breathing hard. "I had to come up with a believable excuse to get out here. I think I have an idea to get you in."

Halcomb glared at Kiefer, then looked at me. "One wrong move, and I will kill him, Jay."

"He already knows what is at stake, and we are going to get him out of here when we are done," I said.

The four of us had to sit close together just to keep warm. Halcomb wasn't at all thrilled at being so close to Kiefer, but begrudgingly put up with it. "So, what is this genius plan of yours?" Halcomb asked.

Kiefer glanced around at all three of us. "We get deliveries of supplies every Monday. Mostly food, medical supplies, basic things. The truck makes its last stop in the town before it comes up here. That would be a perfect place for you to hide. Just get in the crates and wait. I can come let you out."

"That's your genius plan?" Halcomb smirked. "We could have figured that out—"

"Stop," I snapped. "Yes, we could have figured that out, but it might have taken us too long."

Kiefer flushed red in embarrassment. "I am sorry I do not have anything better."

"No, no, do not be sorry." Elvira held her hand out to him. "We appreciate all the help we can get."

Kiefer took his glove off before taking Elvira's hand. "Thank you, Miss. Um... what supplies to you need once you are inside?"

"First, we will need a layout of the castle," I said.

"I thought you might say that." Kiefer's hand was shaking as he gently pulled it away from Elvira, and slid his glove back on. He reached inside his heavy black trench coat, and took out a folded piece of paper. It unfolded into a very large map of the castle. "The food crates will give you the greatest chance of getting inside. There are guards pacing every corridor, except the basement, because there are so few ways someone could sneak inside. Wahler has 'labs' on every floor and level, except the officers' quarters, which are here, in the southern tower. The dungeons are where he keeps his subjects, and the north tower is where the guards' quarters are. The center of the castle is where most of the dissections and such work is done, and it is heavily guarded. This long corridor is on the third level, and where Wahler is most of the day. If you are going to kill him, you can either do it there or in the officers' quarters at night."

"How many guards are there?"

"Ninety. They patrol in three shifts of thirty men each."

"We will need weapons, then," Halcomb said.

"I can get some from the armory for you. It is not too far off from the kitchens."

"We might have an advantage if we can free the prisoners," I said.

"That is unlikely. Many of them are extremely weak, and some of them... just want to die. They've been revived, over and over, by necromancers. I cannot imagine how that feels."

"They are the most evil of witches and warlocks," Elvira added. "Raising the dead for their own benefit and unable to let anyone rest in peace. They will corrupt the minds of the dead as well, until you are nothing but a husk for them to control."

Kiefer nodded. "It is not easy to watch. Or hear."

"They are also dangerous on their own. We cannot leave any of them alive."

"That should be easy when we get ahold of their wands," Halcomb said.

"No, even that will not stop them. They are the only type of witch capable of wandless magic."

"Oh, great." Halcomb paled.

"How many does Wahler have?" I asked.

"Three," Kiefer replied. "They have their own quarters above the dungeons."

"That should not be too bad."

"It would be better not to get too confident too soon," Halcomb muttered. "That and our new friend here might be lying to give us a false sense of security."

Kiefer sighed. "I am being completely honest with you. Unless Wahler has secret witches hidden somewhere in the castle, there are only three right now." He looked all of us in the eye. "I am trusting you to help me. You need to do the same."

"Until there is proof otherwise, I trust you," I said.

Elvira nodded in agreement. Halcomb shrugged.

"Two out of three is better than none," Kiefer replied. He gave Halcomb a look. "I expect an apology when we pull this off."

"You will have to strangle it out of me," Halcomb grumbled.

"We will have none of that," I snapped. "We are on the same side."

"I certainly hope so."

On Sunday morning, Kiefer took me to the location where the truck would be loaded with supplies. It was parked behind a general goods store, the back wide open. Empty crates lay in front of it. They were big enough for a grown man to curl up in, but it wouldn't be comfortable.

"Does the driver inspect the crates before leaving?" I asked.

"Almost never. I can keep him distracted while you and your companions get in," Kiefer replied.

We were hidden in the bushes lining the forest behind the store. The streets were empty, as was the small lot behind the store. Everyone was home, or at church. It was the perfect chance for us to scout where we needed to be. I looked up at the trees, noting they were beginning to change to their lovely fall colors. If we were successful, I'd be able to go home and see Central Park in its full autumn garb. More and more, I found myself missing the little things about home.

"I could feel you were frustrated with Halcomb," Kiefer said, breaking the silence. "You two are close?"

"Yes. He recruited me, actually, and we became friends while I was in training. That made him volunteer to accompany me here." I sighed heavily. "I cannot be too mad at him. He was supposed to just sit at a desk and interview people the whole war, but he knew this was going to be dangerous and involve risks. We talked about this. He apologized for how he treated me in North Africa. I hoped that would be the end of it."

"But this was too far."

"I guess so. We clearly have a different approach to life, but he is still my friend. Possibly even my best friend."

"That means a lot to you."

I nodded.

Kiefer picked up a yellow leaf, turning it over in his hand and gently folding it. "I do not know what it's like to have a friend, much less a best friend, but in my observations of people, I can tell it is something held dear. It is like love, but... a different kind of love." He took his gloves off, continuing to toy with the leaf.

"I have already lost a friend. I do not want to lose another," I said.

Kiefer looked at me attentively. "Was it through an argument?"

"No. It was through death. I... used to be an explorer. I made many trips to Antarctica. When my team and I decided we wanted to go to the South Pole, we made all the necessary preparations, but... nothing can prepare you for the conditions. We lost one team member after he fell in the water, and within minutes of us pulling him out, he died of hypothermia. The rest of us argued about what we should do next, and we settled on going back to our ship. Our leader, Duncan, had lost many fellow explorers over his career, but he had been very close to this group. McIntyre's death affected him in a way I did not think humanly possible. He became withdrawn, maybe even suicidal. He would not eat or rest. One by one, the rest of the team... died. Except for me."

"Do you feel guilty for surviving?"

"In some ways, yes. Not only was Duncan a friend, but he was a father figure to me. I had my uncle, but that was not the same. Because of how I lost my father, I... I couldn't go anywhere without someone knowing the story of what he did and pointing it out. Duncan and the rest of the team treated me like a unique person. When I lost them, I lost that chance to be someone other than 'Morgan's son.'"

Kiefer turned his attention back to the leaf as he thought. "I know Wahler's operation started because of your father, but I did not bring it up because I did not think it would be appropriate. I guess that makes this mission more personal for you."

"It is. Halcomb told me I should not feel obliged to accept it because of my father, but, a part of me does feel obliged. It is not guilt, it is... something I can't describe."

"You do not want his name, and by extension, yours, to be tarnished by Wahler's horrific work."

I nodded. "I know my father had nothing to do with this, but Wahler was 'inspired' by what he saw. Morgan had no intention of getting Conjurus banned from the draft, but that is what happened. I have wanted to fight since the draft was announced. I want to do something with my life. Before this, I was... a refrigerator coolant technician. An average man."

Kiefer smiled at me. "You got your wish by becoming a spy."

"In a way, it was Wahler's work that led me to that. I guess I should be grateful for that."

Kiefer set the leaf down and hugged his knees. "If I had known exactly who you are when we first ran into each other, I would have tried to take you aside earlier. The fact that this is a personal mission for you makes it... different, than if you were just picked for the job by your government. The mission actually means something to you."

"Even if it had nothing to do with my father, I would accept it. Witches have been exploiting the Magicless and Conjurus for almost a thousand years. I do not want to see them collaborating with the most evil of Magicless to subjugate an entire continent."

"I would not say all witches and warlocks are evil," Kiefer said, picking a blade of grass. "There was a witch who lived near us when I was growing up. She did not kill people for potion ingredients, but she did use animal parts. She made health tonics and hair tonics, and she was nice to people. Not a recluse like most witches. I liked visiting her, because she had a mouse familiar. She had a son as well, but he was very shy, like me."

"That would be the first time I have ever heard about such an individual."

"Ones like her are not common, but I wish they were."

"Is she still around?"

"I do not know. I have not seen her in four years. Her son lives somewhere in the Black Forest now, and we have not spoken in a while."

"Is he like his mother?"

"Yes, but he is not nearly as friendly. He is nice for a warlock, but he does not bake cookies and make magic Christmas decorations for people." Kiefer pulled the grass blade tight. "I should probably visit someday, but after we are done with the castle, that will not be possible for a few years. Perhaps we will never see each other again."

"I hope you do," I said. "If you need it, I could help you."

"That would be appreciated, but I do not know how he would feel about seeing me with a Conjurus."

"Then I will just give you a ride there." I grinned a little. "Although I wouldn't mind meeting a different warlock, someone different from the spy in the *Afrika Korps*."

"I knew Wahler sent spies to the Eastern Front, but I did not know he sent some to North Africa."

"Well, this one was in France during the invasion. Apparently he was such a good medic that Rommel requested he be transferred into the *Afrika Korps*. When it was found out he was a warlock, Rommel admitted to feeling betrayed, and I can't blame him."

"I have heard some of the guards talk about how they get nervous at night with the witches roaming freely in the castle with no supervision, but they cannot do anything about it."

I shook my head. "I do not suppose we could count on any of them to help us?"

"If there are any, I do not know who they are, so we should remain cautious. Do not trust anyone until proven otherwise." Putting the grass down, Kiefer put his gloves back on. "Anything else we need to go over?"

"No. You will get us down here tomorrow morning?"

"Yes."

I grunted in pain when I stood up, having sat for nearly an hour. It was still morning, with plenty of time left in the day. We had a plan in place, and I was confident it would work. My fears lay in what we would do when we were inside the castle. It wasn't exactly small, and we were sorely outnumbered. Part of me was worried, and another part of me, that very naïve and adventurous part of me, was excited and looking forward to the thrill of danger.

Something began sinking in the pit of my stomach. I had been excited about Antarctica because of its risks, and those risks had gotten Duncan, Tallor, McIntyre, and Archie killed. It seemed selfish to be excited. Halcomb, Elvira, and Kiefer could get killed. Then again, so could I.

"You look lost."

Snapping out of my thoughts, I glanced at Kiefer. "I was just thinking. Sorry."

"Please, do not apologize. I think a lot, too." Kiefer smiled at me. "What are you thinking about?"

"Is it strange that there is a part of me looking forward to doing this? That there is a part of me that gets a thrill out of this?"

"No, why?"

"Because that is how I felt in Antarctica."

"So? You were not the one who caused your friend to die. You did not push your group to keep going. And it is not like you got a thrill out of watching any of them die. You do not seem like that kind of person anyway. Trust me, I have seen that."

"You bring up a good point, but... I do not want anyone to get killed because I am taking risks."

"Life is full of risks. That is unavoidable. What you and Halcomb and Miss Cristaldi are doing is incredibly dangerous, and there is not much you can do to mitigate that risk. Besides, if you want my honest opinion, I think people who do not take any risks at all are rather boring people, and you are far from boring."

I weakly smiled. "I appreciate that."

"At the very least, I would like to stay in contact with you when we go to America."

"I live in New York City. That is not exactly the quiet life you're hoping for. Upstate is very quiet, though. Perhaps that would be best if we want to see each other in person often."

Kiefer nodded, his smile fading. "Maybe I was being a bit... defensive when I said I wanted to be completely alone. I want to be alone, but I do not want to be... lonely."

"That is fair. I would not wish loneliness on anyone, and I hope you can find new happiness in your new home."

I met back up with Halcomb and Elvira when the sun started to set. The red-orange light turned the autumn forest into a bonfire that gradually put itself out as the light continued to sink into the western horizon. The clouds went from pink to red, and the air became colder and colder.

Inside the restaurant, patrons took turns crouching in front of the fireplace. It seemed strange watching SS officers acting similarly to clockmakers and farmers and tailors. They knelt, crouched, and rubbed their hands the same way, blowing into their fists and adjusting their scarves. They were just as human as everyone else. At least for now. Things could change and these same men could be ordered to raze the town to the ground.

"Did you have a good time with Kiefer?" Halcomb asked.

I couldn't tell if he was being sarcastic or genuine, so I ignored the question. "We have a plan for tomorrow morning, though it requires us to get up at a terrible hour."

"So, we are using the crates?"

"Yes."

"There is really no other way in?"

"No."

Halcomb looked down at the table, then stood up, beckoning for us to follow him outside, where he hissed in my ear, "We are actually trusting this officer."

"We will be right back to square one if we reject his help. I cannot think of another way that will get us directly inside the castle without being seen."

"I still think we could have done this without his help. We taught you back in the manor that there are risks and unnecessary risks. This is an unnecessary risk, as was cozying up to Rommel."

"Rommel was a necessary risk in order to get out of North Africa alive."

"We could have gotten out alive if we did not get caught up in business that was not ours!"

"Why bring this up when you yourself told me that I was right in Italy?"

"Because I thought that would be the end of cooperating with hostile forces!"

"Kiefer is not hostile!"

"How are you so certain that this is not a ruse?"

"Because *I just know!* Do you not trust me?"

"I trust you. I do not trust Kiefer."

"I trust him. If you do not trust him, you do not trust me."

"That is the most absurd-"

"Alright, that is *enough!*" Elvira gave us both a stern look. "I did not come all this way to listen to you two argue! If I have to beat both of you to make you cooperate, I will."

I expected Halcomb to keep arguing, but he gave me a look that I can best describe as "disappointed."

It was difficult to sleep that night with the mission getting closer at every tick of the clock. I found myself watching it when I couldn't focus on anything else. At the very least, I could count on Halcomb to not let whatever gripes he had with me to interfere with the mission. However, I was worried about how he would treat Kiefer after the mission was over. Letting out a quiet sigh, I resumed staring at the clock. We could worry about that when we get there.

I wasn't sure when I managed to doze off, but when the alarm clock began ringing, I felt like I had only slept a few minutes. Perhaps I had. Despite my exhaustion, I forced myself out of bed, and scrambled to get my clothes on. The more I thought about the mission, the less tired I felt. It was really happening. As excited as I was, I tried to keep that to a minimum. A trek through the Antarctic is dangerous, but storming a castle full of highly trained SS men and their necromancers is another.

I had to pull myself from my thoughts as I left my room, buttoning my coat and walking briskly to Elvira's room. "Are you ready to go?"

"Nearly!" she called. "Check on Lester, please!"

"Alright." I went across the hall, knocking on Halcomb's door. "Are you ready to go?"

"In a minute!" Halcomb shouted.

It was less than a minute later when Halcomb and Elvira left their rooms. We were dressed as comfortably as we could, knowing this was going to be quite a lively mission, and that we were going to be cramped in crates for a little while. After grabbing a quick breakfast and cups of coffee, we immediately headed to the spot in the woods Kiefer told us to meet him.

Thankfully, Kiefer was there, his black uniform standing out against the reds and golds of the forest, beckoning us further in. "No one followed you?" he asked as we jogged up to him.

"No," I said.

"Good. Come."

There was no time for chatter as we headed down to the little clearing behind the shop where the truck was waiting. The driver guided two SS-ZA soldiers carrying a heavy-looking crate up a ramp and into the vehicle. There were five other crates nearby.

"I will distract them. Stay here and wait for my signal," Kiefer whispered.

"What will your signal be?" Halcomb asked.

Kiefer pulled an acorn from one of his pockets. "I will throw this across the ground."

Nodding, the three of us crouched in the bushes while Kiefer headed off.

Elvira turned to Halcomb. "Do you trust him yet?"

"Not yet."

I opened my mouth to argue, but closed it. This wasn't the time.

Ten minutes passed before we saw Kiefer exit the shop and toss the acorn onto the cobblestone lot. We quickly left the bushes, dashing down the small hill to the crates. Kiefer gestured to the ones we could fit in, prying the tops off as we approached. Kiefer closed them as soon as we were curled up and as comfortable as we could be inside.

"Watch your fingers, Halcomb," Kiefer whispered, gently placing the lid onto the crate.

"I assume we have to trust you to let us out when we get there?" Halcomb asked.

"Yes. I understand that is not an ideal situation for you?"

"No, it is *not*."

"Then please accept my apologies for putting you in this situation." Kiefer then went around knocking on my crate and Elvira's to ask and make sure we were secure. Once we gave him our approval, he went back into the store.

I was extremely grateful the fruit inside was fresh, though I didn't appreciate the apples digging themselves into my sides and ribs. About a minute after Kiefer left, he returned with the other SS men and the truck driver. He helped them load the crates in the back of the vehicle and joined them in the drive up to the castle.

The drive wasn't very long. The closer we got to the castle, the more nervous I felt. There would be no turning back, no running, when we got there. We wouldn't leave until the mission was complete, until Wahler was dead and we put a stop to his experiments.

It hit me during the ride that we had no idea what we were going to find inside that castle. Kiefer had mentioned that the Conjurus prisoners often begged for death, that they were dissected like frogs in a classroom. I couldn't doubt that we were going to see things no human being should ever see.

Chapter 11

When the truck stopped and I heard shouting in German, I knew we had arrived at the castle. The slightest mistake could get all four of us killed. I stayed as still as I could as the crates were unloaded. Everything depended on Kiefer now. This was where we would learn if he was friend or foe and either put Halcomb's suspicions to rest or confirm them.

The crates were set down in a cool room with a stone floor. I couldn't see much through the cracks in the wood other than lots of grays and blacks and flickering torches on the walls. Relief washed over me when I saw Kiefer kneeling in front of my crate, but he quickly stood up when someone marched into the room.

"Good morning, *Standartenführer*," Kiefer said.

My view through the crack in the wood was my first time seeing Wahler in person. He looked incapable of smiling, unless he was watching someone writhe in pain. He was almost as pale as an ice-variant, likely from keeping himself inside the castle for most of the time. There was a chestnut wand on his belt, and he pulled it out as he paused in front of Kiefer. He didn't return the greeting, and the room was suddenly engulfed in silence. Only the crackling of the torches could be heard.

"I hope you are not here to ask for anymore favors, *Untersturmführer*," Wahler said.

"No, *Standartenführer*."

"Good. You have a simple task today; I am getting my potion ready for mass-testing on the Eastern Front, and I need you to supervise the draining of blood from prisoners."

"Supervise? Sir, that is not something that needs to be—"

Wahler held up his wand to Kiefer's neck. "You were not assigned to me to question orders, you were assigned to follow them. Now, if I tell you that you are going to supervise this task, you are going to supervise this task. Is that understood?"

Kiefer's eyes were darting between Wahler's and the floor. "Yes, *Standartenführer*."

"Good. Put these crates in storage and come to the dungeons as soon as you are done."

Kiefer didn't look down until Wahler and his guards left. He remained silent until bringing each crate, by hand truck, into a dark storage room. Smoked and salted meats were hanging from hooks above us, and there were shelves full of canned foods and rations. After making sure he was alone, Kiefer opened the crates. "Is everyone alright?" he whispered.

"A little cramped, but doing well," I said, wincing as I crawled out of the crate.

"What potion was Wahler talking about?" Halcomb asked, popping his joints.

"Something to keep tank and vehicle parts from freezing. Wahler's hoping a success will further validate his work with High Command," Kiefer explained.

"And winter is approaching fast," I added. "What do we do now?"

"Go to the dungeons and shoot the son of a bitch," Halcomb muttered.

"The dungeons are heavily guarded," Kiefer said. "You would be shot before you even reach him." He thought for a moment, rubbing his chin and pacing. "There is a hidden stairway behind the last shelf in this room. It was how the vampire's slaves delivered food to prisoners without being seen. Not even Wahler knows about it."

"Then how do you?"

"A book." Kiefer made eye contact with Halcomb. "If I was your enemy, I would have turned you over by now. Do you believe me when I say I am on your side?"

Halcomb let out a sigh while looking at the floor. He glanced at Elvira and me before returning his gaze to Kiefer. "If I apologize, will you accept it?"

"Of course. Now, when you reach the bottom of the stairs, there is a passage way that leads to what looks like a dead end. There will be a sewer grate on the floor. Climb down and look for a row of torches on the wall. Some of them will have small rocks tied to them. Follow those torches to a ladder. That ladder leads right up into the dungeons. You will know you're there if you can hear screaming."

"Right. What do we need to watch out for while we are down there?"

"In the hallway or the sewer?"

Halcomb shrugged. "Both, I guess."

"The sewer is clear—well, aside from the obvious. There will probably be guards standing near the grate. I will do what I can to get them away."

"Once we are in the dungeons, how do we eliminate Wahler?" Elvira asked.

Kiefer looked at me. "Do what you did to me in the forest. Threaten him and keep him from getting out of your grip, but do not kill him. The guards will not shoot as long as you use him as a shield. I think that is the best way we can go about this."

"Seems easy enough," I said. "Hopefully we will be out of here before sundown."

"I hope so." Kiefer looked me in the eye. "That is something I have not done in a long time. I do not want to regret it."

The spiral staircase leading down to the passageway was dark except for the flashlight Kiefer gave us. We kept quiet, and I prayed no one could hear the rapid pounding of my heart. Anything could go wrong when we get out of the sewer. When we got to the bottom of the stairs, I wondered where exactly we were in the castle. We couldn't feel any drafts, and the air was stale and stuffy. There were small piles of black ash and soot on the floor underneath the torches, which hadn't been lit in many years. Rats scampered away from us as the light touched them. We turned the flashlight off every time we drew close to walking under a floor grate, hoping and praying no one up above would see it.

It was quiet for the most part aside from the dripping of water in parts of the sewer we couldn't see. We looked for a ladder and listened for screaming. As much as I prayed we didn't hear any, I knew it was inevitable. This wasn't a dream. We actually were in a horrible place, where evil was rank and innocent people died. There was no hope of the suffering here ending until we took action.

The first sound we heard wasn't screaming, but the barking of orders from Wahler, followed by the sharp sound of him slapping someone. Then we saw the ladder and the grate above it. My heart was in my throat as we gathered around the light shining through the grate. Quietly, I breathed a sigh of relief when I saw Kiefer. He briefly looked down at us and smiled.

"I will cut the son of a bitch open myself to get every last drop," Wahler was saying. "This potion will make High Command take me seriously, and there's nothing I want more than to make my influence felt across the Reich. I do not want anyone or anything standing in my way." He snapped his fingers. "Go get meat hooks from the kitchens. If I have to do this the messy way, I will."

"Yes, *Standartenführer*," Kiefer replied.

We could sense the fear from each other. None of us could bring ourselves to speak, but we all knew one of us had to go up and see if we could get to Wahler.

"I will go," I whispered.

"Jay, it is too risky. Wait for Kiefer," Elvira said.

"Who knows how long that will take?" Halcomb muttered. "Besides, I do not think Wahler is alone up there."

"That is why it will be best for me to go," I replied. "Stay here. I will signal you when it is safe."

Halcomb opened his mouth to say something, then closed it. He and Elvira moved further back into the darkness. I wanted to look like I was the only invader if I was caught. I didn't want to put them in danger.

When I was at the top of the ladder, I listened for footsteps, then lifted the grate. Wahler was at the end of the hall, back to me. I disappeared back under the grate when he started to turn toward me. My heart beat faster and faster as he paced toward the grate. He stopped just in front of it as Kiefer came back, holding several meat hooks.

"Hang up that corpse and put a bucket under it," Wahler ordered.

Kiefer stammered. "S-Sir—"

"If I hear you cry about it, I will put a scar on your other cheek. Is that clear?"

"Yes, sir." Kiefer sounded scared and defeated.

There was a sudden clattering sound. The meat hooks had fallen to the floor as Wahler took Kiefer by the shoulders and shoved him up against the wall. "You were sent to me because you are a pathetic embarrassment to the SS. If I have to beat you into submission, I will, and I will not hesitate. You are in no position to question my orders. If I tell you to go hang up a corpse, you will go hang up that corpse."

No response.

"It is entertaining to watch you squirm, Kiefer. It makes me wonder how you survived training." Wahler was silent for a moment, and I assumed it was because he was watching Kiefer writhe in his discomfort. Then he said, "Go. Hang up that corpse. I do not want to hear another word out of you unless I ask for it."

Kiefer went into the prison cell. I watched as Wahler walked past the grate and shouted, "Guards! Get the subjects from cells five and six and take them to the laboratory."

I heard four sets of footsteps march down the length of the dungeon hall followed by the loud clanging of the cells being thrown open. My blood ran cold when I heard the panicked screaming and begging of two men, followed by the hard *thunk* of the guards knocking them unconscious. Next was the sound of heavy footsteps and bodies being dragged along the floor. When Wahler followed them, I lifted the grate again.

My emotions were telling me to run after him and strangle him, but my logic said that would only get me killed in the process. Climbing out of the grate, I peered into the chamber where Kiefer was hanging up the corpse. He was shaking, but his expression was blank. At the same time, he looked like he was holding back on how he really felt. He barely noticed me coming in, but eventually turned to face me. "Did you hear everything?" he asked.

"I heard Wahler berating you." I was about to apologize for how Wahler treated Kiefer, but stopped. What was the point in apologizing? It wouldn't make things better and Kiefer already had my sympathy. An apology would be pointless and redundant. "You will be free of this place soon," I replied instead.

"Now do you see why I have lost hope?"

I nodded.

Kiefer was silent as he continued his work. It wasn't easy watching him lift up the corpse, and I could tell it wasn't easy for him to do. Eventually, he said, "Am I a coward for not having dealt with Wahler sooner?"

I shook my head. "It would have been suicide."

"Yes, but... it would have been heroic."

"Maybe, but you have a lot to lose."

"I have nothing to lose. I do not communicate with my family anymore. I am an embarrassment to them."

"You should not think of yourself that way."

"No?"

"No." I glanced over my shoulder. "What do you recommend I do when Wahler returns?"

"He will not be alone. He will have two guards with him. The only time he is alone is at night. Everyone else stays in town, but Wahler and the necromancers stay here."

"So I should go back into the sewer?"

Kiefer nodded.

"Why bring us this early, then?"

"Because it would be harder to bring you in at night. It would be far more suspicious." Once the corpse was strung up, Kiefer turned away from it. He maintained eye contact with me, but looked like he was struggling to do so. "Keep hiding. Keep listening. I will find you when Wahler goes up to his quarters."

Right when I was about to turn to head back to the sewer grate, we heard Wahler and his two guards walking in. Kiefer gestured for me to get under a table with a bloodstained cloth covering it. As I crawled under, Kiefer went back to looking busy as Wahler entered the room.

The guards were dragging two unconscious prisoners with them. Wahler directed the process of hanging them up by their ankles before sticking tubes and needles into them. The tubes led into a series of jars on a table. I watched the tubes turn red as blood flowed into them, and every fiber of my being cried out to make it stop.

As much as I cursed myself for not acting, I knew it would be irrational. I could be killed. Kiefer could be killed. Even if I killed Wahler, there was no way of stopping this entire operation afterward. It would have all been in vain.

I paused to think. The most important part wasn't just to kill Wahler, but to sabotage White Raven so the Nazis could see it as pointless to continue. As dangerous as the idea seemed, I thought of telling Halcomb and Elvira to split up and go to various parts of the castle to destroy whatever they came across that was related to Wahler's work. Yes, that could work, couldn't it?

Wahler looked at Kiefer, who was avoiding eye contact with everyone in the room. "I expect you to be on your best behavior this afternoon. We have a visitor coming."

"A visitor, sir?" Kiefer asked.

"Doctor Griebel. You remember he was here a few months ago, documenting my findings on ice-variants."

"Yes... I remember him."

"I know he is not as smart as he tries to make himself out to be, but until Himmler decides he is not useful anymore, we have to put up with him. He should have been removed a long time ago, but that is not up to me, is it?"

Kiefer shook his head. "No, sir."

"That was a rhetorical question. Now, all I ask is that you do not reduce yourself into a blubbering mess when Griebel arrives. I could care less if you bawl like a baby in front of me, but I do not need him telling Himmler about your behavior. You know what will happen to you if you are removed. I do not think you want to be sent to the front in Russia, do you?"

"No, sir."

"I thought so. Any outburst from you and you will hang here with the corpses all night."

Kiefer didn't respond.

"Have I made myself clear?"

"Yes, *Standartenführer*."

"Good. Go prepare the guest quarters and then come back down here. I have other things for you to do."

Kiefer clicked his heels together. "Yes, *Standartenführer*." He left the dungeon. Blood drained from my face when I realized I was alone with Wahler and his two guards. About a minute later, another officer entered the room.

"You wanted to see me, sir?" he said.

"Yes. Was my contact serious when he said that Lexis was murdered in North Africa?"

"Completely serious, sir."

"Murder. And... who murdered him?"

"A Conjurus, sir. An ice-variant. More specifically, an American spy named Jay Loalin. Field-Marshal Rommel allowed him to carry out a witch-hunt after two soldiers were killed for their kidney stones."

"Loalin... A relative of Morgan's, I suppose?"

"Possibly, sir."

Wahler was silent for a moment. "What else? What was an American doing in North Africa? Are they preparing for an invasion?"

"We never learned what his mission was, sir. Your contact was not able to get close to him."

More silence. My heart was in my throat. Were there *two* warlocks in the *Afrika Korps*? Perhaps more than two?

Wahler tapped his wand on the table as he paced, thinking. "This is certainly a first for my operation. I knew most of the military officers were not in favor of integrating warlocks into their ranks, but I did not think any would resort to killing them. We will have to be more careful."

"Do you plan on... doing anything about the field-marshal, sir?"

"No. A field-marshal is too high-profile, and until I have gained validation with High Command, killing an officer without permission from the *Führer* could land me in serious trouble. I will send another warlock to North Africa with orders he does not do anything stupid to reveal his identity. What the hell was Lexis doing killing soldiers?"

"According to your contact, he was making acid potions to sell to a witch in Tobruk."

Wahler fell silent again. "So his own greed revealed who he was. In the presence of a Conjurus, no less. See, that is the danger of working with witches and warlocks. They look out for themselves and no one but themselves. Lexis was not dedicated to me or the Reich."

"No, sir."

Nodding, Wahler looked at the tip of his wand. "When you take leave for the night, I want you to compile a list of local warlocks and give it to me. I will talk to them personally. Be friendly to them. Try to appeal to them. Forcing them will only give us another Lexis. I want loyalty, nothing short of complete, devout loyalty."

The officer clicked his heels. "Yes, *Standartenführer*."

Before the man could leave, Wahler held up his hand. "What became of Jay Loalin?"

"He escaped the camp shortly after Lexis was killed, sir."

"A shame. I would have liked to have had the opportunity to have him here. But it makes no difference. You are dismissed."

"Yes, *Standartenführer*." Spinning on his heels, the officer left the dungeon.

I thought I was going to be sick. What could Wahler possibly want with me? Taking a deep breath and trying to think clearly, I swore under no circumstances could I allow Wahler to capture me. Nothing good could come of it.

I was thankful Wahler hadn't been a warlock since birth or he would have been able to sense my presence in the room from the moment he walked in. He did his gruesome work with the prisoners' bodies, draining their blood as thoroughly as he could.

Honestly, I had been praying that the two brought in earlier had already expired, but at some point, they awoke. They panicked, screamed, and tried thrashing around. I curled up under the table, covering my ears. Their crying and howling and begging piercing my brain and soul. A dull ache started in my chest, and it gradually intensified as I lay there, doing absolutely nothing.

The two men began moaning about the cold. I had been told that when an ice-variant says it's too cold, it means death is just around the corner for them. Wahler hadn't reacted much to the sounds of human suffering. He simply watched the blood continue to drain from the bodies.

"I still need more before I can start making a batch of potion," he mumbled, likely to himself.

One of the prisoners' last words were, "You heartless son of a bitch." And I agreed.

For a moment, I felt like the real heartless son of a bitch for not doing anything. I could have killed Wahler there, but I had been paralyzed with fear. Even long after Wahler ordered his guards to dispose of the bodies in a mass grave on the castle grounds, I was cursing myself, questioning myself. This was the whole reason I took this mission, and I couldn't bring myself to do it when the time was right.

Was the time right, though? Kiefer said it would be better to kill Wahler at night because he was alone. It would be easier to get away, and no one would find Wahler's body until morning. That made sense to me.

I kept telling myself that it would all end soon, and then we could go home. As I lay there, tears rolling down my face and the screams of the dying echoing in my mind, I wanted nothing more than to go home.

Kiefer finally returned to the dungeon. For a moment, I didn't understand why it took him so long to set up the guest quarters, but after witnessing Wahler slowly kill two innocent men through the loss of blood, I don't blame Kiefer for stalling.

"What took you so long?" Wahler asked. "Did I not mention that I have other things for you to do?"

"Y-You did, sir. I was making sure everything was perfect for Doctor Griebel. You know how he is with everything being in the right spot."

"I do not care if he wants the damn bed perfectly made up and the wine set exactly in the center of the tray! I will not be his servant! Now, I have a very delicate task for you." Wahler handed Kiefer a bucket. "Fill this with olives and bring it to the potion lab up on the first floor. I'm ready to begin"

Kiefer nodded. "Just... fill this? No specific number?"

"I would have given you a number if I wanted it. Get out."

I was beginning to feel cramped lying under the table, but I didn't dare move until Wahler left the dungeon. Once he was out in the hallway, I crawled out, my legs somewhat stiff. I limped over to the door, checking to make sure I wasn't being watched. When I knew I was clear, I dashed over to the grate, opening it as quietly as I could before dropping down to the ladder inside.

Halcomb and Elvira emerged from the darkness. "Jay, we were starting to think something happened!" Halcomb hissed. "What took so long? Did you kill Wahler?"

I shook my head. "Not yet. We will have our opportunity later tonight. He will be alone and a lot more vulnerable."

Halcomb didn't look certain about what to say next. "Well... shit. You went out there for nothing."

"No. Kiefer told me it would be best to wait. Wahler has his guards with him. Trying to kill him now would be suicide. Plus, we might have another target on our hands."

"Who? Or what?"

"Someone called Doctor Griebel."

"I have never heard of him."

Elvira shook her head. "Not familiar to me, either. What did you find out about him?"

"Not much. He is 'documenting' things Wahler has learned about ice-variants, and according to Wahler, he is an idiot. Kiefer is also very uncomfortable with him."

"Do you think we should kill him, too?" Halcomb asked.

I nodded. "I do not know if he is the top scientist on this, but I certainly would not waste the opportunity."

"It could help set the Nazis back in their research," Elvira said.

Halcomb thought for a moment. "Fine, but I am turning around and going home the minute you suggest we go kill Himmler."

The castle gradually became colder and colder as night covered the landscape. When the last truck left, silence fell over the castle aside from an occasional shout from a guard to his companion in a watchtower.

We didn't stay in one place the whole day, fearing that could get us caught. When we finally had some alone time, Kiefer told us all we needed to know about Dr. Griebel.

Griebel had been assigned to the ZA and White Raven after Wahler proposed his outlandish idea of creating a super-human out of all the Conjurus variants. However, Wahler wouldn't be given the resources he needed until he proved Conjurus could actually be useful in the war effort, and Griebel was ordered to ensure Wahler was staying on task. Wahler interpreted that as he wasn't being taken seriously and so he loathed Griebel's presence.

They were both tasked with bettering the German race, but they both had different ideas as to how to go about it. Griebel believed in destroying the "undesirables." Wahler favored "breeding them out" and not wasting the resources on destruction when they could be used in creation. He was, in a sense, trying to be Victor Frankenstein.

Conjurus hybrids are already incredibly rare. One with more than two powers is unheard of. In fact, it's never been recorded. It's been explored in fiction and various so-called academic journals, but it doesn't exist. If Wahler were to pull this off, he would make history. At the same time, I don't think we're meant to have more than two powers. His attempts could likely fail spectacularly.

When the time came, we were able to freely move about the castle under the cover of darkness, dodging ZA guards. Wahler had a nightly routine that involved staying up and reading until 2100. I proposed waiting an extra hour to make sure he was fully asleep. Halcomb looked like he wanted to argue, but he also looked like he didn't have the energy to do so. We took advantage of the time and quiet to go to the kitchens and have something to eat. We didn't realize how hungry we were until biting into apples taken from the crates we smuggled ourselves in. Kiefer stood watch, warning us whenever a guard approached. Despite me offering, he refused food for himself. He had been punished with starving for a day after sneaking food for one of the guards, so he didn't want to be seen eating.

"The guards will surely sound the alarm long before Griebel gets here," Halcomb said. "We might not get the chance to kill him."

Kiefer glanced over at us. "That is a good point. Wahler's death will be a huge blow to the ZA in general, but I think killing Griebel will ensure White Raven is ended for good. He is the only other person who knows the inner workings of the project. That will give the Allies time to invade Europe. High Command already does not have a lot of confidence in the project."

"It also brings up another question," I said, a cold feeling settling in my stomach when I thought of the conversation I heard earlier between Wahler and one of his aides. "Wahler keeps his warlock spies in line. When he dies, they will have no direction. They could just start killing indiscriminately."

"That depends on what his successor will do with them."

"Do you know who his successor is?"

"*Obersturmbannführer* Walther Kaschel. He is currently working on another project near the town of Würzburg, I think."

"Do we need to worry about killing him too?" Halcomb asked.

"That's a bit too far out of the way," I replied.

"Killing Wahler will definitely send the ZA into chaos," Kiefer explained. "Kaschel will take over, yes, but it will take time to reorganize."

"Hopefully the spies will simply flee into the wilderness," Elvira said.

"Or they keep weakening the German armies from the inside," Halcomb added.

"Not every German is a heartless killer." I gestured to Kiefer. "You want him to be butchered by a warlock?" Kiefer had many opportunities during the day to turn us in if he was really playing with us. I still couldn't understand why Halcomb was so reluctant to trust him.

"Jay, I am not saying I want Kiefer dead, but I am warning you that this habit of trusting the enemy is going to get you killed," Halcomb said, sternly yet calmly. "We got lucky with Rommel and Kiefer. You do realize Lehning wanted us both dead when he found out we were spies, right? What if we were caught by Lehning alone, without Rommel to stop him from shooting us on the spot—"

"I know we got lucky! I can think on my feet, you cannot!"

"Can we stop arguing, please?" Kiefer fretted.

"Why are you still arguing about this?" Elvira hissed. "This is all part of being a spy! We are not always going to be faced with easy decisions. No mission is going to run smoothly, or as planned. A plan is a roadmap, and there are multiple ways to get from one place to another. We still have our destination in mind, don't we?"

Silence fell over the kitchen. Kiefer shook his head before taking in a deep breath and saying, "Alright, we must discuss how we are going to do this. I suggest we wait until Griebel is here and kill them both on the same night."

"Does Wahler keep the same routine when Griebel is here?" I asked.

"Yes. Griebel tends to sleep later, usually around 2300. The guest quarters are in the same tower as Wahler's. We cannot have any screaming from either of them, or gunshots."

"That will be easy for me," I said. "I can just put an icicle through their skulls."

"Do you want to just deal with both of them, then? We will figure out an escape route."

"I think it will be for the best. It will keep the rest of you out of danger."

"Oh, we will still be in danger. We will not be out of danger until we are out of Germany," Halcomb said with a snort.

"Still, I do not want you to get hurt, or worse."

Halcomb, Elvira, and I found a secluded place to hide and sleep for the rest of the night. We slept against a cold stone floor and wall. Like the night in the forest, Halcomb and Elvira were sleeping close together, trying to keep each other warm. I remained separate from them, trying to get some sleep. My mind remained active, though, making sleep almost impossible.

Did I really trust too quickly? I thought back to every relationship I've ever formed in my life. My mother, my uncle, my grandparents, my cousins, my team in Antarctica, my coworkers at the refrigeration plant, Laurel, Halcomb, Colonel Stafford. All of them were good people. I had good reasons to trust them.

It dawned on me that I had never really been given a reason not to trust someone, or that someone I was talking to wasn't making it obvious that I couldn't trust them. Perhaps they could see right through me, and happily took advantage of my kindness.

As I lay there, my thoughts turned to a conversation among relatives on Christmas Eve when I was a boy, about my father. It had been eight years since his death, and many of them still found it odd that he wasn't there. I can't remember every word said, but I remember my grandparents saying Morgan was a natural leader. Anyone who doubted him could be persuaded to trust him.

I wanted to be the same way, and for a long time, it worked. I thought that I could win someone over just by trusting them, making them feel validated, that someone was listening to them. It never occurred to me that someone can easily manipulate that and that I could be trusting the wrong person. At least Lehning had been clear from the start that he couldn't be trusted.

I had no doubts that Kiefer could be trusted, but I could understand why Halcomb didn't think he could be trusted at all. He's part of the SS.

They're trained to be cold and merciless. Kiefer only joined to avoid bringing shame and humiliation to his family because as a civilian, he was nothing more than a peculiar loner.

Things could have ended differently. I understood that. Kiefer could have easily been pretending or he could have just shot me outright in the woods. It's scary to think about, but it didn't happen.

I jumped when I heard the tapping of steel-toed boots against stone and readied myself to throw ice in the face of whoever was coming. When I saw it was only Kiefer, I released my breath and lay back down.

"Are you alright?" Kiefer whispered.

"Yes, I am trying to sleep," I said.

"But you are too stressed."

Over the last several days, I had noticed Kiefer pointed out such observations as statements rather than questions, and the only reason I never questioned it was because he was right. I was stressed. I was thinking a lot. I couldn't settle down. "How exactly do you know that?"

"I watched you toss and turn through a sewer grate upstairs, and I could feel something... as if something was writhing in my stomach."

I sat up, looking over at Halcomb and Elvira to make sure we hadn't roused them. "And you're not a telepathic warlock?"

Kiefer shook his head. "I cannot read thoughts, just emotions, and it is not something I can control. It is... ever-present, and it does not always feel like a gift. At times, it feels like a curse. I am around awful people all day. I feel... I constantly feel hatred and anger. But I also feel sadness. I feel confusion, stress, and uncertainty. I feel everything from everyone around me, especially pain. The reason I stole food and gave it to a guard one day was because I felt his pain and stress from hunger. He did not know it. He just thought it was a random act of kindness."

"It is amazing you have not gone mad from this."

"I have come close several times. When I get overwhelmed, I do not feel like screaming and yelling. I feel like... doing nothing at all. I feel drained, and empty. I can feel my expression going blank and I want to hide until it passes. I cannot take in any information. Not even simple things like names or dates."

I had never heard of such a phenomenon before. "Has anyone here witnessed that from you?"

"Some of the guards have. They've used the word 'melancholic' with me. Wahler has witnessed it and he seems to enjoy when I do not have an expression on my face. Sometimes I think he would be perfectly happy with cutting my eyes out and sewing my mouth shut. Sometimes I think that's what he and others want to do with every person in Germany—turn them into emotionless, heartless... freaks." Kiefer glanced around and picked up a smooth stone from the ground, pulling his gloves off to toy with it. "If this is what it takes for me to not be an embarrassment to my own family, I guess I am better off gone."

I wasn't sure what that meant. Did he mean what we discussed several days ago, when he told me he wanted to flee to America? Or did he mean something else? "Gone as in—"

"At first, I thought 'gone as in dead.' I battled that for a long while, but one day, one of the guards here announced he was getting married. His joy and happiness... felt so light and powerful at the same time. For once, I did not feel a heavy sensation in my chest. For once, I did not feel like I was cursed."

"You saw there is still good, even in dark places."

Kiefer nodded. "I want to feel that again. Actually—" he gestured to Halcomb and Elvira, "I have noticed they're becoming rather close."

"They do have to keep warm, you know."

"Oh, I know, but there is something else. He is protective of her. She can talk him out of an argument."

"You think they like each other?"

"Only time will tell of that. Relationships are delicate things at first. It takes both members to strengthen it. That is why I'm not married. Well, that and the woman I genuinely cared for is gone."

My heart sank. "Gone?"

"Disappeared. I think. Possibly dead." Kiefer focused on the stone in his hands. "Because she and her family are Jewish. We saw each other in secret for a long time. Even before Hitler came to power, a relationship like ours was not encouraged. Her family would not have approved and neither would mine. But that did not matter to us. She was the only person in the world who knew about... my ability. It was wonderful to not keep it to myself anymore. It was wonderful to feel joy from another person. It is... hard to describe what I felt around her. We talked about everything. She did not think it was possible for someone to think so much about the little things in life, but she liked it. She also liked how I gave her a chance to be alone and be herself. When I said I loved her, I meant it."

"Why did you not run away together and find somewhere you could be together?" I asked.

"We planned on it, but we were not certain where to go." Kiefer gripped the stone tightly, suddenly staring blankly ahead. "I still remember I was at the library that day, looking at different maps. Despite the distance, I thought it would best to run to Switzerland. We would be safe there. When I was finished, I went to her home and found it had been ransacked. Everyone was gone and someone painted a Star of David on the doors and windows. I asked their neighbor what had happened and she told me the Gestapo came through and took them away. She did not know where." Tears rolled down Kiefer's face. "I prayed that they had merely been deported. Sent away somewhere else. Well, they were sent somewhere else, but not somewhere they could start a new life."

"Where were they sent?"

"To hell. That is the best way I can describe it. There are... camps designed to exterminate anyone the Reich has deemed undesirable. The Jews, the Slavic peoples, the physically and mentally disabled, communists, capitalists, Catholics, and everyone else who does not or cannot fit their ideal of a perfect people. They must be destroyed or enslaved."

I had known that Hitler implemented various policies to remove certain people from German society, but this was the first I had heard about the death camps. "How many camps are there?" I didn't want to ask what went on in these camps. It couldn't be a "camp" if they were mass grave sites, where they just shot hundreds of people and dropped them in a massive hole in the ground like animals. A camp implies buildings and long-term stay. Were they starving these poor people to death? Were they working them to death? It certainly didn't sound like a summer camp. Honestly, it sounded like a perversion of the whole concept of a camp.

"I do not know. There are probably hundreds at this point. The more people the Germans capture in Russia, the more space they need to keep them." Kiefer looked back down at the stone. "I should not have let myself be forced into the SS. At the same time, maybe I could have found Miri. But... I would have to endure so much hell to get to her. I do not know if I could do it."

I touched Kiefer's shoulder. "I do not know if there's anything we can do to help. If there are hundreds of these camps, it would not be easy to find her."

"I will not ask you to. It is too dangerous." Kiefer drew in a breath, visibly drained from recounting all this. "The only thing we can do is hope Europe is liberated soon. And it is possible she is already dead. I doubt it, though. She was young and healthy. She is probably being worked to death in a factory."

"We have to do something—"

"We are doing something. The sooner we set back the Nazi war machine, the sooner they can be defeated."

"Then why do you want to flee when this is over? You did not tell me you had a girlfriend. You cannot just abandon her!"

Kiefer suddenly looked hurt. "Have you not listened to anything I just told you?"

"I listened to everything. You love this woman. You should save her."

"How am I supposed to know such an effort will not be for nothing?"

"You do not. But you have to try."

"Is it worth the suffering? If I get myself assigned to one of those camps to look for Miri and find out she is not there, I have to suffer. I have to feel the pain, the death, the sickness, the lack of hope, the hate, the anger, the depression, all of it."

"It is worth it if you get her back."

Kiefer let out a soft sigh, shaking his head. "If you knew exactly what I go through every day, you would understand why it's not a task I can undertake."

"If you love her that much, you can do it."

"Jay, you do not understand, and it is not your fault." Kiefer looked at me, pleadingly. "Can we drop this, please?"

I was fine with that, considering I couldn't think of anything else to say. One part of me was astounded at Kiefer's fear. Another part of me agreed with him—I had no idea what he went through on a daily basis. I can't imagine what it's like feeling what everyone around you feels. That doesn't even sound possible. Yet, I didn't think Kiefer was lying.

Speaking of which, I thought back to Halcomb, and looked over at him. Curiosity overcoming me, I glanced at Kiefer. "Can you tell when someone is lying to you? Or when you can trust someone?"

Kiefer nodded. "Not all the time, but, yes, I can tell when I can trust someone."

"How can you tell?"

"When I do not feel uncomfortable around them."

"How can you tell if someone is manipulating you?"

Kiefer looked up, working his jaw as he thought. "How do I explain it? Listen to your own thoughts and feelings, not just what the other person is telling you. Do you feel something deep inside screaming at you? Do you feel a strange, uncomfortable sensation in your stomach? Does something inside tell you 'this might not be right?' Little things like that. Why do you ask? Because of Halcomb?"

I nodded. "I have never been manipulated before, or trusted someone I shouldn't have trusted."

"You are lucky. Be grateful for that. You will never forget the day you found out the person you thought you could trust turned their back on you. You will never forget the fact that they used you. I hope you never have to go through that, but I also hope it only takes you one lesson. Some people never learn."

Again, I nodded, and anxiety gripped my chest. Was that how I was going to learn? The hard way? How do I learn so it never happens?

Chapter 12

I managed to fall into a dreamless sleep at some point after Kiefer left our little hiding spot, and awoke when I heard voices through the small cracks in the stone holding the walls together. One was Wahler's. Another was his aide, the same one who told him about Lexis's death, and the voice of a man I didn't recognize.

Sitting upright, I found a crack wide enough for me to see through. I saw black ZA uniforms and a white lab coat. Another crack higher in the wall let me see that the coat belonged to a short man with dark hair that was beginning to thin at his temples. He wore silver-rimmed glasses and his face was covered in uneven stubble. I assumed he was Dr. Griebel.

He and Wahler exchanged greetings, *heil*ed Hitler, and began talking about Wahler's work before they even started walking down a long corridor lined with helmeted ZA guards. I noticed Kiefer in Wahler's entourage.

"You said this... potion is ready for field testing?" Griebel said.

"Yes. I finished a batch last night," Wahler replied.

"Good. A couple of generals on the Eastern Front have requested samples."

"Oh? Did they sound confident in it?"

"I would not say they sounded confident. A few in particular said they do not care if this is the result of witchcraft as long as it works."

"It will work. I promise."

"Yes. Now, my question for you, *Standartenführer*, is can you adapt a formula that works on soldiers and horses?"

Wahler stopped, turning to face Griebel. "I can try. You do realize there is an extreme amount of risk in this."

"I do, and we have millions of test-subjects for you to choose from in the extermination camps."

Wahler laughed. "No. No, no, if the people in those camps are subhuman as you say they are, how are we going to get an accurate result?"

Griebel sounded stunned. "*Standartenführer*, are you suggesting we... test on our own people?"

"Yes. Do not worry, it will be voluntary, and I will not conduct it unless I am certain it will be safe."

They were soon out of hearing range, and I shook Halcomb and Elvira awake, telling them what I just heard.

"If this potion works on tanks and vehicles, they are going to escalate it to humans and horses," I whispered. "We cannot let the samples leave the castle."

"How do you propose we do that?" Halcomb asked, rubbing his eyes. "The dungeons are well-guarded, aren't they?"

I thought quickly. "Slash the tires of all the trucks outside. That will buy us time."

Halcomb raised his hand. "I'll—"

"No, let me. I am smaller. I can hide easier," Elvira interrupted.

I was hesitant for a moment, then said, "Alright. Just be careful."

"Please," Halcomb added.

"I will. Don't worry about me." Elvira adjusted her jacket and stood on her toes to give Halcomb a kiss on the cheek. "You two be careful as well." She squeezed both my hands. "Good luck."

"Good luck to you, too," I said. When Elvira left, a sinking feeling started in my stomach, and all I could do was pray she succeeded, unhurt.

"What do we do now?" Halcomb asked.

"Wait for her," I replied. "Everything rests on Elvira now. I want to hear what Wahler and Griebel are talking about."

Halcomb and I left our hiding place to find that most of the guards weren't at their usual posts; they were off guarding Wahler and Griebel. That gave us easier access to the castle, but not by much. We still had to dodge individual guards patrolling corridors and standing in front of doorways, forcing us to get creative with our route to the dungeons. We eventually settled on using the sewers again once we figured out exactly where we were.

Coming to the spot we hid in the day before when I made my first attempt to kill Wahler, Halcomb crouched in a dark area away from the grate. He had an anxious look on his face as he switched back to English. "I don't like the thought of Elvira out there by herself. None of us should be going anywhere in this hellhole by ourselves."

"Ah. I thought it was because you like her," I said, jokingly.

Halcomb smirked a little. "If you want me to be honest, I do like her, but how did you know?"

"One, I've noticed you two always sit close together. Two—and you won't like this—Kiefer's noticed."

"Oh, now how is *that* possible? He hasn't been around us very long."

"Have you noticed how strongly he reacts to other people's emotions?"

"A little."

"Apparently, he can feel them, like he's experiencing them himself, and he's not a warlock."

"Odd." Halcomb looked up at the sewer grate. "I kinda wanted to wait until I was alone with you to say something."

"About what?"

"About Kiefer. If he hasn't turned us in by now, then... I guess I can trust him."

I smiled. "I'm glad you do, now."

"Don't take it lightly. I'm still worried you're going to trust the wrong person one day, and it'll get you hurt. I know I didn't express it very well, but that's what I was worried about. You."

I nodded. "Does that mean we're still friends?"

"Definitely. We never stopped. At least, I don't think we did."

"You acted like we stopped."

"I know. I'm sorry. Just... if something happens to us here, I want you to know that."

"We'll all get out of this alive. I pr—"

"Don't promise it."

"But—"

"Just don't. We don't know if we're going to get out of this alive, and I don't want you to feel guilty like you did after Antarctica." Halcomb gave me a stern look. "You're going to try your best, I know, but this isn't something you can promise. You're a magical being, but you're not unstoppable."

We fell silent when we heard the voices continue above us, starting with Griebel. "...How do we apply this potion practically? We have hundreds of tanks across the Eastern Front and if this works we will need a method of getting this to everyone."

"I can always make more, but I think it might be necessary have a dedicated witch or warlock in every division," Wahler said.

"What is it with you and wanting to put witches into the *Wehrmacht*?"

"If we are going to embrace witchcraft, then it is also necessary for the soldiers and officers to get used to them."

"And how do we keep them from killing our men? You know how they are."

"Let us take this one step at a time, Doctor."

A sudden cold feeling passed over me when another figure joined the group. They were dressed in a black shroud, with the hood over their head. There were gnarled hands coming out of the sleeves, white as snow but mottled with the red of broken blood vessels, and the ZA guards seemed to be uncomfortable in the figure's presence. A harsh voice said, "If we are to become dominant in Germany, it will take much more than just integrating us into the military."

"I was already aware of that, Rentarus," Wahler said.

"That's a necromancer," I whispered to Halcomb.

"I can tell," Halcomb whispered back. "He seems more evil than Wahler."

"If you were already aware of that, then are you aware of the steps we must take after you are done with killing half of Europe?" Rentarus asked.

Wahler fell silent. "We discussed what will happen after the war."

"We did, but after some thought, I have come to the conclusion that it will not be enough to simply let witches come out of hiding. They must be fully integrated into society, to teach those who are able to learn."

"I am certain we can arrange for witches to become part of the Hitler Youth."

"No. A person must be taught from the minute they are able to hold a wand. You know this. This is why most of the SS failed. Magic is not something anyone can learn. It is insulting that you arrogantly think that being the master race means you can simply learn magic at your will. We must teach it young, and those who are too old or unwilling to try should become nothing more than cattle for us to use."

The way Rentarus said "cattle" reminded me of Lexis. It was already disgusting that the Germans were trying to kill everyone who didn't fit their physical and mental demands. This was just as bad. Now they were planning on killing everyone who couldn't perform basic magic.

"Where does it end?" I whispered.

"What?" Halcomb asked.

"Where does all the pointless killing end?"

Halcomb thought for a moment. "It ends when the good people in the world stand up to it, and that's what we're going to do tonight. We're going to set this project back to give the rest of the Allies a fighting chance."

I nodded, and suddenly I felt as though the fate of everyone in Europe rested on my shoulders.

Wahler, Griebel, and Rentarus continued discussing their plans for after the war. Griebel interjected with, "We have to win the war first. If this potion helps in beating back the Soviets, I think we'll be granted a little more freedom with this project."

"It is going to take much more than a glorified lubricant to win," Rentarus said.

There was a tense silence for a moment and then Wahler replied, "A glorified lubricant? You yourself this was impressive for someone who started practicing witchcraft as an adult."

"I said it was impressive you were able to make a potion without it exploding and killing you in the process. I did not say what exactly you created is impressive. In fact, it is entirely amateur and shows you are far too cautious."

"Cautious?"

"If you were serious about improving the chances of your people to win in the Soviet Union, you would have created a potion that turned your soldiers into cryomancers. That would have been impressive."

"And it would take years and resources that I do not have. That is why I started small."

"We do have plans for creating potions for soldiers," Griebel added. "As *Standartenführer* Wahler said, it will be long and difficult, and it is important that we make sure they can take it safely."

"As long as you do not make any mistakes, Wahler, the potion you create will be safe," Rentarus said.

"I really do not appreciate you doubting me, Rentarus," Wahler hissed, his tone changing sharply.

"You still have potential, but you are wasting it by playing around and not making anything of value. You and the doctor can do what you want with this child's play, but when you are ready to make something useful, come see me."

Rentarus left, and Wahler said to Griebel, "Wretched old fool."

"I do not trust his kind," Griebel replied.

"Necromancers are highly skilled. If we are going to learn anything about sorcery, they are the best in the business."

"They are selfish and arrogant—"

"You are one to talk! All you do is cut limbs off prisoners and throw them in boiling water out of so-called scientific curiosity! I would have the resources to impress Rentarus *and* High Command if you were not squandering it all on torturing people for your own amusement!"

"You know the importance of the Final—"

"It is a waste of time and resources. I have a brilliant plan to create a better German. We can eliminate the inferior peoples by breeding them out. If our genetics are so superior, then why not use it to our advantage, and why not add something spectacular in the process?"

"Your plan is bold and far too risky. That is why High Command has not given you what you wanted. If they like your potion, maybe you will get what you want, but for now, you must be patient." Griebel sighed. "Even Himmler agrees with me that you are extremely reckless and need some reining in. Perhaps allowing you to create the ZA was a mistake."

"I think the rest of you are afraid. You love having control over everyone and terrorizing them. If you were to start creating instead of destroying, no one would be afraid of you anymore. Tell me, would you rather have several small groups of people afraid of a group of non-magical men with rifles, or the entire world shaking in their boots at the idea of fighting an army of men with every magical power known to us? I think long-term. You do not."

"For the moment, Wahler, we must think short-term. You have a brilliant mind and we would like you here and now."

"I am here and now, and now I have had enough of your idiocy. Kiefer, take our esteemed guest to his quarters."

"He's insane," Halcomb whispered.

I didn't have anything to say in response. Staying perfectly still, I kept listening.

"You are all dismissed," Wahler said to the guards. "I would like to be alone."

We heard the boots of the guards as they left the dungeons. A few minutes later, Kiefer returned. "Griebel told me to tell you that if your potion fails to win over High Command, he will find a post for you on the Eastern Front."

Wahler didn't say anything at first. "He does not think this is at all possible, does he?"

"I believe he thinks this is all a circus trick."

"A circus trick." Wahler laughed a little. "Are you joking?"

"No, sir."

"Very well. It means he will be among the first to be dismembered and his parts sold as potion ingredients and ritual pieces when this is over. He will be completely useless to us."

"Sir, surely not everyone incapable of magic will be... murdered over that."

"Only those putting up the biggest fight. You have already heard me discuss with Griebel how much I think the extermination camps are a waste of time and resources. We could have been creating something, rendering the inferior races extinct over the course of several generations of breeding new and better Germans. But, no. Everyone else is too impatient. Perfection cannot be achieved overnight, and they fail to see that."

"It is possible that they will see it eventually."

"The problem with that, Kiefer, is that everyone in High Command is as stubborn as an ass. It would take a miracle for even one of them to see that my work is worth their time and attention."

In some ways, listening to this gave me a sense of relief. German High Command wasn't taking Wahler seriously, which meant he probably would never get the resources he needed to create his superman. At the same time, this didn't make him any less dangerous. He was still slaughtering ice-variants, and he would continue to do so until ordered to stop or until he ran out and the necromancers could no longer revive the bodies.

I stood still in the darkness of the sewer, wondering how all of this stemmed from Wahler simply seeing my father's power on the battlefield. I wondered what could have been changed, if anything.

As the sun began to set, I was prepared to kill Wahler in his sleep, but it wasn't going to be as simple as I hoped. Elvira was successful in slashing the tires of all the trucks in the lot outside the castle, but much to our dismay, we had failed to take into account the fact that some of those trucks are used to take most of the guards into the village for the night.

The castle was put on high alert when the cause of all the tires being flat was discovered. Guards were sent into the woods and the castle itself was scoured for infiltrators. All three of us remained hidden in the sewer.

Eventually, some of the ZA men marched down to the village on foot to interrogate the civilians. When Kiefer told us, a look of guilt came over Elvira's face.

"They are going to hurt innocent people over something I did," she said.

Kiefer reached out to her. "It is not your fault, Miss." He took off his gloves and gently squeezed Elvira's hands.

"Slashing the tires was my idea," I said. "If anyone is to blame for what happens to the citizens of the village, it is me."

Kiefer shook his head. "I don't want anyone to blame themselves. The ZA has been tormenting the village since long before you arrived. Something like this was bound to happen sooner or later." He looked back at Elvira. "I do not want people to be hurt any more than you do, but this had to be done. We cannot let that potion leave this castle."

Elvira nodded, clearly unhappy, but said, "Very well."

Reluctantly, Kiefer let go of Elvira's hands. His expression of unhappiness mirrored hers. "I have to go before anyone notices I am gone. Stay here until I say so." He dashed toward the ladder leading out of the sewer.

When he was gone, Halcomb looked at me and Elvira. "We should have known this would happen."

"Even if we did know, we had to do this," I said. "I have one shot to kill Wahler, and that is in a few hours."

"What do we do about the necromancers?"

"I am not powerful enough to deal with necromancers, and I do not have the training either. I doubt they will stay after Wahler dies. You and Elvira just think about putting together an escape plan, and make sure Kiefer knows."

We were forced to hide not even ten minutes later when we heard German voices echoing through the tunnels. None of us spoke, or even breathed very hard, as we dashed ahead of them, toward the hidden staircase between the kitchens and the sewer.

As far as I knew, only Kiefer knew about the staircase. My heartbeat quickened when I saw beams of light flashing through the cracks between the stones and heard one of the guards saying, "There is no one else besides us in the castle. Who slashed the tires?"

"I think it was children from the village," another said.

"They know better than to disrespect us! Only a fool would do such a thing."

"Oh, please, you were a child once. I am sure you did stupid things like the rest of us did."

There was silence, followed by a third guard saying, "If it was not a spy or one of the villagers, then one of us is a traitor."

"I doubt it. We have all known each other for a year. I cannot think of anyone here who would turn on us."

"Perhaps one of the necromancers, then?"

"This is too mundane for them. Hell, they probably would have turned the trucks into frogs or something like that."

Their voices faded as they continued through the sewer. Even after we were certain they had left, we stayed put.

Over an hour later, Kiefer came down from the kitchens. "Are you alright?" he whispered.

"Fine. You?" I asked.

"Anxious, but alright. Wahler arranged for another SS unit to come with new tires. They will not be here until tomorrow afternoon. Good job."

"What about the villagers?" Elvira asked.

"I do not know. Most of the men are still down there. I think most of them will stay for the night." Kiefer smiled a little. "By tomorrow afternoon, we'll be out of here."

"That will be relief. I cannot wait to get out of here," Halcomb said.

I looked at Kiefer. "You will have to ditch the uniform. Do you have civilian clothes?"

Kiefer nodded. "Yes. How much should I bring?"

"Just one set. When we leave, we will have to move as quickly as we can. We cannot afford to carry much baggage. Just take whatever you think is important, because you will not be coming back."

That hit Kiefer hard. "I know I said I want to go to America and live out the rest of my life in peace, but..."

"This is still home to you," Halcomb said.

I was astounded he was the one to speak up, but, in all honesty, it made sense. Halcomb left his home state in order to start a new life on the East Coast. Granted, it wasn't as drastic as leaving one's home country, but it was still a big change.

"Yes. Yes, this is still home to me, and... I do not know how I will adapt to leaving." Kiefer made eye contact with Halcomb.

"We will be with you every step of the way," I said. "And we will help you start learning English as well."

Kiefer nodded. Behind his eyes, though, I saw fear. I couldn't blame him for being scared. This was going to be a massive change for him, but if he was going to leave the Nazis behind, this was the way to go.

Chapter 13

It wasn't until ten o'clock at night when everyone remaining in the castle had retreated to their quarters. There were a few guards out, pacing the long hallways that were only lit by lanterns and torches.

I left Halcomb and Elvira in the staircase to head up to Wahler's quarters. My heart was pounding as I crept through the oppressive darkness of the castle. Whenever I saw a ZA guard's face illuminated by the flickering light of a torch, I remained still, listening and watching.

The lack of sound aside from the light crackling of the torches burning and the tapping of the guards' boots on the stone floor made the castle feel much bigger and emptier than it really was. At times, I felt like I was the only person there.

The tall southern tower was where Wahler slept, right at the top. The tower was mostly composed of a massive stairway and small rooms. I found the rooms were empty and dark, and not one guard was to be seen after I had entered the tower. It was just me there, aside from Wahler at the top.

I walked slowly and quietly, not wanting to make any noise. The loudest thing at that point was my own heart, beating faster and faster the closer I got to Wahler's chamber. The stairs seemed to go on forever, until they stopped at a wooden door. There were torches on the wall, and a small window gave me a view of the forest and village below. The moon was shining through clouds as they passed by, and the trees and buildings were black silhouettes against the midnight sky.

Turning to the door, I peered through the tiny barred window. It was dark aside from a few candles, and the only movement I could see was from the flickering flames and the rhythmic breathing of the bed's occupant. I noticed Wahler's coat was hanging off the bed's headboard, and the bright red of the Nazi armband on it stood out like a sore thumb in the darkness.

Taking a few deep breaths and praying, I wrapped my hand around the doorknob. To my surprise, the door was unlocked. I didn't know why. Perhaps Wahler was convinced he was untouchable here. I turned the doorknob as slowly as I could until I could push the door itself open. My heart nearly stopped when Wahler groaned and shifted in his sleep. Something fell to the floor. I panicked until I saw it was a book Wahler had been reading in bed. I remained still until I was certain the sound hadn't roused him.

Releasing my breath, I approached Wahler, though not before taking a look around the room. I honestly would have thought Wahler would have chosen the master bedchamber to be his. Frankly, I'm not sure if it was a matter of personal preference or security. After all, without the proper knowledge, an assassin would have looked in the master bedchamber. At the same time, I noticed Wahler had few possessions. There were no photographs of family or loved ones. The bookshelves were composed of guides to various aspects of witchcraft. I expected that to be what had fallen on the floor, but when I knelt down to look, I saw it was a diary.

As a child, I had been taught the importance of respecting someone's privacy by not touching their diary. It is that person's space to express their thoughts in the written form. Uncle Redvar told me that reading someone's diary without their permission is as heinous as murder. I was still tempted. I wanted to get inside Wahler's head. There had to be more to him than what I had seen so far. At the same time, I was afraid of what I could find.

I resisted. I had a job to do. First, I had to find Wahler's wand.

Where was it? I searched the nightstand, bookshelves, and even his uniform. It was nowhere to be found. Sighing, I could hear Halcomb's voice in my head telling me to just get this done. If I'm quick, Wahler won't feel a thing.

Frost covered my fingertips. Counting in my head, I reached down and grabbed Wahler's neck, squeezing my eyes shut. I felt him thrash, then something jabbed my own neck. Opening my eyes, I saw Wahler was awake, and putting his wand up against my throat. He was shaking with cold, and starting to turn red.

"If you kill me, I will kill you in the process," Wahler hissed.

Part of me felt he was bluffing, but I also wasn't sure. I wanted to go home to Laurel. I wanted to make sure Kiefer started his new life comfortably. Reluctantly, I loosened my grip. I had to get that wand.

Wahler sat up in bed. "Now, I want to know who you are. You are obviously an ice-variant. Are you here on a vengeance quest?"

"I am here to end the suffering of everyone you have tortured here. That is all you need to know."

Wahler grinned and nodded. "I must applaud you for sneaking in here undetected. That is a feat of brilliance."

I made the mistake of looking down at his wand one time too many. Wahler adjusted his grip, and said, "Do you like it?"

I swallowed hard.

"It's a pity the Conjurus do not use wands. They have such a wide range of uses, many more than you could ever imagine." Wahler looked over his wand, then back at me. "But you could not handle that kind of power. It is why your people have been at war with witches for the last thousand years."

"It is not the power itself. It is what people like you and the necromancers will do with it," I said.

"Me? Please, my friend, I am the least of your worries. I do not seek destruction. I seek the opposite, in fact."

"Yes, but your efforts to create a new race will result in the destruction of others."

Without warning, I was hit with a blast of heat powerful enough to send me off the bed and into the wall. Falling to the floor, I was overcome with a weakness similar to being woken up in the middle of the night with a terrible flu. I couldn't even lift my head to look Wahler in the eye.

Wahler got out of bed, adjusting the band of his robe before walking over to me. "Are we done with dodging my earlier question? Are you going to tell me who you are? Or am I going to have to force it out of you? I know what hurts people like you, but I really do not want to have to waste the resources on one would-be assassin. I will, though, if you do not talk."

I was sweating profusely. Every pulse of heat ached terribly. "What... What have you done?" I grunted.

"Nothing permanent. I will gladly prolong it if you do not start talking."

It felt like fire was searing through every inch of vein and artery in my body. Struggling not to scream, I said, "My name... is Jay Loalin."

I wasn't sure what to expect after that. I knew Wahler was looking for me after hearing about what happened to Lexis, but I didn't know what he wanted from me. Did he want to kill me? Torture me? Attempt to replicate what my father had done at the end of World War I? Whatever it was, it wasn't going to be pleasant. My mind was a swirling mess of pain and panic. My entire body was burning. My clothing was soaked with sweat. Amidst the cries of pain in my head, I was afraid Wahler would find out that I was not alone.

Wahler stood over me for some time. He paced around me, expressionless as I continued to suffer. Eventually, I got to the point where I couldn't hold back any longer; I started grunting and groaning in pain, and tears streamed down my face.

"Am I to assume that you are Morgan Loalin's son?" Wahler asked.

"You would be correct," I said.

Nodding, Wahler continued, "You bear a strong resemblance to him. I should have seen it when I opened my eyes. Did you know I witnessed to your father's last stand? Is that why you came to kill me?"

I tried to breathe evenly as cold steadily began to pulse through me again. "I am disgusted that this is what your fascination with us turned into. Why? Why devolve into torture? Why become obsessed with creating something that cannot exist? Why use us as tools? *Cattle*, as your necromancers call us. Yes, that is why I came to kill you. I do not want this to be what my father's legacy is tied to. I do not want this to be what *my* legacy is tied to!"

"Your legacy, and your father's, will be tied to something incredible when my work here is finished. First, I was fascinated, and then I was inspired. I do not want to be the most powerful warlock. I want to *create* the most powerful warlock."

"It is not possible," I hissed. "Hybrid Conjurus are already incredibly rare. None have ever been recorded with more than two abilities."

"It might take time, but I will find a way." Wahler sat on the floor across from me.

I looked him in the eye. "What now? You are not going to kill me?"

"Oh, I do not know what I want to do with you. If this were the army, I would have to shoot you for being a spy, but since this is not, I can do whatever I want with you. For the record, I do know that you murdered Lexis in North Africa. That I may have to punish you for. I just can't decide how."

My strength was gradually coming back, but I didn't want Wahler to know that. My mind was racing to figure out what to do. How do I get his wand? How do I get out of this alive? I kept telling myself not to look at his wand or he would figure out what I was up to, so I looked at the floor instead.

"Was it you who slashed the tires of all my vehicles?" Wahler asked.

The question took me by surprise. "Yes," I said.

"You are working alone, then. Interesting, considering you had a companion in North Africa. Where is he? Is he still in North Africa?"

"Yes. I went on alone. He was sent to a POW camp."

"So, you escaped and you left your companion behind. I find that... most unheroic. Your father died to save his men, yet you could not be bothered to break your friend out with you. Do you not think he would be disappointed in you?"

In hindsight, I'm glad Wahler fell for my lie, but I was still overtaken with rage. "He would be proud of me for going on despite the danger. I left my friend behind for his own safety. He has no magic."

"I see." Wahler fell silent again, toying with his wand and continuing to stare at me. "Your friend would have been completely useless, then."

I could see now that Wahler was trying to get me angry. He was enjoying this for some reason.

It didn't take long for him to give up. He lifted my chin to look me in the eye and said, "I hope you understand I do not want to kill you. Why would I? If I met your father today, I would be honored to be in his presence, for he inspired me to do what I am doing today."

"I do not think he would be honored to meet you."

Wahler smirked. "Regardless, I may not kill you, but you will not escape anytime soon. You can bear witness to my creation."

When I felt a refreshing coolness spread through my body, I resisted the urge to stand up, try to snatch the wand away from Wahler. He would see that coming. He probably knew that's what I wanted.

"Strange. I would have thought you would have tried to escape by now," Wahler said. "You are smarter than I initially thought. You can recognize when things are hopelessly against you, so you do not waste your energy."

I refused to look him in the eye at that point. I didn't want him seeing and mocking my anger.

"At the same time, I am getting the impression you want me to take pity on you. You have clearly never been hit with a crippling heat spell like this before. It must hurt. It always does the first time." Wahler grinned a little.

Though I wasn't looking Wahler in the eye, or at his wand, I was looking at his chest and stomach. I should have thought of it earlier, but I thought it wouldn't have killed him instantly. An icicle through any part of his torso would catch him off guard, hopefully long enough to take his wand.

Up until that point, I had thought and talked about killing him. He was evil and it should've been easy, but here I was, hesitating. But I had to stop. I was here with the mission to kill him. Killing him would end the madness that was White Raven. It might not bring back the prisoners he tortured and killed, but it would prevent others from suffering the same fate. It would prevent the Third Reich from gaining any edge over the Soviets. It would be better in the long run.

Drawing in a breath, I pretended like I was just starting to recover from the effects of Wahler's spell, and began trying to sit up. Wahler watched, not taking his eyes off me for a second. My heart pounding faster and faster, I reached behind my head, running my fingers through my hair. I didn't want him seeing the frost forming on my hand as I focused on conjuring an icicle.

"If you are worried about being mistreated while you are my prisoner, you do not need to," said Wahler. "You will be well-taken care of. That I can promise you. You will be witness to history, the start of an era where your people and mine do not have to hate and hunt each other anymore, because you will be one and the same."

I could hear Halcomb screaming in my head that I needed to act and stop thinking. I had already disappointed him several times throughout this mission. This was definitely not a place where I could afford to disappoint anyone. I took one more breath and brought my hand around.

Wahler's eyes widened with shock as a loud *crack* echoed around the room. For the first time, I saw this man had felt fear. He gagged and coughed. Blood was mixed in his saliva, and he dropped his wand. I grabbed it swiftly, but without taking my eyes off the icicle protruding from his stomach. He doubled over and I saw had gone right through his torso, with several inches of bloody ice sticking out of the left side of his back. The melting ice and blood dripped from the sharp tip, and soon the floor behind Wahler was covered in water droplets full of red swirls.

"You son of a bitch!" Wahler hissed. He looked down at himself, and tried pulling the icicle out. He let out a shout of pain and scrambled to grab his wand from me, cursing.

I stood up, finding it hard to look at him as he struggled. Every movement hurt him. Blood was gushing out from around the wounds in his back and stomach, and the ice was slowly melting.

"Damn you, Loalin..." Wahler grunted. "Do you think this will solve anything?"

"My only regret is that the people you have tortured weren't here to see this!" I shouted. "My father would not have wanted this to be the result of his actions in France! He died saving his platoon! You are going to die a monster!"

Tears were rolling down Wahler's face. "My goal was to prevent more bloodshed."

"By causing more bloodshed and hurting innocent people in the process?"

"And is that not what you are doing here?"

"I am getting rid of one to save many. You killed many. You tortured many. You enlisted a bunch of fucking necromancers to help you!"

"I still fail to see how you are morally superior, Loalin. The way I see it, we are both trying to end this war, but we just have different ways of going about it." Wahler looked torn between emotions. He was angry and scared at the time. He kept squirming and twitching, and I wasn't sure what he was trying to do, until I realized he was trying to crawl toward the telephone on his nightstand.

Without hesitating, I grabbed Wahler by the collar of his robe, and dragged him back over to me. He cried in pain, and it was then I decided he had suffered enough.

I don't look back on these memories fondly. I understand the necessity of killing Wahler, and I don't doubt he was evil, but what does it say about me for letting him suffer instead of killing him outright? I didn't prove anything by screaming at him. I had lowered myself to his level. I made him suffer as he had made so many ice-variants suffer.

Whether or not he deserved it is not my question to answer.

He seemed to know what was coming, and his breathing became heavy and rapid. "Please! Please, Loalin, no!" he begged.

He was in such a panic, it was difficult to hold him still. I didn't want to miss or else he would just keep suffering. Not wanting to hesitate more, I threw an icicle into the back of his neck. His muscles relaxed instantly, and he became a literal dead weight in my grip. Dropping him, I stepped back, watching blood pool under Wahler's corpse. He was lying face-down, and I couldn't bring myself to try looking in his eyes. I was afraid of what I would see, and I didn't want to regret my actions. Releasing my breath, I told myself there was no way I could have talked Wahler out of ending his work. He wouldn't have listened. After everything I heard from him and Griebel and Rentarus, I'd be a fool to think I could change Wahler. It wouldn't be possible.

The only sound in the room then was the ticking of a small clock on the nightstand. It was almost midnight, and I still had to kill Dr. Griebel.

Feeling sick just looking at Wahler's body, I sat down at his desk. I couldn't just sit and think about what happened. This had to be done. I shouldn't feel sorry. None of the ice-variants he's tortured and killed would feel sorry. Kiefer wouldn't feel sorry, not after all the abuse he's put up with over the last year or so.

I stood despite the nausea, and left the bedroom. I didn't want to make any of the mistakes I made with Wahler. Before going into Dr. Griebel's quarters, I broke Wahler's wand and tossed it out a window into the bushes below. At least with Griebel, I didn't have to worry about him using magic. Like Wahler, he was fast asleep, but unlike Wahler, Griebel slept on his side. That certainly made it easier to put an icicle through the back of his neck. He had no idea what hit him, and I preferred it that way.

Before I left the room, I spotted a leather-bound book with a letter on top of it addressed to Field-Marshal Keitel and *Reichsführer* Himmler. It read as follows.

"Attached to this letter is a collection of Standartenführer Fritz Wahler's research in ice-variant Conjurus and witchcraft. I still believe that this is a waste of time. Not that long ago, I did not believe in witchcraft. Having seen it for myself, I know now that is real, but it is not something we should toy with. It is dangerous and impractical. Our goals are to exterminate the inferior races and make living space for Germans in the East. Wahler's plans would severely hamper that. We cannot have that space if we simply wait for races to go extinct through breeding. That could take several generations and render this war pointless.

"However, that is not my decision to make. I am presenting my argument against it as a scientist and loyal follower of the Führer. If Hitler himself says that Wahler's research may continue, then I will do my best to carry out his wishes."

The book itself was full of detailed descriptions on ice-variants' powers and the different applications of them in potions, as well as the results of Wahler's gruesome experiments. Without giving it a second thought, I took the book with me. This couldn't fall back into the Germans' hands, and we certainly couldn't let it get to Hitler. The first chance I had, I planned on setting the book on fire and making sure there was nothing left.

I jogged down the steps of the tower, and dodged the guards again in order to get back to the others. As I went, I couldn't believe I had accomplished this. Then again, I told myself, we still needed to escape the castle. Only then would I have accomplished this mission.

When I got to our hiding place, I found Halcomb and Elvira sitting close together, and Kiefer standing and facing the wall. Kneeling in front of Halcomb, I whispered, "Wahler and Griebel are dead."

"We know," Halcomb said. He pointed at Kiefer, then his gaze turned to the book. "What's that?"

"All of Wahler's research. Griebel was going to send it to the OKW and the SS. I am not going to let that happen."

Halcomb smiled. "I cannot believe you did it." He hugged me tightly. "I knew we could count on you!" He helped Elvira stand up. "We should leave before they find the bodies."

Nodding, I walked over to Kiefer. He was staring at the wall. I wasn't sure what to do, as his expression was blank. I tapped his shoulder, and he jumped, shrinking away from me. "D-Do not do that!"

Embarrassed, I said, "Sorry. We are leaving now. Are you alright?"

Kiefer wrung his hands. "Could I talk to you in private?"

"We do not have a lot of time."

"It's important. I'm sorry."

I looked over at Halcomb. "Go. Wait for us in the village."

"What the hell are you doing? We have to go now!" Halcomb hissed.

"We will catch up as soon as we can. Just go." I looked back at Kiefer. "Alright, what is it?"

"I knew when you hurt Wahler. You stabbed him—" Kiefer pressed his hand against the upper left side of his stomach, "here, didn't you?"

I nodded.

"And then you let him suffer."

Another nod. "If that caused you distress, I... I apologize."

"Do not apologize. When he finally... died, I felt a weight lift off my chest. I suddenly felt... liberated. I no longer felt fear. I do not feel tied to anything anymore. I feel like I can go and live my life now." Kiefer squeezed my hand. "Thank you. I... I cannot even begin to express how grateful I am." He made a gesture like he wanted to hug me. Shrugging, I let him. He squeezed me tightly, and I could feel his gratefulness washing over me. "I also want to say thank you for trusting me. That... means a lot to me."

"No problem," I said. Patting his back, I slowly pulled away. "We had better go. Either the guards or Halcomb will kill us if we do not hurry up."

Kiefer quickly got changed into civilian clothes before we left the castle. He looked much happier not wearing the dreary black of the SS uniform, but his smile quickly faded as we headed up into the kitchens. "Jay?"

"What?" I asked. The last thing we needed was another holdup.

"The prisoners. What are we going to do with them? If we leave them here, they will be slaughtered when the guards discover Wahler and Griebel are dead."

Kiefer did make a fair point. At the same time, the entire town could be razed come morning. Whichever route we went, it was likely innocent people would die. Taking a moment to think and sigh, I said, "What do you suggest we do?"

"We free the ones who are not being starved. Most of them have to be force-fed, but, the majority of them are healthy. They will be able to fight their way out and give the weaker ones a chance to escape."

"And how many of them are hundreds or thousands of miles away from home? We cannot exactly take them with us."

"They are ice-variants, Jay. I have heard many of them mutter that they want to kill the guards. Most of them can defend themselves. There are plenty of local resistance groups that can take them in. Either way I cannot bear to imagine them stuck here."

I didn't want to see these people shot for something I did. "How do we get them out?" I asked.

"I have the keys." Kiefer held up a large keyring.

Nodding, I turned to follow Kiefer down the secret stairway to the dungeons. The guards were still making their rounds, completely unaware of what had transpired above them. I kept watch while Kiefer crept forward with the keys. Not every cell was occupied. In fact, only eight were occupied.

Looking in through the bars, I saw the prisoners were curled up on their cots, asleep. Two were lying awake, and one was sitting upright, staring. His neck bore a long scar. My guess was that he was used as a bleeder for Wahler's potion, and then healed since he didn't die outright. There was still something human in his eyes, so he couldn't have been a necromancer's husk. He tilted his head when he saw Kiefer. "What do you want? It is after dark, is it not? You should be asleep."

Kiefer gestured for him to be quiet as he unlocked the cell. "We are freeing you."

The man didn't respond at first. He seemed to suspect that this was a trap.

"Wahler is dead," I said.

That got the prisoner's attention. "Is he? What killed him?"

"I did."

A vengeful look crossed the man's face. "It is a pity you did not drag him down here for us to deal with. If he wants to treat us like animals, let us return the favor."

Kiefer unlocked the cell door. "All we ask of you now is that you go home."

"I cannot go home if I do not know where I am."

"We're in a castle, in a village some distance outside of Munich," I said. "Where are you from?"

"Austria. Can you guarantee safe passage?"

Kiefer shook his head. "Your best chance is to find a resistance group or head to Switzerland."

The prisoner nodded. "That is better than nothing."

We went around freeing the others. Some were collected, like the first, but others were more than ready to exact their revenge on the guards. As we fled the dungeons, we could hear screaming, ice cracking, and guns firing. Kiefer was covering his ears as we went and his breathing was heavy as we made our way back to the kitchen exit. We dashed out into the cold darkness of night, the sounds of battle inside the castle becoming muffled.

"Come on, we need get out of here!" I grabbed Kiefer by his arm, pulling him toward the bushes surrounding the castle. The hill was dangerously steep. We carefully climbed down, though frantically looking around for any signs the SS-ZA had discovered our presence.

"Jay! What the hell took you two so long?" Halcomb snapped at us as we lowered ourselves into his and Elvira's hiding spot.

"We freed the prisoners," I said.

"You just let them loose? With no idea how to get out of the castle? The ZA will round them up and shoot them!"

"At least they can put up a fight! I do not want them bearing the blame for my actions!" I shouted.

"Can you two not argue for two minutes?" Elvira stepped in between us. "We need to leave before the Germans figure out what has happened."

"We might have to walk to Switzerland," I said. "That is over two hundred miles from here." I thought for a moment before looking at Kiefer. "Do you know anyone in the resistance circles around here?"

"I do not know anyone personally, but I know the Gestapo office in the village has been trying to get ahold of names and places. We could search their records." Kiefer pointed toward the lights of the village. "They set up in the village's police headquarters, just west of here."

The village was completely silent after we made our way down from the castle. I was extremely grateful to get away from that place, but I didn't realize it until we were at the base of the hill. The anxiety of potentially getting caught, and the horrors I witnessed, were still fresh in my mind, but something was telling me I didn't have to worry about it anymore.

As much as I knew this was far from over, I felt like I had gotten further than I had in Antarctica. Killing Wahler was the equivalent to actually reaching the South Pole. Now, we just have to make our way back to the ship anchored off the frozen coast. Only instead of fleeing an oppressive winter, we were fleeing an oppressive group of people.

I could only pray that the village didn't have to endure any retribution because of what we did in the castle. Frankly, for a government that claims it wants to lift the German people up, and proclaims them all as supermen, they have no problems slaughtering them when they don't step in line. Seems a bit counterproductive in my opinion.

The silence was very welcome as we headed through the streets. I kept glancing over my shoulder at the castle, kept listening for the sound of trucks roaring down the hill toward us. Then again, that couldn't happen since all the tires had been slashed. The fear was still there, though, and probably wouldn't leave until we left the village entirely.

The Gestapo office was a flat brick building that sat near the village marketplace. I could remember overhearing some of the townspeople quietly whispering how they could never get used to the presence of the Gestapo monitoring every little thing, right down to transactions for milk or butter. Others really had no input. Either they didn't care or were too afraid to say anything.

The four of us ducked into the bushes across the street from the building. Kiefer peered out through the branches. "Stay here," he whispered. "We are not alone."

I wasn't sure what he meant until seeing the gray-clad guard pacing behind the gates with a rifle slung over his shoulder. Kiefer looked at me. "I am going to distract him. You knock him unconscious."

"Go," I said. "We do not have a lot of time."

Nodding, Kiefer waited until the guard had turned around before sneaking out of the bushes. Less than a minute later, the guard was facing Kiefer. "Hey, what are you doing? It is long past curfew."

"I know," Kiefer said. "I could not sleep. It is such a lovely night."

The guard was forcing himself not to smile and laugh at Kiefer. "You should pace in your own home instead of being out here."

"There is not enough space." Kiefer walked closer to the guard. "You seem like you would like to go to bed as well."

The guard rolled his eyes. "Anyone up at this hour would want to go to bed."

"I am tired, yes, but so are you."

The guard gave Kiefer a quizzical look. "Yes, but why is that any of your business?"

Kiefer shrugged. "I feel bad for you; that is all."

"Nonsense. Everyone in this damn village hates us. We should raze it to teach the rest of Germany a lesson. These resistance groups keep spreading lies about us. If we could get our hands on them, it would make things a lot easier."

"Perhaps."

While they talked, I snuck up behind the guard, forming a hailstone in my hands. He was completely unaware of me until he said, "Why is it so cold—"

I struck him over the head with the hailstone with a hard *whack*, and the guard fell to the ground. Halcomb was quick to run from the bushes and pick up the guard's rifle and search the unconscious man for ammunition. Slinging the rifle over his shoulder, he pulled the guard's Walther P38 from its holster and handed it to Kiefer before pulling two extra magazines from one of the pouches on the guard's belt and handing them over as well. He kept the rifle ammunition for himself, shoving it into his pockets.

We dragged the unconscious guard into the building and locked him in one of the holding cells with a cloth around his mouth and his hands bound behind his back. Kiefer and I went into a large office with shelves packed full of documents, while Halcomb and Elvira found a hiding place for the keys. I was certain there was no way we could find the files we needed, but Kiefer knew exactly where they were. Without even searching very hard, he walked up to a shelf near the office's obscenely large portrait of Hitler and pulled a thick folder off of the third shelf from the top.

"How did you do that?" I whispered.

"I am not sure," Kiefer replied. "I have only been in here a couple of times, but I remember distinctly where each of the folders go." He lay the folder on the desk. "Hmm... ah! I have seen this man around here. A tailor named Peltzer. He is under surveillance for breaking curfew and being seen in the woods with people not from this village. He has been suspected of possessing weapons, but his home has been searched several times and they found nothing. No weapons, no Allied propaganda, nothing."

"You think he will help us?"

"It is worth a try." Kiefer closed the folder. "He lives a block away from the inn I saw you in when you first arrived, in the northern part of the village."

As he put the folder back, Halcomb and Elvira entered the office. "Well? Anything?" Halcomb asked.

"Yes. A tailor," I said. "Where did you put the keys?"

"Buried in the garden."

"Good enough. It will keep them busy for a few hours."

"My only regret is that we will not be here to watch them tear this place apart looking for them. I am ready to go find this tailor."

The moon was still high in the sky as we jogged up the cobbled streets to Peltzer's home. I looked up at the castle again. Lights were on in some of the towers, and I could only imagine the chaos going on inside. We hadn't seen any of the ice-variants yet. Either they took off into the woods behind the castle or they hadn't escaped at all.

The house was attached to several others, lining the entire street. There were automobiles parked on the side of the road, as well as several empty wagons. There was silence aside from the wind. Turning to look around, I noticed a couple of houses had Stars of David painted on the doors and windows, as well as notices tacked to the doors that I couldn't read from where I was standing. Some of the windows were broken, and something about them felt like they weren't occupied.

Kiefer knocked on the door of a house on the corner of the street. When there was no response, he knocked again. After the third time, we heard someone walking down the stairs. A middle-aged man with dark blond hair, gray eyes, and a maroon bathrobe pulled back the curtains, gave us a confused look, and then went to the door.

"Well, you do not look drunk and you do not look like you have anything to sell, so what are you doing here?" the man asked.

"Are you Mr. Peltzer?" Kiefer asked.

"Yes. Why does that matter to you? You are not the Gestapo again, are you?"

"No, but we do have some questions to ask you, because we need help getting out of Germany."

"I want to know this is not a trap."

Halcomb spoke in English. "Does this sound like a trap to you?"

Peltzer folded his arms over his chest. "You are Americans. How did you—"

"Not out here," I said.

We were let inside, and all the curtains were closed before Peltzer turned any lights on and had us sit at the kitchen table. He still looked wary of us. "Before we begin, how did you know about me?"

Kiefer raised his hand. "We searched the Gestapo's records for anyone they suspected to be part of any local resistances. I am... was with the SS."

Without much warning, Peltzer grabbed a rolling pin from the counter. Before he could bring it down on Kiefer's head, Halcomb jumped up, getting in between Peltzer and Kiefer, who had crawled under the table. "Do not! Put that down, now!"

"That animal deserves to be beaten to a pulp for everything he and his disgusting ilk have done!" Peltzer shouted.

"He is going to be beaten to a pulp if the SS find out he betrayed them. I did not trust him at first, either. I was so certain that he was going to turn us over to Wahler and his men while we were up in that castle, but now we are here."

The house was silent. Kiefer had come out from under the table, and stood behind me. "It is not like I had much of a choice," he said, voice shaking a little. "Not where I came from. I was already seen as completely useless and unable to provide for Germany as a whole. My entire neighborhood thought I needed to be... disciplined. What better place for that than the SS?"

"You didn't run away like any sensible person would? So, not only are you a murderer, but a cowardly one as well?"

Kiefer's hands were shaking. "Do *not* call me a coward! I have suffered enough over the last several years! I refuse to let anyone else push me around anymore! I let that happen once, but I am not letting it happen again! If you refuse to help us, then we will get to Switzerland on our own!"

"We are all on the same side," Elvira said. "We might come from different places, but ending the war is the goal for all of us here." She glared at Peltzer. "Kiefer risked his life to help us. He earned our trust. Besides, his knowledge of how the SS works could be beneficial to you."

Peltzer finally put the rolling pin down. "Alright, but I want you out of my house as soon as we are done. I do not need the neighbors hearing you."

He led us into his study, which was immensely disorganized. I imagine that was to throw off any Gestapo agents who came in. There were books stacked in columns as tall as a grown man and papers scattered all over the desk, some covered in cigarette ash. The hearth was full of ash that I later found out were remnants of papers Peltzer didn't want the Nazis getting their hands on. The shelves were threatening to buckle under the weight of papers and books, as well as an old ceramic statue of a gray rabbit holding a sunflower.

Peltzer dragged a chair over and shakily climbed up to take the big rabbit down. He turned it over and pull a rolled-up map out of its bottom. After handing the map to Halcomb, Peltzer put the statue back and slowly climbed back down. "I had to hide that after I started marking it up. This has every known hideout of the resistance in the Munich area. I personally have no ideas of how to get you to Switzerland, but the group to our west—" he pointed to a little town called Königsdorf, "has a woman who regularly goes to the Swiss border to meet with a sympathetic farmer and get supplies from him. Her name is Jette Fehrenbach."

"Jette Fehrenbach," I repeated. "Is she in charge or just a member?"

"She and her husband run their branch together. Their son is fighting in the Soviet Union."

"They sound like very brave people," Elvira said.

Peltzer nodded. "Ask around for Karl Fehrenbach. If they want to know who sent you, give them my name and say that the rabbit showed you the way." He gestured to the statue on the shelf.

"What is the easiest way to get to Königsdorf?" Halcomb asked.

"Head west along the railroad tracks. It is only a few kilometers away. If you head out now, you will reach the town by morning." Peltzer rolled up the map to put it back in the rabbit. "I wish you the best of luck."

"We will not forget you for this," I said.

Peltzer looked over at Kiefer. "I am taking a big risk trusting you. Do not break it."

"That is not the first time he has heard that," Halcomb said. "Come on, everyone."

Chapter 14

It was still quiet when we finally left the village, and we certainly didn't want to stick around to see how long it would last. After finding the railroad station, we started following the tracks west, walking at a quick pace.

Kiefer was enjoying the walk. It was clear he hadn't been outside and free in a long time. He was happier than I had ever seen him before, but that didn't last too long. For part of the walk, he was very talkative, in awe at the vast open space that lay between the railroad and the mountains to our south. But, when we were several miles away from the village, Kiefer stopped rather suddenly and started pacing in a circle, holding his head.

"Are you alright?" I asked.

"Yes. Yes, yes, I am alright. I am perfectly fine." Kiefer kept pacing.

Halcomb looked over his shoulder. "We cannot stop now!"

I dropped back to assist Kiefer, but he recoiled when I touched him. He was shivering and looked as though he was about to cry. "Kiefer, you need to speak to me. What is going on? Are you hurt?"

Elvira jogged over to us, which made Kiefer step back. "There is no need to be scared, Soren, you are alright."

Finally, Halcomb joined us. "Kiefer! We cannot stop now! The SS and Gestapo will be combing the village for us by morning, and we need to be as far away as possible!"

Kiefer stared at him for a few seconds, but didn't respond. He went back to pacing and holding his head.

"What do we do?" I whispered.

"Give him space," Elvira replied. "Let him do what he needs to do. He is probably traumatized after how Wahler treated him."

She was right. Kiefer had never been in a place where he wasn't being watched and berated all the time. According to him, he hadn't felt safe ever since the last time he was with his girlfriend.

This lasted around five minutes. Kiefer paced, then stopped, and took his hands away from his head. He shook them for a few seconds, then sat down in the cold grass, hugging his knees and rocking back and forth.

"Maybe we should just take him by the armpits and drag him with us," Halcomb whispered.

"How would you like it if you were in his position?" Elvira asked.

"I do not understand what he is doing. If we were in a public place, he would be looked at as insane. He cannot do this every time he is upset."

"He has probably never been allowed to for that very reason," I said. "This is probably why he was seen as useless by his family and neighbors, and why they pushed him into the SS. I also wonder if he is so used to being in enclosed spaces that the sight of a wide-open place—like the field we are in—is upsetting."

"I understand that, but why... do this? Why pace around and act like he has got bats in his brain?"

I shrugged. Admittedly, I agreed with Halcomb that we couldn't sit around here forever, not when we knew that we didn't have long until the ZA men in the castle found Wahler and Griebel's corpses.

Eventually, Kiefer stopped rocking, and slowly stood up. He walked over to us, giving each of us a stare before turning to keep heading west. "We can go now."

Not wanting to stand around any longer, we kept going, but it wasn't too long after when Halcomb broke the silence. "What happened back there, Kiefer? You completely lost yourself."

"I do not know," Kiefer replied. "I... I have done that since I was young. Whenever I become... upset or excited, I feel like I have no more control. I have to stop altogether, and then I do what you just witnessed. I cannot talk or think clearly, I do not want to be touched, and I can hardly process anything other than what I am doing in the moment." His face reddened. "I am sorry you had to see that."

I shook my head. "You do not have to apologize. We just want to know what led to you acting like that."

"I realized I was free from the SS, and that I was going to be free from the Nazis as a whole. And then I realized that I have never felt free before. It is so... overwhelming. It is... not something I can describe in words." Kiefer covered his face. "Whenever I become overwhelmed, I do not know how to talk about it, because it does not feel like something I can verbally describe, and then I do not understand why I can think so much but cannot communicate in a way other people can understand. Why can I understand how other people feel just by being around them, but I cannot describe how I feel to them?"

I wasn't sure how to respond to that, only because I personally haven't had much trouble describing how I feel to others. The only thing I could compare it to was how I don't always like talking about Antarctica. I was there, the person I'm talking to wasn't, so they don't understand how I felt and why we did the things we did.

But that's just one incident. For Kiefer, it's everyday emotions, and it's extremely frustrating.

We kept walking, and I stayed alongside Kiefer, who was still rattled over the fact that he was no longer under Wahler's control. Everything throughout his day was planned for him. He was at Wahler's every beck and call. He had no time for himself. Now, he had no idea how to take care of himself. He had so many choices ahead of him and it was understandably overwhelming.

"I am glad you and Halcomb and Miss Cristaldi did not yell at me or beat me for my actions back there," Kiefer said. "I know Halcomb was upset, but he had a good reason to be."

"I am actually surprised he stood up for you at Peltzer's," I replied. "He did suggest just dragging you along with us, though."

Kiefer suddenly took on a distant stare. "I do not ever want to be touched when I am lost like that. Even if you are trying to comfort me. Miri... had to learn the hard way."

"What happened?"

"My mother would try to force me out of it by beating me. Usually with her fists, but she would also use whatever item she had in her hands at the time. It never worked. In fact, it made it worse. A few weeks after I started dating Miri, I had a moment where I was upset over something that had happened at my apprenticeship. I started pacing around, wringing my hands, holding my head. She tried to help by getting me to sit. I fell to the ground and started frantically trying to get away from her. I was so frightened that she would leave when I came out of it. It was the fact that she did not that convinced me that we were meant for each other."

"She loved you despite your faults."

Kiefer nodded. "Even if she is already dead, I do not think I could ever find someone else that willing to put up with me."

Kiefer had gotten flustered when I brought up going to save her. I wasn't sure I wanted to go back into that, but I did say, "Perhaps we will get a chance to save her."

"I hope so. It will take more than four people to free a single camp, and I understand you all want to go home."

"Yes, but—"

"Do not trouble yourself with this. That is all I ask."

I nodded. As hard as it was, I decided not to say anything further about it.

As the sun began peeking over the trees and mountains behind us, we could see the church steeples of Königsdorf. Having gone several nights already with very little sleep, I wasn't opposed to the idea of taking the day to get some rest, but Halcomb certainly was.

"If the opportunity arises, we will rest, but not now. We are so close to getting out of here that I do not want anything else holding us back from going home," Halcomb explained.

"I could sleep right here on my feet," Kiefer moaned.

"We could use rest and food," Elvira said. "Getting our energy back so we can keep going is just as important."

Halcomb sighed. "Alright. We should find the Fehrenbachs first, though."

The town was just as quiet as the village outside Munich. With it being so early in the morning, it was no surprise that no one was up and about, and we waited for the sun to come further up before we started searching for the Fehrenbach couple.

There must have been an airfield nearby, because most of the uniforms we saw were the dark bluish-gray of the *Luftwaffe*. That's not to say there wasn't an SS presence. They were certainly around, and Kiefer muttered something about feeling an "unpleasant presence".

After exploring the town for a couple of hours, we started asking around for either of the Fehrenbachs. Eventually, an old lady running a candy shop pointed us in the direction of a farm on the southwest edge of Königsdorf. As we left the shop, a squadron of SS men, led by a very tall and intimidating officer who was missing his right eye, were headed down the street. The old woman behind the counter gestured for us to move further in so we weren't seen. "They do not like strangers from out of town," she whispered.

"That is what I felt," Kiefer said to me. "From the officer with the eyepatch."

I watched the officer lead his men. He glanced at the townspeople occasionally, but ultimately didn't pay them much attention. At the street corner, he divided the men up into groups of two, and sent them off in different directions.

"It looks like they are just patrolling," Halcomb said. "We will be fine if we stay out of their way."

"Sounds good to me," I replied.

We waited until the men left, then exited the shop. I imagined Kiefer was paranoid about being recognized, but I highly doubted anyone within this particular unit would even know who he was unless a notice had been sent out to find him.

The cobblestone path turned into a well-worn dirt one as we headed west, coming across a small farmhouse at the end. To our south, snow-capped peaks stretched as far as the eye could see, and the forests were adorned with autumn colors.

A dark-haired woman stepped outside the house, bundled in a long jacket and scarf. She looked at the ground as she approached us, before stopping and trying to decide which of us to focus on. "What can I help you with?" she asked.

"We are looking for Karl and Jette Fehrenbach," I said. "The rabbit showed us the way."

The woman's shoulders relaxed. "I am Jette. Please come inside." She waited until we were all inside before saying anything else. "Karl is in town but he will be back for lunch. That phrase originated just outside of Munich, yes?"

"A Mr. Peltzer helped us," I replied.

"Jay and I are OSS agents," Halcomb explained. "Elvira is an Italian contact and Kiefer is an SS defector. We are trying to get into Switzerland to go home."

"I see." Jette escorted us into the living room, a small but cozy space with a lit fireplace and portraits and paintings all over the wall. A big clock stood near the north-facing windows, which Kiefer took an interest in.

"We were told you go to the Swiss border regularly," Elvira said. "Is that still the case?"

"It is. Would you like something to drink? You all look tired."

"I have not had coffee in a very long time," Halcomb replied. "If you have any, please."

"I think we could all use some coffee," I said. A heavy weariness seeped into me almost as soon as I sat down. After being on the move for the last several days, I hadn't considered food, water, or sleep. Being safe and comfortable awakened me to my own needs, and I would have gone to sleep right there if it weren't for the perky smell of coffee coming from the kitchen.

Jette was kind enough to prepare us a breakfast as well. The house was soon filled with the savory smell of cooking eggs and potatoes and onions and bacon, and the sweet smell of cinnamon rolls. For the first time in a while, we were comfortable to talk about other things.

Elvira told us stories about her father's days as a witch-hunter. Halcomb discussed hitchhiking from Illinois to Washington. Kiefer talked about his first date with Miri. I worked up the courage to talk about an adventure from Antarctica. Up until then, I hadn't thought about Antarctica or Duncan or my father in quite some time.

Though it felt like it had happened days ago, I realized not even twelve hours ago, I had killed Wahler. His words about how he planned to create a better German were still echoing in my mind, but it was comforting to know that wasn't going to happen, especially since I had stolen his research.

His journal, along with Griebel's note to Keitel and Himmler, was still in my knapsack. Frankly, the last thing I wanted was for another twisted mind to get their hands on it. Excusing myself from the table, I opened my knapsack and pulled the book out, walking out into the living room and kneeling in front of the fireplace. After stoking the fire for a bit, I tossed the book inside.

"What was that?"

Jette's voice made me jump. Rubbing my face, I turned to make eye contact with her. "*Standartenführer* Wahler's life's work," I said. "His research into ice-variants and attempts to create a human capable of all Conjurus powers along with witchcraft. We were sent to kill him, and we succeeded just last night."

"Karl and I had been working to help Conjurus flee Munich after Wahler arrived. I did not know that was what he was doing."

I nodded. "Unless someone else tries to start over, there i nothing left. Surely the Allies could invade Europe before such a creation ever comes to fruition."

"I would hope so." Jette fell silent for a moment. "I just want my son back. The reports from Russia... I have my doubts as to how accurate they are. My only comfort is his monthly letters."

"Where exactly is he?" I asked.

"Not too far outside of Stalingrad. I did not want him sent to Russia. I would have rather he stayed in the Netherlands or be sent to North Africa." She sighed. "If the Western Allies open up a second front, I pray Rudi is sent there. I would rather he be captured by the British than the Soviets."

"I hope that doesn't happen," I said.

Before we could go back to the dining room, someone knocked on the front door. Jette motioned for us to stay out of sight while she answered the door, but then called for us to come out when she brought the visitor in. We hesitated when we saw it was a *Luftwaffe* officer, a lieutenant to be exact. He was lanky with thick dark blond hair, and blue-green eyes. Given his rank, he was probably young, but his face bore lines that I could only guess were from stress.

"He is safe," Jette told us. "This is Hans Gensch, one of our 'inside agents'."

She turned to Gensch. "I was not expecting to see you until later. Is everything alright?"

The lieutenant gave a nervous grin. "Yes, everything is alright, but we are going to need to be on alert for a bit."

"Why?"

"The SS are searching the area for resistance members. An SS officer was killed in a castle near Munich last night."

"That was us," I said. "I am Jay Loalin."

"It is a pleasure to meet you, Mr. Loalin." Gensch shook my hand. "You are in good hands here. No harm will come to you as long as you do what Karl and Jette say. They have saved many lives the last few years."

"I believe it. We are looking to get to Switzerland. Halcomb here and I are part of the OSS."

"Ah, American. I knew you were starting to get involved, but I did not realize they were already sending agents over here."

"Yes. We were sent to assassinate *Standartenführer* Wahler."

"So, the ZA wants your heads on a platter. Then you came to the right place." Gensch took off his coat, and I caught a glimpse of something thin, shiny, and wooden hanging from his left sleeve.

I tensed, clenching my fists and letting ice form on them. "Are you a warlock?" I asked, eyes narrowing. We hadn't had one pleasant experience with a witch or warlock so far on this mission.

Gensch suddenly looked embarrassed. "Yes. Why?"

"You are not one of Wahler's spies?"

"No." Gensch studied my face a bit. "You are a cryomancer, or ice-variant, correct?"

I nodded.

Gensch held up his hands. "I know. We are supposed to be bitter enemies. Cats and dogs, right? I take it you have never heard of the League of Gentlemen Sorcerers and Lady Witches? Ah, right, you are American. We do not have a branch over there. Not yet, anyway."

I raised an eyebrow. "The what?"

"The League of Gentlemen Sorcerers and Lady Witches. It is a bit of a mouthful, I know. They are a group for witches and warlocks looking to change the relationship between themselves and Conjurus and the Magicless. They are relatively new, about twenty years old, I think, but they quickly became a force to be reckoned with because the witches who do not want to be associated with evil now have group of like-minded individuals to turn to."

Halcomb interjected, "Honestly, that name sounds more like the name of a country club."

I winced, expecting Gensch to take some offense to that, but instead the pilot burst into laughter. I gave a sigh of relief before turning to Elvira and asking, "Did you know about this... League?"

Elvira shook her head. "No. Father never mentioned them." She looked at Gensch. "When did this League form?"

"Late 1922, I think," Gensch replied.

"That explains it. My father was a witch-hunter. He retired just a few years prior to Mussolini coming to power."

"There is a lot of background that I will not bore all of you with," said Gensch. "Just know that I'm not going to cut your hearts out in the middle of the night and leave on a broomstick." He smirked again. "I do have one, though, but nothing beats a Messerschmitt 109."

"I only learned recently that there are harmless witches in the world, and I did not know they had banded together," I said.

"I would not call them harmless, not with all they've been doing across Europe. Trust me, we have no intention of teaching members of the SS-ZA how to use magic, not when we know what they will do with it."

After dealing with Wahler and Lexis, it was definitely a relief to be seeing a wand that wasn't pressed up against my throat, but there was still a part of me that was anxious around Gensch, even if he was the exact opposite of how I've always thought witches and warlocks act. He wasn't cold or dour, but he was mischievous, in a fun way rather than a malicious way.

Out of everyone in our group, I was surprised Elvira took a liking to Gensch, asking him about what it was like being a warlock. Even Kiefer sat listening to the two of them, and he would later tell me that it was because he felt comfortable in Gensch's presence, but he couldn't explain why.

Halcomb and I left them to talk to Jette and help her clean up after breakfast. She said that if the SS weren't searching for us, she would have waited a day to take us to Switzerland in order for us to rest up. Instead, we would leave that night.

"The sooner the better," Halcomb said.

"The one thing we have on our side is that the SS does not know exactly who killed Wahler," I said. "We were never seen in the castle."

"Yes, but Kiefer disappeared after the killing. They will assume it was him."

"How did you kill Wahler?" Jette asked.

"I put two icicles in him," I explained. "One in his stomach, the other in the back of his neck."

"Wounds make by ice are somewhat different to wounds made by, say, a knife. Their shapes, for instance. Plus, if Wahler's group has been working with ice-variants for some time now, surely they would know the difference."

"And Kiefer is already known not to have any magic."

Halcomb shrugged. "I still think they will find a way to blame him."

"The SS are not stupid. Besides, he is guilty of treason and aiding an enemy agent. They would be correct to assume that."

Jette nodded. "If there is one thing we have learned over the last several years, it is that the SS are not stupid. Brutish thugs, yes, but that combined with intelligence is terrifying."

"Speaking of that," I said, "who... is the chief SS officer here? The man with the eyepatch. We saw him on our way here."

"Captain Adalwin Derichs. The last thing we want is him on your scent. He is the perfect example of what I was just talking about. An absolute brute, but very smart. We have tried assassinating him several times. Each time, he catches on and foils it. Unless something brilliant comes up, we have given up."

"And he has not found you?"

"No. Not yet, anyway. He knows someone here is trying to kill him, but he has been unable to figure out who."

I glanced in the dining room at Gensch. "I imagine you have had help."

"A lot of help. We would not be able to conduct our operation if we did not have Gensch on our side. Smuggling in ingredients for healing potions is easier and less suspicious than trying to get specific medicines."

I had never thought of witches being helpful. The impression that I had gotten since I was a child was that even neutral witches weren't keen on helping others. I started to wonder if witches were experiencing the same cultural shift that Conjurus were, with many moving closer to the Magicless and living similarly to them while keeping their magic. Gensch certainly seemed like he had lived among the Magicless for a long time, if not his whole life.

Halcomb pulled me from my thoughts. "Given how small this place is, I am surprised you have not been caught."

"It is a miracle," Jette smiled, taking a towel to dry one of the dishes. "I just hope it stays that way."

Karl Fehrenbach returned to his home a few hours later to find all of us standing around a large map. "Jette, dear, who are all these people?" he asked.

"OSS agents. They need to get into Switzerland," Jette replied.

"Ah." Looking a bit more relieved, Karl hung up his coat. "Hello, Hans."

Gensch waved. "Do you have anything interesting to report?"

"SS and Gestapo are crawling all over the place. More than usual."

"That would be because of us," Halcomb said. "We killed an SS officer in a castle outside of Munich."

"Well, I'd say a congratulations are an order." Karl shook Halcomb's hand, then mine. "Please, introduce yourselves."

Somewhat shyly, I pointed to myself and Halcomb before saying, "Jay Loalin, Lester Halcomb." I gestured toward the living room. "Elvira Cristaldi, our Italian contact, and Soren Kiefer, a defector we picked up at the castle."

"You must have quite the story to tell."

"We do."

"With many twists and turns," Halcomb added, "including Jay sweet-talking Erwin Rommel into letting him hunt a warlock."

Karl raised an eyebrow, looking at me intently. "You had a face-to-face conversation with Field-Marshal Rommel?"

I nodded.

"And you did not assassinate him?"

"No, sir," I said. "That was not our mission. And the British have already tried to do that without success. Our mission was to get to *Standartenführer* Wahler, and we had to go to Africa to get information on his location from a German defector. A warlock who Wahler planted was killing German soldiers to acquire kidney stones—"

"For an acid potion?" Gensch asked without looking up from the map.

"I think so." Giving Gensch a curious look, I asked, "What else would he have needed? He took kidney stones from both soldiers, and the liver and gallbladder from one of them."

"Any citrus fruit, and a cup of dead bees, although I can only guess that he would have gotten the bees by trading with local witches."

"Based on a conversation I overheard Wahler having with one of his aides, that is exactly what was going on. It is what gave him away."

"That is no surprise," Gensch replied. "Wahler must not have been giving his spies good incentives. Hard to blame them, especially after being uprooted from their homes and forced to be part of some master plan to get everyone to become a witch."

I imagined it was harder for Gensch to maintain his life than any Conjurus. The Nazis were hell-bent on learning witchcraft. Any witch could be torn from their home and forced to teach sorcery. The consequences for saying no were probably dire. "How exactly have you been able to avoid being caught as a warlock?"

Gensch shrugged. "It is not hard." He lifted his left arm. "I stitched a couple of bands inside my sleeve so I can hide my wand, and I have lived around Magicless for so long that I know how they behave, and act accordingly. It is certainly easier for someone like me than it is for the Conjurus."

I wasn't about to disagree with him on that.

The conversation didn't continue after Karl knelt in front of the map between Jette and Gensch. "I take it you are trying to get into the OSS office in Bern?"

"Yes," Halcomb replied.

"Getting there will be easy. Just follow my wife's instructions. Do not try to deviate from the course. Do not make any foolish moves until you are inside Switzerland. We will try to keep the SS and Gestapo off your trail for as long as possible. Get some rest for now. You will leave in a few hours."

We got our rest on couches in the living room and library. I wasn't sure how much time had passed, but I awoke to hear Karl, Jette, and Gensch talking in hushed voices.

"... We have to get them out of here soon," Gensch was saying. "I cannot believe Derichs has enlisted the help of a necromancer."

"Not just any necromancer. One of the ones who was in the castle Wahler was operating out of," Karl replied.

I sat up on the couch. After rubbing my eyes and putting my boots on, I got off the couch and walked over to the kitchen. "What is going on?" I asked.

"We will leave soon," Jette said. "Like Karl said earlier, do exactly as I say. We do not need a necromancer following us."

"What about Karl and Gensch?" I looked at Gensch in particular. "Do you have any idea how dangerous necromancers are?"

"I do," Gensch replied. "That is why I am staying here. Do not worry about me."

"Go wake up your friends," Jette said. "We will pack what we need and go."

Nodding, I went back into the living room to shake Halcomb. He woke up Elvira while I went into the library to find Kiefer asleep on a couch with a book by his head. I was a bit nervous in waking him because of what had happened on our way there, but the last thing I wanted was for us to be delayed. Gently, I shook Kiefer awake. He shivered violently before opening his eyes, and then stretched. "Is it time to go already?" he asked.

"Yes. One of Wahler's necromancers is helping the local SS find us," I said. "Jette told us to pack only what we need."

"We need everything we have," Kiefer replied.

"Then pack all of it!"

After our bags were packed, all the lights in the house were turned off. Gensch put out the fireplace with his wand, and headed upstairs to hide. Karl hugged his wife tightly, whispering, "Please be careful, dear. Just come home safely."

"I will be alright," Jette replied. "I am more worried about you and Hans."

"We will be alright as well. Go. Get these people to Switzerland."

Letting go of her husband, Jette threw on her scarf and jacket before picking up her backpack. A second later, Gensch came back downstairs, holding an unloaded MP40 and three magazines. "Do not forget this." He handed Jette the gun.

"Thank you, Hans." Jette turned to me. "Do you have everything, Jay?"

"Yes," I said. "We are ready whenever you are."

"Alright. Go. Just run. I will catch up."

I headed out the door with Halcomb, Elvira, and Kiefer close behind. The sun was just starting to set, and the air was bitterly cold. I could sense it was going to snow that night. The grass was becoming a dreary brown color, and many of the trees had dropped most of their leaves. That was bad. The last thing we wanted was anyone hearing us.

We were jogging down a dirt path into the shedding forest when Jette caught up to us. She got in front, turning to face us as she walked. "Alright. We are going to follow this path to a stream running through the center of the woods. We will cross it and keep heading south. Whatever happens, keep going south."

Looking over my shoulder, I could still see the outline of the farmhouse in the deep red and dark blue of the sky. Karl and Gensch faced certain death if they were caught, and Gensch definitely so. He wasn't just a traitor. He was a traitor in uniform. At the same time, he was a warlock. Was he going to face death, or forced to teach at an SS hideout? I imagine he would prefer death. Then again, the few hours I knew him on this mission told me he wasn't going to accept death. He was going to get out of whatever his punishment was somehow, and there wasn't a doubt in my mind that this League of Gentlemen Sorcerers and Lady Witches would help him to the best of their abilities.

It didn't stop me from fearing for him and Karl. They shouldn't have to risk their lives to help us, but that was normal for them.

Chapter 15

Darkness and cold shrouded the woods. Kiefer was whispering something about it being so cold he was in pain, but there really wasn't anything we could do about it. We had to keep going.

At least when we were following the railroad, that was a sign of civilization. Here, the untouched forest was all we could see, and aside from Jette's compass telling us we were heading south, it felt like we were going nowhere in particular. We were in a place of nothingness.

The only thing that would have made it worse would be to remove the trees and bathe the landscape in ice and snow. Replace the mountains with towering, monstrous glaciers. Turn the sky a depressing shade of gray. Make the place into Antarctica, where only ice-variants can survive.

My thoughts lingered on Antarctica for most of the walk. The endless trudging felt similar to my team's expedition to the South Pole. I shuddered at the thought, despite knowing that anything could happen. It was possible one or more of us could die, and it wouldn't be my fault. At the same time, there wasn't a doubt in my mind that I would blame myself for the deaths of anyone on this mission. I didn't want a repeat of Antarctica. I never do. I wanted all of us to go home safely.

"Do any of you hear something?" Kiefer asked, breaking the silence.

"Other than wind and owls, no," Halcomb replied. "Why?"

"I hear footsteps in leaves."

"That is probably just us."

"No. It is very faint."

"It is probably an animal."

"It is not fast enough to be an animal. It sounds human."

Jette looked over her shoulder at Kiefer. "Can you tell how far off it sounds?"

"It is far off, but getting closer."

"Then we need to hurry. We are almost at the creek."

We started jogging. I could hear the footsteps, too, then we heard German shouting. "There! I see movement up ahead! Fire!" There were loud *cracks* from behind us, and bullets whizzed by our heads.

"Get down!" Jette hollered, ducking behind a bush. She pulled her MP40 from her backpack, shoved one of the magazines in and pulled back the charging handle, shouldering the gun, and raising the sights to her right eye. Halcomb unslung the K98 and dropped to his stomach nearby.

Elvira was lying behind Halcomb. Kiefer had drawn his pistol and was firing in the direction of the SS men shooting at us. When a helmeted man's head appeared in the bushes, I flung an icicle at him. He didn't even scream as the ice speared his brain.

The forest had come alive with banging and screaming as two more SS men were shot. Snow had begun to fall during the firefight. Halcomb's hand was almost a blur as he pulled back the bolt on his rifle, firing at the slightest sign of an SS soldier in the forest. Jette threw the magazine to the side when her gun was empty and swiftly replaced it with a full one. "Jay! Do you have any tricks that could slow them down?!" she asked.

The only trick I could think of was creating a blizzard of diamond dust, which isn't something many ice-variants can do simply because it isn't something we would have to do on a regular basis. Uncle Redvar isn't particularly good at it, which is why we only practiced it for a few hours during my training. I had to try something, though.

Stepping away from my companions, I drew in a breath as I let the coldness of the air fill me. Snow swirled around me as frost formed on my hands. I repeated the steps I so vaguely remembered. *Focus on your magic, let your temperature fall, and imagine thousands of shards of ice surrounding you.*

A faint fog had enveloped the area surrounding us, and snow and ice had started dancing around me. The Germans were shouting that they couldn't see. I clenched my fists and made a pushing motion. Ice and snow swept toward the SS men. It covered the trees and bushes, and some of our pursuers stood up in a panic. Their faces were bloodied from being struck with sharp ice, and I could imagine that some of them had even lost one or both eyes. A few tried running away, only to be shot.

A familiar face stepped forward when the ice began to clear. Captain Derichs. My energy was drained. I struggled to build the magic to produce an icicle. He pushed one of his wounded compatriots out of the way as he aimed his pistol at me.

"*Jay, no!*" Halcomb shouted. He fired a round at Derichs, missing the big man's head by just a few inches. Derichs fired a round into my left shoulder before getting back to cover. I was blinded by an explosion of pain spreading across my upper torso as I fell to the ground. Blood soaked my jacket, and the wet warmth swiftly melted the frost on my hands. All I could feel was the sensation of every muscle, tendon, and nerve being ripped apart in my shoulder.

I would have rather been hit with Wahler's heat spell again. I was fighting every urge to scream, but it came out anyway. Halcomb knelt by me and tried to lift me up. A burst of pain seared through my shoulder. There was no way I could be dragged all the way to Switzerland.

"No! Just go!" I grunted.

"I am not leaving you here! Are you insane?" Halcomb snapped.

"I said, go!"

"We can finish them off!"

Something pushed aside the bush separating us from the Germans. Halcomb and I both looked and saw it was a black-shrouded figure, holding an old, twisted staff. His face and hands were gnarled, and not from age. He looked down at me with contempt before turning his gaze to Halcomb.

"You are going to hell, you son of a bitch!" Halcomb growled as he swung his rifle at the necromancer.

Rentarus' expression didn't change as he waved his staff, shoving Halcomb aside with an invisible force. Halcomb picked himself up, and with one final look between me and the other members of our group, who had begun running, took off after them.

Rentarus turned to Derichs and the remaining SS men. "Leave them. This is the one we came for." He touched the tip of his staff to my chest. I howled in pain as I was held down long enough for two of the Germans to handcuff me. Rentarus yanked me into a standing position, paying no attention to the fact that it was excruciating. It's a miracle I didn't pass out, though the ripping feeling was extending to my entire left side.

We walked through the woods, all the way back to Königsdorf. Blood was covering the left side of my torso, and I couldn't stop crying out in pain. Rentarus and Derichs paid no mind as we walked through the sleeping town to the SS headquarters. I tried to stop the bleeding with my own powers, but Rentarus would whirl around and slap me each time I did. By the time we entered the office, both sides of my face were a deep red from crying and being slapped repeatedly.

"Take him downstairs," Rentarus ordered, calmly.

Derichs and his companion dragged me down to a cell with a tiny barred window near the ceiling, where I was strapped to a chair. Rentarus put a red pendant around my neck. "So long as that is on you, you are powerless," he said. "No more than a common Magicless."

I was shivering, weak, and riddled with unimaginable pain. When I sat down, I realized the bullet had gone right through my shoulder. My back quickly became sticky with blood when it pressed against the back of the chair. A web of pain had stretched across my torso. My throat was raw from screaming. All I could do was grunt, and moan.

"One more sound from you, and I will render you mute."

I struggled to look Rentarus in the eye. It is shocking what dark magic can do to a person. His face was horribly twisted, worse than any Picasso painting. His eyes were so bloodshot that I couldn't even say "the whites of his eyes" anymore. The irises were a sick yellow color, like they were deeply jaundiced. His skin was paper-white, and he looked to be nothing more than skin and bones. Every vein was visible, and I felt sicker the more I looked; I could actually see his veins throbbing. My stomach turned each time I looked, but what could I look at? Everything about Rentarus was completely inhuman.

He stared intently at me. He never smiled, never gloated about the fact that he caught me. "I was not expecting my search to take such a short amount of time. All I ask is that you try not to deny that you killed *Standartenführer* Wahler." He touched the tip of his staff to my cheek. "That pathetic prisoner squealed as soon as I was able to get my hands on him."

I assumed he meant the man from Austria we freed. "What happened to them?"

"The prisoners at the castle? I am sure you will be happy to know that some got away. Others did not."

I cursed myself in my head.

"You, on the other hand, will answer everything I want to know."

"And if I do not?"

"I will make sure you die slowly and painfully here. The most resistance I expected to face were from fools within the German Army unwilling to embrace the greatest chance of their lives to become more powerful than they could have ever imagined. I was not expecting anything from the outside."

"Well, I am sorry to disappoint you," I grunted.

Rentarus' expression didn't change. "I will admit, your sneaking into the castle was impressive. Then again, you had help."

Rage boiled over inside me, mixing with the intense pain in my shoulder. I grit my teeth, trying not to let one sound out. Every muscle ached with the restraint.

"It is no secret *Untersturmführer* Kiefer disappeared with you after Wahler's death."

"Leave Kiefer out of this!"

"Kiefer is none of my concern. If he is captured, he will face the consequences for treason, but catching him is not my job. My job is you, Mr. Jay Loalin, son of Morgan Loalin, the entire reason we are here, in this room tonight. I will handle your consequences for destroying any hope had for witches and Conjurus to end their pathetic rivalry."

"Oh, spare me your arguments!" I shouted. "Wahler gave me the same sad story about how he wanted to end the bloodshed! You, and especially you, just want more people to use in your disgusting rituals! You want an endless supply of cattle! You want to destroy over a thousand years of culture and the people within it!"

Rentarus smiled, but it was small and condescending. "Wahler was weak. Everything he said to you about wanting to end the war and the killing was true. On a different day, in much different circumstances, the two of you could have been friends. His ambition and bullheaded defiance were what made him a terrible student of witchcraft. It was his intelligence and willingness to even try such a wild experiment that made me think there was hope for him. His work is still valuable, and I know you took it." He held out a pale, bony hand. "Where is it?"

"Burned. I burned the book, and the letter Doctor Griebel was going to send to Keitel and Himmler. No one should ever have that research. Wahler's work is finished, and will not be restarted." My rapidly beating heart was sending more blood to leak from the wound on my shoulder. Everything around my shoulder still hurt, but my left arm was steadily becoming numb.

Rentarus remained expressionless, but he did let out a sigh. "A pity. Almost twenty years of work, lost."

I managed to look him in the eye, relishing his defeat. At the same time, I desperately wanted to go home. I was tired of being on the run. I had achieved my goal. I completed my mission. Wahler was dead and he couldn't hurt anyone anymore. "What will you do with me, then? I am not useful to you if I cannot tell you where that damned book is."

"You are right, you are not useful if that book is gone. You are still a spy, though, and that is out of my league. The SS will deal with you, but, in exchange for catching you, I would like whatever is left of you." A strange and terrifying glint appeared in the necromancer's eyes. "Everything. Your skin, bones, blood, organs. It would be a pity for all of that to go to waste."

A shadow appeared behind Rentarus. Arms folded over his chest, Derichs stepped into the cell. "All you did was lead us to him. When we are finished with him, we will decide if you get to keep his remains or not."

Rentarus looked over his shoulder at Derichs. I expected him to kill the captain for daring to question him, but he simply said, "Very well, but I will not tolerate such insolence again. You barbarians asked for my help, and this is how I am repaid?"

"We never came to a decision on what you would get out of this. Now, leave. I would like to question the prisoner." Derichs watched Rentarus storm out of the cell, then walked in, grabbing a chair and sitting across from me. Despite his eyepatch, and the scar on the bridge of his nose, Derichs was more pleasant to look at than Rentarus. I could at least look him in the eye. He looked over his shoulder, then reached over to yank the pendant from my neck. "I don't appreciate being called a 'barbarian.'"

I didn't respond. As soon as I felt my powers start to come back, I tried clotting the wound on my shoulder.

"Sergeant, bring me a first-aid kit and a bucket of water," Derichs said, looking over his shoulder at a man standing outside the cell.

I raised an eyebrow. "Why?"

"Because I am not going to let that necrophile kill you."

"I killed one of your own. You have no reason to help me."

"You will still be punished, but I hate necromancers more than I hate anyone else. I do not care if Himmler himself says they are going to help us win the war. They are the scum of the Earth. I want you healthy so you can be sent to a labor camp." Derichs nodded to the sergeant when he delivered the kit and bucket. As he set to work washing the caked blood from my shoulder, he looked me in the eye. "Conjurus, right?"

I nodded.

"This will sound dark to you, but, I assisted with removing several dozen of you from Königsdorf a few years ago, sending you to labor camps all across the Reich."

"We hunt necromancers, and yet you participated in such an act? Surely, that would make us allies."

Derichs sighed, putting the bloody rag in the water and wringing it before putting it back on my shoulder. "After what I went through, I would be happy not to see any more magic in any form. All of you—witches, Conjurus, necromancers—can be slaughtered for all I care."

"What happened?"

There were several long moments of silence before Derichs answered. "I was a werewolf."

"'Was?'"

He nodded. "I was cured a few years ago, after suffering for almost fifteen years. I was bitten in the forest, near where we found you. I managed to hide it for a few months before my family realized what was going on." A look of barely concealed rage manifested in Derichs's left eye. "First, they tried to cure me by going to a witch. That witch was no ordinary witch—"

"A necromancer?"

Derichs nodded, not even caring that I had interrupted him. "That swine killed my father."

"I am sorry."

"Do not give me any petty apologies."

"I—"

"Shut up."

I bit my lip. "That sounds horrible."

"'Horrible' does not even begin to describe it. I was an outcast living in the woods for fifteen years. I joined the SS despite being cursed, because of the promise of being able to exact my revenge." Derichs tightly wrapped a bandage around my arm. "I was not even sure I would be able to hide my lycanthropy. That worried me for the first year I was an officer. They would probably either kill me or turn me into a living weapon of sorts."

"How were you cured, then?"

"I do not know. Someone who knew how to make one must have caught me in the woods while I was transformed, because I do not remember anything other than waking up in the forest with no clothes on and the taste of metal in my mouth."

"A local witch must have brewed a silver potion," I said. Grunting as the bandage was tightened, I added, "And your thoughts did not change after that?"

"No, because curing me did not change the fact that this had happened in the first place. I could have been on the front lines, away from this place, but because this happened—" Derichs gestured to his eyepatch, "I am relegated to petty domestic duties."

I shook my head. "You do not have to be vengeful forever."

"Come talk to me when you've been hurt and abandoned multiple times. Be grateful I hate that necrophile more than you, or else I would have shot you as soon as I walked in. The last thing I want to see is his ugly excuse for a face smiling in satisfaction." Derichs left the cell, but returned a minute later with a scarf. He untied my left hand, and watched me wince in pain as he gently pulled it around to my front. Stars exploded in my vision, and tears streamed down my face. Right as I thought I wouldn't be able to take anymore, the movement stopped.

The scarf was a makeshift sling. Derichs knotted the ends of the scarf as tight as possible. He also made sure my good arm was secure behind the chair so I couldn't try to escape. "If it makes you feel better, Rentarus will not come in here tonight. You will be sent off tomorrow morning." Derichs put the pendant back around my neck, likely to keep me from escaping. "Get some sleep."

I wasn't sure how to feel about Derichs. On one hand, he probably wished I had died out in the woods. On the other, he saved my life, or, at least, extended it by a few weeks. I imagined he was going to send me to one of the death camps Kiefer mentioned. I was going to be worked until I dropped. That, to Derichs, was preferable to being shot and mutilated for potion and ritual pieces.

I've been fortunate not to encounter any werewolves. They're extremely rare in a city environment. Every story I've been told describes them as vicious monsters, cursed to transform every full moon, cursed to slaughter anyone who crosses them in their wolf form. Their only cure is a silver-based potion, which is why whenever there's a story about stolen silver, the culprit is almost always a witch. I wouldn't be surprised if it was Gensch who cured Derichs in this situation.

It was impossible to sleep with the amount of pain and emotion coursing through my body. I struggled to sit comfortably. My right shoulder was sore from being tied behind the chair. I was weak from the magic of the pendant. I can't remember ever being in this much pain after a journey in Antarctica. Then again, I wasn't shot and tormented by a necromancer at any point. Something like this was to be expected when I took this mission, but I didn't think it was actually going to happen.

At least everyone else got away. That was my goal. I didn't have a repeat of the South Pole. I was going to be the first and only person to die, instead of someone else.

I ended up falling asleep at some point. My body gave up on trying to stay alert for any opportunities to escape. To be honest, I hadn't had any real rest since the mission started. Even in North Africa, it was impossible to sleep with the fear that the Germans were going to somehow figure out that Halcomb and I were spies. Even after we were found out, we were constantly afraid Lehning was going to disobey orders and execute us in the middle of the night.

When I reawakened, I found I had been plunged in complete darkness. Part of me wondered if I was still asleep and experiencing a dream, but when the pain in my shoulders surged through my body, I was certain that I was indeed awake. The guards had turned all the lights off. There was moonlight spilling in through the tiny window, casting shadows of myself in the chair.

I wanted desperately to lie down when I became more awake. The soreness had spread from my arms and shoulders to my legs, and I joked to myself that if I lay down, I wouldn't get up for a long time. Comfort was impossible, but I tried to adjust myself, wishing the night would end already. I had a better chance of escaping a labor camp than I did escaping this cell.

For a moment, I thought I was hallucinating. The lock on the cell door unhooked itself, and dropped to the floor. Unsure of what to make of this, I lowered my head, convincing myself that I was exhausted and seeing things. A figure stepped forward, opening the door, and I heard a familiar voice say, "Jay? Are you alright?"

I looked up to see Gensch standing in front of me, in civilian clothes. Relief washed over me like a tidal wave, but that relief was tinged with pain just from moving slightly. "In a lot of pain, but mostly alright," I said. "H-How did you get in here?"

Gensch smiled before holding up his wand. "Magic." He set about untying my right arm. "I distracted the guards by casting a familiar, then broke in."

"I never thought I would ever be thanking a warlock for saving my life."

"Well, I imagine you have quite a story to tell us." Gensch helped me stand, which was incredibly painful. I couldn't move my left shoulder at all. "How did this get bandaged and put in a sling?" Gensch asked.

"Surprisingly, that was from Captain Derichs," I grunted. "He hates necromancers more than anything else. He was going to send me to a labor camp instead of letting Rentarus have his way with me."

"I see." Gensch fell silent as he helped me out of the chair. "Steady now. Hopefully the guards are still busy."

"If you hadn't come, I would have tried to escape from whatever camp they were going to send me to," I said.

"To be honest with you, Jay, I highly doubt they would actually send you to a labor camp. You're still a cryomancer, even though Wahler's dead, the ZA is still around. They would not just throw you away. Far from it. You would be taken to another castle somewhere here in Germany, and there's no guarantee you would be rescued."

"Even though Derichs—"

"Please, don't tell me you actually trust Derichs to tell you the truth. He hates you. He might not have shown it because he hates the necromancers more, but he's not going to change his tune on magic folk."

"Give what he told me, I assumed that he would rather not see the ZA use me at all."

Gensch shook his head. "If you were sent to a labor camp, the doctors would find out what you are pretty quickly. There would be nothing anyone can do to stop them from sending you to a ZA facility."

I nodded a little, not wanting to think about what could have happened to me if Gensch hadn't rescued me. Never once in my life did I think I would owe a warlock my life.

We went around to the back, where Halcomb was waiting with a large broom behind the bushes. He looked relieved to see me, and I had never seen him very emotional before. I never thought it was in his character, but I guess I meant something to him. Even after all the times we argued, he cared. He looked like he was trying to hold back tears, and he wasn't doing a very good job at hiding it. He gave a heavy sigh before putting his arms around me. "I knew you would still be alive."

"He refused to go on into Switzerland without you," Gensch explained.

"We started this together and we are going to finish this together," Halcomb said. "I am not leaving you behind if I can do something about it."

"Even though I told you to go on?" I asked.

Halcomb shook his head. He jumped when we heard German shouting and bushes rustling as the SS guards were leaving the woods that bordered the town, jogging back toward the building. "We can talk when we reach Switzerland."

"Yes, we should go before they see us," Gensch replied. "Can I have my broom back, please?" He took the broomstick from Halcomb, swung one leg over it, and sat on it before tapping it with his wand. The broom began floating. "I take it you have never ridden on a broom before, Jay?"

"No," I said.

Halcomb helped me on. A broomstick isn't exactly comfortable, nor is it really made for holding more than one person with such poor balance. I had to hold onto Gensch with my good arm while Halcomb held on from behind. A chill shot through me when a siren began wailing. A voice shouted a second later, "The Conjurus escaped! Find him!"

Halcomb cursed when a couple of the guards dashed around to the back of the building. "Take off, damn it!"

"Stay calm," Gensch said with a grin. He waved and pointed his wand at the guards. One of them skidded to a halt and nearly fell on his rear when the large, ghostly form of a blue jay sprang forth from Gensch's wand. The guards were so badly spooked that they turned and sprinted as fast as they could back toward the building.

Gensch put his wand in his belt before pulling the broom up at a slight angle. We went slowly at first, like the initial climb of a roller coaster. "Alright, hold on tight," Gensch said.

"You had better not drop us," Halcomb grumbled.

"Why do you think I told you to hold on?"

We climbed a few more yards upward before Gensch gently tugged on the broom to go faster. Surprisingly, a broom is quite smooth in flight. We were quite high above the trees, looking down at the houses and farms and church steeples of Königsdorf.

"I wish we could have just taken this to Switzerland," Halcomb commented. "That would make things a lot easier."

"But I am the only person with a broom," Gensch replied. "My plan was to escape with Karl on this if the SS got too close to the house. Try to imagine putting six people on a broom."

"We could have done it in trips," I said.

"It is too risky and would take too much time."

We left the town behind, and the forest opened up below of us. The mountains bordering the two countries loomed ahead, growing larger as we approached. I looked over my shoulder to see if anyone was trying to follow us, but somehow, I felt as though this was all over. The mission was complete. The Nazis were far behind us, and it would be a long time before we ever saw them again, if at all. Still, I kept fearing that we would soon be followed by planes. As we got closer to the mountains, a sense of relief combined with exhaustion began creeping over me. This really was all over.

The peaks of the mountains were gorgeous from such a height. After having my magic restrained by that pendant, it was a great relief to feel cold again as we raced by the snow-capped mountaintops.

"Welcome to Switzerland, gentlemen," Gensch said, glancing over his shoulders to smile at us.

Halcomb gave a heavy sigh of relief. "It is over. It is fucking over."

I would have reached over to squeeze his shoulder if we weren't riding a broom. All I could do was smile and take in the gorgeous view around us. We cleared the mountains and a wide view of lakes and rolling meadows spread out before us. The lakes were surrounded by villages and cities of homes built close together. There were clock towers and churches and all manner of shops clustered close. Instead of fearing whether or not we would be pursued by the Nazis, I felt welcomed and relieved, more relieved than I ever have been in my life.

I was aware of how well-guarded the Swiss are. Frankly, it's amazing Gensch's broom wasn't shot down, but I wouldn't be surprised if it was simply too small to be seen, or if the Swiss were used to seeing witches on their brooms. I just hoped the Germans didn't take advantage of that. Then again, it's not like a Magicless can use a broom to fly.

We gradually began flying lower and lower as we approached Bern. I hadn't even realized it took us several hours to get there, but when I did, my shoulders, legs, and hips began aching. I'll never know how I managed to sit on a broomstick for all that time, but I'll take that ride over being stuck in Wahler's castle or Derichs's office in Königsdorf again.

It was early in the morning when we landed in Bern. The residents of the city were still asleep and we did our best not to cause a ruckus when we got off Gensch's broom. Halcomb was struggling to contain his excitement and relief at being out of Germany. He immediately fell to his knees and kissed the ground, breathing, "Hello, Switzerland!"

Gensch stayed on his broom, looking a little sad, but smiling at the same time. I held out my free hand, asking, "I take it you are not staying?"

"No," Gensch said. "I have to get back before my squadron starts wondering where I am. I would stay if I could." He shook my hand. "I hope we can work together again someday."

"I hope we can meet when the war is over," I replied. "You are the first... good warlock I've ever met."

"I am honored."

I let go of his hand, glancing over my shoulder at Halcomb, who had finally gotten off the ground and was heading down the street to look for a map. Looking back at Gensch, I asked, "Did you know Captain Derichs was a werewolf?"

Gensch nodded, his expression sobering further. "I was the one who cured him. It is a long story. Why do you ask?"

"He told me. It is why he hates all magical beings, witches and Conjurus alike."

"His story is tragic, no doubt about that, but I do not find it to be a good excuse for him to want all of us exterminated. He played a major role in helping to deport every Conjurus in Königsdorf, and then he began performing night raids on every known witch and warlock in town, pulling them from their homes and beating them senseless. If they died, that was a bonus. It did not matter if his victims were men, women, or children. He and his goons would break into their homes and destroy every magic relic they came across. Wands, cauldrons, brooms. Anything."

"How did you avoid it?"

"I had already joined the *Luftwaffe* when it started. I was a broom-racer, after all, so flying seemed very natural to me. That, and I was already aware of how badly the Nazis wanted witches to teach their knowledge. I was already used to hiding what I was."

"Is that why you joined the League of Gentlemen Sorcerers and Lady Witches?"

"I was already a member. My parents were among the founders."

"And... I take it the OSS can contact the League if we ever need assistance?"

"Absolutely. Do not hesitate. Just have them send a message to MI6. They will put you in contact with the League."

"How can we thank you for all you and the Fehrenbachs have done for us?"

"Just go home safely. We will see each other again." Gensch gently patted my shoulder before taking off on his broom. He circled the city once, waving to us, and then flew north toward Germany.

As I stood watching the sky, Halcomb said, "Come on, Jay! Elvira and Kiefer are waiting for us!"

When we met up with Elvira and Kiefer at the OSS building, I was immediately driven to a nearby hospital while Halcomb debriefed with Director Allen Dulles himself. I slept for hours upon laying down after being treated, and I imagined the others were eager to get some sleep as well.

Halcomb's meeting went long into the following morning, so I didn't see him again until the afternoon. He came into my room looking refreshed and smiling as he sat in a chair next to my bed. "How are you feeling, Jay?"

"Still a bit sore," I said. "I was told my shoulder is broken. It'll take a few months to heal."

"I'm sorry. That'll put you out of action for a while," Halcomb replied. "At least you're alive." He glanced around, making sure we were alone. "I... I wasn't going to leave you behind, even if it cost my life."

"You were the one going on about doing this with minimal risk."

"I know, but what would it say about me if I left someone—more specifically, my friend—to die in an enemy country? That, and you're the first person I've gotten close to in a long time, the first person I've trusted in a long time with my secret. I know you would have done the same for me."

"I most certainly would have." I tried to sit up in bed. "What exactly happened after I was captured?"

"Jette kept leading us to the Swiss border, as planned. When we arrived, she went to get the farmer she usually meets, and Kiefer was in complete hysterics. Elvira tried to calm him down, but he wouldn't let anyone touch him and sat under a tree crying. We had to wait for Swiss soldiers to show up and take us to Bern, but I didn't want to wait to rescue you. Leaving you in Germany just... didn't sit right with me. Most spies are expected to commit suicide when they're captured. I knew you wouldn't, and despite all my training stating that I can't become emotional, or attached to anyone, I... I just couldn't leave you behind."

"No one got hurt, and the mission had already been accomplished," I said. "You didn't do anything wrong. At least, I don't think so."

Halcomb shook his head. "I certainly don't believe I did." He was quiet for a moment. "I was prepared to rescue you alone when Gensch found me running through the woods. He was on his way to tell us that you were being taken to the Königsdorf Gestapo office. I'm not one to pass up opportunities, so we went back to the town together. It would've taken hours without him, and who knows what would have happened to you by then." He bit his lip before looking me in the eye and saying, "Brooms are uncomfortable. I don't understand how witches use them regularly."

"I completely agree with you," I said, grinning a little.

"Thank you. Anyway, after everything you've told me about witches, I was a bit nervous about trusting Gensch, but... he's a good man. I guess not all witches are psychopaths bent on controlling every little thing on the face of the Earth."

I shook my head. "No. I hope to meet more like him, and less like Lexis."

"Same."

We sat in silence for several long minutes. It was nice to just sit and think. We didn't have to run anywhere, or do much of anything. Now that I wasn't fearing for my life, my thoughts returned to home, to Uncle Redvar and Mother and Laurel. I knew I couldn't tell them where I had been, or what I had been doing, and I feared that would cause a rift to form between us. I feared it would cause me to live alone for the rest of the war, however long that would last. At least my actions would help shorten the war.

At least now I had friends I knew I could discuss my experiences with. At least now I would never be alone.

Still staring up at the ceiling, I asked, "What will become of us when we go home?"

"Probably nothing. You still can't tell your family what you've been doing the last month or so," Halcomb replied.

"I know. I just... don't know if I should return to New York, or stay with you in Washington. I wouldn't mind doing more for the OSS."

"Honestly, I wouldn't mind your company, especially since..." Halcomb trailed off, looking at the floor.

"Elvira's going back to Italy?"

Halcomb nodded. "Yes. I've already said goodbye, and we admitted that" he took a breath, "that we care for each other. Now I'm afraid for her, and will be afraid until the war is over."

"You're afraid of going crazy if you go home and are alone with nothing but your thoughts."

"Exactly. I know we have to deal with Kiefer as well. I'm sure Colonel Stafford will want to meet him and learn as much as he can from him about the SS."

"No doubt about that."

"Kiefer has also expressed wanting to learn English."

"Good. We'll just have to find a tutor who can keep up with his intelligence."

"And put up with his eccentricities."

I smiled, shaking my head. "He's not that strange."

"I will have to respectfully disagree. Regardless, he'll be happier in America. I want to see him happy, because he's been through a lot."

"Same here." I adjusted myself again, trying to stay comfortable. "Speaking of going to America, when will we be heading back?"

"In a day. We'll be flying to Britain first, then back to Washington."

"I don't want to sit in this hospital that long."

"Good luck convincing the doctor to let you go." Halcomb gave me a warm smile. "Are you any good at chess?"

"Not really. I haven't played in years."

"Perfect. I'm terrible."

Halcomb didn't have a chess set, so he went and bought one from a local artisan. By that afternoon, we were struggling to get through one match. I was feeling better by then, but still sore and tired from the whole ordeal.

Kiefer joined us about an hour after we started playing, and long after I started wondering where he was. He looked rested and happy, but there was a hint of sadness in his eyes. "Elvira is on her way back to Italy," he said. "I am surprised you did not see her off, Lester."

"I said my goodbyes," Halcomb replied. "I do not think I could sit with her in the airport. All I would do is try to convince her not to go back, but

I know how much her family means to her. It would be selfish for me to get her to come to America with us."

"You miss her, though."

"I do. Stop pointing out the obvious."

Kiefer gave him a small smile. "You will see her again."

"I certainly hope so." Halcomb went back to staring at the chessboard.

Kiefer stood over his shoulder, and rubbed his chin. "You have five different opportunities to put Jay's king in jeopardy."

"You know how to play chess?"

Kiefer nodded. "I've never played myself, but I used to watch some of the guards play when they were off-duty at the castle."

"Don't help him!" I said. "It's more fun for us to be terrible together."

"The game would last forever, though. Besides, I can help both of you." Kiefer sat on the bed next me. "See, you have a few options to protect your king, Jay. You know you can move the queen, right? And this rook is perfectly poised to take Lester's knight."

The rest of the match basically played out like Kiefer was playing against himself. Frankly, it was interesting watching his mind at work, and humorous watching Halcomb get frustrated with the fact that Kiefer had ruined our fun. Overall, I enjoyed us not being constantly threatened and finally having a chance to bond with each other.

In all honesty, I would do this adventure all over again, both for the adventure itself and the friends we made along the way. I can rest easy now that I set out to achieve something monumental, and didn't lose my companions. I would have liked to have Elvira with us when the three of us went out to a lakeside restaurant that evening, but I was content with the fact that she was going home.

It was nice seeing Halcomb more relaxed for once and talking to Kiefer as an equal rather than a dangerous animal to be feared. Kiefer had worked hard to earn Halcomb's trust, but I doubted this would mean Halcomb would become more open to accepting any German who claimed to be on our side. I knew he was right in saying that I needed to be more cautious in who I trusted during missions, because if I trusted the wrong person, it could get myself or a lot of other people killed.

Upon retiring to our hotel rooms that night, I reflected on the journey. Despite the fact that we are enemies, I found myself missing the German soldiers we lodged with in North Africa. To a small extent, I missed challenging Lehning, if only to see him become enraged. I did have to remind myself that Rommel and Altschul mentioned that Lehning had a bit of a tumultuous past, and that he wasn't angry and bitter for the sake of being angry and bitter.

While I was in Switzerland, the private conversations I had with Rommel feel like strange dreams, because they shouldn't have happened. I was amazed that I had managed to speak with a prolific figure in such a personal and intimate manner. He was a high-ranking officer, and I was a scrappy spy disguised as a German private. I have a feeling any other officer would have had me shot, but I also wondered if Rommel had only been kind to me because I had information he wanted, and we were dealing with a common enemy. At the same time, I never once felt like I was being used. He did seem genuinely curious about Conjurus as a whole. Our encounter was certainly a once-in-a-lifetime occurrence, and I doubted I would ever see Rommel again aside from newspapers and reels at the cinema.

I also wanted to go back to the Conjurus village in Italy someday. Having been raised around Magicless, I had yet to experience the life of Conjurus who still chose to live apart from the people they adamantly claim to protect. I remembered the conversation with Amadeo about how the village took in witches from Russia, and how I mentioned it was strange to have witches and Conjurus living together in such close proximity.

That brought me to Karl and Jette Fehrenbach, and Hans Gensch. When I was a child I was taught that very few witches could be trusted, and I remembered saying once to my mother that I doubted I could ever befriend a witch if the things I was told about them were true. Granted, those things are true, but I had learned not all witches are like Lexis and Wahler. There I was, hoping I can see Gensch again, because I wanted to satisfy my curiosity about what life as a witch is like.

There was also a part of me that wondered about Captain Derichs. I agreed with Gensch that the one-eyed SS man's story was tragic, but that his way of dealing with that tragedy and subsequent trauma was unreasonable. In the process of dealing with monsters, he became a monster himself. I felt sorry for him, but I also hoped he would be brought to justice for hurting innocent people.

I did agree with Derichs on one thing, though: necromancers are truly despicable. Rentarus is still at large and free in Nazi Germany. While he may not care about me anymore, he was probably going to move on to something else, something just as wicked as his work with Wahler. I didn't want to make it my mission to hunt Rentarus, but I also didn't want the Magicless Allied soldiers to have to deal with him. A simple witch is one thing. A necromancer is something else entirely, and I planned on discussing that with Colonel Stafford when we returned to the States.

Over the next several days, I did my best to start teaching Kiefer English. In London, he listened to the people around us, picking up random words and phrases and repeating them to himself. On our flight back to the United States, he was trying to practice sounds that don't exist in German, like "th" or "w." It was interesting how something so simple to Halcomb and I was a struggle for him. Then again, Kiefer has the same problem with his own emotions.

The return to Washington felt good and strange all at the same time. I only lived in the city for a few months, but it felt like home. It certainly felt like home after being constantly chased through the wilderness of Europe and North Africa for the last several weeks. Being able to slow down was a blessing. I knew I was safe there.

Unfortunately, Kiefer didn't feel safe. He became anxious and scared as we departed the airport and headed through the city on foot to meet up with Massey, who was waiting near the Willard Hotel. "Everything feels very big," he said. "There are so many people, and so many emotions. Everything feels different."

"Different in a good way or a bad way?" Halcomb asked.

"Both."

"We are going somewhere much quieter," I said. "It will be alright."

"Am I going to be questioned? I do not want to be questioned right now."

"You will not be if you do not want to. Our commanding officer would like to meet you, though. If you can at least say 'hello,' that'll be good enough for now."

So Kiefer practiced saying "hello" in English during our ride out to the mansion. Going back to the mansion was certainly strange. The last time I took the drive there, it was at the tail-end of summer. The trees were just starting to turn. Now, they had all fully turned. Some had already dropped their leaves. The ground was covered in a blanket of warm colors. The winds were colder. There were fewer pumpkins in Phineas Calmont's fields. As we pulled up to the big garage, I saw there were women on the porch, and men discussing a rifle out on the range, just like when I first arrived.

Miss Robyn Marrow answered the door when we knocked. We were greeted with the smell of something baking in the kitchen. I assumed it was apple pie, and upon looking in the kitchen, I saw it was many apple pies, sitting neatly in rows inside the ovens. It was a comforting smell, and I looked forward to having a slice.

The three of us headed to library to sit and wait for Colonel Stafford, but as soon as we entered the doorway, the colonel jogged down the stairs, calling, "Lester! Is that really you?"

"Yes, sir, it is," Halcomb said. "How are you?"

"I was just about to ask you the same thing." Stafford was beaming, grinning from ear to ear. "Congratulations on a successful mission, gentlemen. Come on up to the study, and let's talk."

As we headed upstairs, Kiefer hung back, staring into the library. Halcomb paused on the stairs to say, "You, too, buddy."

Shyly, Kiefer nodded before following us.

We sat around the table in the same study we were briefed on the mission in over a month before. Stafford had slices of apple pie and pumpkin-chocolate milkshakes waiting for us. "This is a story I've been waiting to hear since I was telegrammed that you both made it to Switzerland." He looked at Kiefer. "And am I to presume that you are the defector the boys picked up?"

Kiefer nodded. He held out his hand, saying, in English, "Hello."

Stafford smiling, taking Kiefer's hand and replying in German, "Hello, son."

"I am not your son."

"No, no, it is an expression of affection." Stafford laughed. "I usually do not condone betrayal, but to betray a group as brutal as the SS, I must commend you."

"I never wanted to be a part of the SS in the first place, sir. It is... It's a long story."

Stafford nodded. "We can hear that story at some point today, I promise." He looked at me. "And I see you must have picked up German pretty well, Jay."

"That and Italian are almost all I've heard for the last few weeks," I said. "Anyway, I can say we followed the initial plan as closely as we could, but—"

"There were some detours," Halcomb said. "Would you believe us if we said we met Erwin Rommel and had to hunt a warlock in the regiment we were assigned to?"

"Please, gentlemen, start from the beginning," Stafford replied.

So, we recounted our adventures in North Africa and Europe. It was nice to see the colonel listening with the same enthusiasm a young child has when listening to his grandparents tell stories from when they were children. He did occasionally ask questions, but I think Halcomb and I were as clear as we could possibly be.

When we finished the story with our arrival in Switzerland, Stafford was quiet for a moment. "Absolutely incredible. I'm very pleased with both of you. I can see I made a good choice in bringing you aboard, Jay, and letting Lester accompany you. There will be other work for you two." He turned to Kiefer. "Your knowledge of the inner workings of the SS will be helpful in winning the war. Whenever you are comfortable, I would like to ask you some questions. Regardless—" Stafford held out his hand, "welcome to your new home."

"When can we expect more work?" Halcomb asked.

"Soon, but you two need to rest, and I am not sending Jay anywhere with a broken shoulder."

I was glad Stafford was encouraging me to rest, but at the same time, I was looking forward to my next adventure. After our debriefing, Halcomb was asked to stay behind. He was going to get some rest as well, but since he was uninjured, he could start another assignment much sooner.

It was disheartening knowing we would be separated, but it wasn't exactly our choice. I just hoped Halcomb and I would see each other again soon. I left the room, Kiefer in tow. He was shaking a little, so I walked with him outside. I would be out of action for some time, and I hoped I could use that time to help Kiefer adjust to life here. We walked out to the pumpkin patch, where Kiefer knelt in front of one of the bigger pumpkins, examining the vines and leaves and commenting on how beautiful and healthy the pumpkins looked.

I let him fuss over the pumpkins, as it seemed to calm him down. As I paced, I noticed a familiar figure strolling toward us with a big grin on his face. "Altschul?"

"Loalin!" Altschul reached out to shake my hand. "It is good to see you again!"

"It is good to see you as well. I take it you have been treated well here?"

"Absolutely, my friend. I have been assisting with other magic-related missions over the last few weeks, and I am thinking about getting my own home near here once I speak enough English. It is such a lovely area."

"It is." I frowned as a thought crossed my mind. "What about your parents?"

Altschul sobered. "There is nothing I can do. I asked if there is a way we can get them out of Germany. Robyn mentioned getting in contact with one of the POW escape lines, but that will take time."

"If they can get to the town of Königsdorf, there are people there who can help them get to Switzerland. A Magicless couple and a warlock."

Altschul nodded a little. "I will bring it up. Anyway—" he put his hands in his pockets, "I have been told you killed Wahler."

"I did."

"It is a start, but we still have the rest of the ZA to worry about. They are going to get desperate if the war continues to stay out of Germany's favor, and that means many more innocent people are going to get hurt."

"I agreed to stay a part of the OSS after I heal."

"Good. I cannot go back, obviously, but I will gladly help you in any way I can."

"I would appreciate that. Thank you."

Altschul's grin returned, and he looked at Kiefer, who was still kneeling in front of a pumpkin. "And who might you be?"

Kiefer looked over his shoulder at Altschul. He was quiet for a moment before standing and holding out his hand. "Um… Soren Kiefer. I-I was former… SS-ZA, under Wahler. I helped Jay and his friends break into Wahler's castle."

Altschul shook Kiefer's hand. "You have no idea how grateful I am to you for helping them. I had to witness some of Wahler's… experiments in Poland, and I could not let it continue."

"I saw a lot of his work as well," Kiefer replied. "And I should thank you for getting them on that mission. I would have never had the courage to run away from the Nazis without them."

Altschul gave a nod before releasing Kiefer's hand. "Where is Halcomb?" he asked, turning to me.

"Colonel Stafford is discussing his next assignment," I replied. "He will probably be off somewhere else while I recover."

"I am sorry to hear that. You two make a great team."

"It will not be all bad—well, I will be worried about him, but at least I can spend time with you two and help you get settled."

"That would be nice. Perhaps we can learn English together, Kiefer."

Kiefer glanced up at us. "Might we get to know each other first?"

"Of course," Altschul replied.

I smiled a little before saying, "Kiefer is a bit shy, but you will have a friend for life when you earn his trust and loyalty."

"I would certainly appreciate that, and I am sure he would as well."

As we were about to head inside, I noticed Halcomb jogging out to us from the mansion. "Jay, good news, I—" He stopped when he saw Altschul, and cleared his throat before switching to German. "I did not expect to see you here, Altschul."

Altschul shrugged. "I had my choice of staying in Britain or coming to America. I chose America, and I am glad because it means I will be able to work with you more often."

"Well, I am glad you were not just another Nazi rat, if you would like me to be honest."

I elbowed Halcomb in the ribs sharply. "We knew he was on our side."

"It is alright, Mr. Loalin," said Altschul.

"Anyway," Halcomb turned to me, when Altschul and Kiefer strolled away, "I have my next assignment. I'll be going to Gibraltar in a week to help track patterns of German U-boats in the Mediterranean."

"That sounds dull compared to what we just did," I replied with a smile.

"I requested something a little duller. Besides, if I'm going to do something exciting, I'd rather have you there convincing me to take more risks than necessary."

"Regardless of what you're doing, at least you're doing something for the war effort."

"Exactly. If I see Sergeant Prisk and his men, I'll say 'hello' to them."

"I appreciate that."

Halcomb looked lost for a moment. He stared off into the east, at the rows of buildings that made up Washington, then he turned back to me. "I know I'm the cautious one, but I'll still be extra careful so we see each other again."

"So will I," I said, holding out my hand.

Halcomb took it. "So long, Jay."

"So long, Halcomb."

After shaking my hand firmly, Halcomb turned to head out to Massey's waiting car, and I walked back to Altschul and Kiefer as the sun started to set. This particular path had ended, but I had a feeling there was a much longer journey ahead of me.

www.ingramcontent.com/pod-product-compliance
Lightning Source LLC
Chambersburg PA
CBHW011928300726
48970CB00008B/2610